ELTHEA'S
REALM

John Murzycki

ISBN:
ISBN-13:
978-1542365192

ISBN-10:
1542365198

To Mom and Dad, thanks for always being there when I needed you and for giving me the space to find my way. Love you always.

Contents

We never knew they existed. Nobody witnessed their birth or anticipated they would lay claim to our world. If we had looked at all, we would never have imagined they could evolve in such implausible circumstances.

One good, the other evil — two races who were mortal enemies before they ever ascended into awareness. Theirs was a hatred for each other bred into their very soul. They have been battling long before this, and it is only a matter of time until their conflagration spills over to engulf us all. Thus far, their clashes have been contained on Earth's technology network, where the typical implements of war have played no part.

But that is about to change.

The opening salvo of the conflict is before us. And curiously, it involves five rather ordinary people who have been unwittingly drawn into the struggle. Their resolve will be tested like never before. And whether they win out or not, our world may never be the same.

This is their story.

CHAPTER ONE

Warning Signs

The words drifted across the screen as if challenging me to make sense of them. I still couldn't understand why I had received this.

Priority Communication for Philip Matherson: Immediately provide all information on The Utopia Project. This is not a request. Do not ignore this notice.

"What the hell," I muttered, rereading it on my cell while trying not to jostle other passengers as I walked up the ramp from the transit station at Government Center.

I hadn't thought about the Utopia Project for years now. Why would anyone be interested in that college assignment?

I glanced at the sender: Bot105.

A fake name? Most likely the message is spam, or worse, a virus — far too many of them lately.

Just a stroke of luck, I decided, that the words meant something to me. It must be eight years since I helped write that paper.

I paused a moment to consider sending a message to Matt Tyler, my team leader on the course called The Utopia Project. But what would I say? I hadn't spoken to him for at least five years. Like the other members of the utopia team, we had drifted apart as we each moved on to our careers.

Besides, I had enough to worry about right now. I felt my job wasn't going well and the last thing I needed was something else to derail me.

First things first, I decided as I made a mental note of my priorities: top of the list was getting my job on track; which related to the second, paying the rent and having enough money left over to do some fun things; third was getting a girlfriend, at least a serious one; and somewhere way down the list was maybe figuring out this odd message about the Utopia Project.

I still continued to fret about it as I strode to my cube deep within the bowels of the Boston Federal Building. This particular room was large, with a maze of crisscrossing aisles and a mass of cubes, each one identical to the others. However, if you knew the rules, you understood the obvious differences in the cubes. My cube, which was located squarely in the center of the room, contained occupants who were lowest on the totem pole. Further along the edges, particularly along the less traveled paths, were those people with either seniority or a grade or two higher in rank. Then there were the ones along the window row — the most senior of the cube dwellers. I didn't even want to think about the hard-walled office people; those were out of my reach, at least for the foreseeable future.

I glanced at my nameplate before stepping into my space. Fortunately, there was no title, only the name. No way they could fit Fourth-Level Assistant for Reviews and Reports. At least that's what I seem to recall was written in my employee folder. Most co-workers typically called me the 'rewrite guy' when referring to my job. Either that or 'Phil, the nice guy,' which I wasn't sure was a compliment or an indictment of a dull personality.

I suppose there were worse monikers.

I stabbed the power-on button on my workstation and waited for the start-up screen so that I could log-in before grabbing a cup of coffee. But rather than the familiar blue and red image of the department logo, I was greeted by a stark gray background with a message scrolling across the screen.

You have been warned once Philip Matherson. We will tolerate no further delay. Give us all information on the Utopia Project.

I felt a queasy feeling in the pit of my stomach.

The words repeated on a loop as I gaped. This morning's text could have been random. But this?

The scrolling message only abated after I executed a forced shutdown on the workstation. This was a secure government facility. How could such a thing happen?

As I waited for the station to restart, I chewed on my fingernails, a bad habit I had recently acquired. Startup seemed to take longer than usual, but finally the screen came up with our official department logo. I exhaled, realizing I had been holding my breath.

Whatever was happening, I hoped this was the last of it.

~ ~ ~

Later that same afternoon Tommy Sullivan's voice boomed from the opening of my cube, "Hey Phil, gonna join us tonight at the Pub?" A native of Southie, he rarely spoke quietly.

The Parker Pub was located conveniently across the street from the office. Having a drink or two after work with a few cube-mates had become a ritual lately. If only some of the more attractive girls would join us, it might be more interesting. Nevertheless, I often tagged along.

"Aren't you jumping the gun?" I replied. "It's only three." I eyed him with a smirk. We could always count on Tommy to have a good time. My immediate inclination was to tell him that I should do something a little more productive. Instead, I answered, "I'll try. But right now I have a bunch of reports to finish."

His face took on a puzzled expression. "Why? You nevah bothered finishing 'em before."

He had me there. Forcing a chuckle, I said, "Figured it was about time."

He shrugged. "So maybe we'll see ya there."

I turned back to my screen. This was another day down the drain — another routine of writing and editing reports; summarizing documents that I doubted anyone would ever read or care about.

The thought gave me pause as I reflected on the high hopes I had in a career not all that long ago. Maybe those stupid messages this morning put me in this mood. The reference to The Utopia Project had reminded me of my college days; a time when I was full of optimism and knew I was going places. That was seven years ago, and now my dreams were a distant memory.

I couldn't help wonder. When had the magic faded from my life?

I pushed the sullen thought away and decided to check my e-mails before finishing this report. I never knew when some other tedious assignment might find its way to my inbox.

The e-mail in red immediately caught my eye. I hadn't ever remembered receiving an e-mail here at work highlighted like this. I paused a long moment before opening it, still skittish from the messages this morning. It appeared innocuous enough except for the color. The subject line was

New Regulations, and the sender was Department Head. Chiding myself for being a namby-pamby, I clicked it open.

Respond immediately with all information on The Human Response. If not, your life will be in danger.

My heart beat faster. The Human Response was the name my team had given to our utopia paper.

I might be able to convince myself that the other messages were some bizarre fluke — even the computer glitch this morning. But this? It was becoming clear that someone wanted something from this paper — a college project from years ago.

"This doesn't make sense," I mumbled as I stared at the message, taking particular note of the words 'your life will be in danger.'

That evening I didn't join my coworkers at the Pub. Neither did I take the T at my usual spot a block from the office. Instead, I decided to walk to Park Street or even as far as Back Bay Station — give me a chance to clear my head.

The brisk evening air helped calm my nerves as I navigated through the heavy foot traffic as office buildings emptied out. It was chilly for early April, but I didn't mind, especially now that the teeth of winter had passed. As I crossed Arlington Street, my cell rang, causing me to miss a step.

Of all people, it was a call from Matt Tyler from the utopia project team. Somehow I knew this call was one of those watershed moments in life, an irrevocable step that once taken could not later be undone. Just as the other messages today, I understood that this was no accident.

"How's it going, stranger?" I said tentatively, not knowing what to expect.

He laughed warmly. "Yeah, I guess it's been a while hasn't it? Sorry about letting things go for so long." His voice immediately brought me back to happier days — a time with such zeal and energy in my life.

"Great to hear from you, even if unexpected. What's going on?" I wondered if this was just a coincidence. My first impulse was to blurt out a description of the messages I had received, but he might think I was a little deranged.

"I want to get the utopia team together. It's been quite a few years now, and well, I just thought it was time."

Maybe it was the strange messages from today, but something in his voice told me he wasn't saying everything. I was once good friends with Matt. I knew if he left something unsaid.

Not sure how to respond, I answered, "When were you thinking?"

"This weekend."

It had been at least five or six years since I had seen anyone on the utopia project team, so his request surprised me. "Oh, that soon?"

He laughed easily. "Yeah, it's spur of the moment. I have a place in the Berkshire Hills in the western part of the state where everyone can stay." A long pause threatened to become uneasy as I considered his invitation. Into the silence he added, "It's been way too long Phil. I miss you guys."

I stopped walking as people flowed around me. All I could think about were the messages I received. And now this call from the leader of our utopia team. "Matt, this is damned strange you calling. Things are going on that made me think of you as well."

He considered this. "All the more reason for us to meet soon. But let's not talk about it on an open line."

What the hell was he saying? Open line? I thought he was going to explain, but instead, he added, "I think it will be good for everyone on the team to come together. It may be serious." The words sent a chill through me. "Please try Phil. We need to do this."

That sealed it. I told him I would. He said he would text me directions and details. As I ended the call, I looked up at the fading light of the early evening sky. This has been one hell of a strange day.

~ ~ ~

After the bizarre messages and Matt's unexpected call, I was looking forward to a quiet evening. But as I opened the door to my studio apartment I was suddenly alert.

The place looked like a hurricane had hit. Everything in the room — clothing, books, sofa cushions — was strewn everywhere. My heart pumped faster. What if the burglar was still inside?

"Hello," I shouted. "Who's there?" And then added, "I'm calling the police."

Silence greeted me.

I stepped tentatively across the threshold into the room, all the while feigning a call to the police.

After a few feet, it was clear nobody was hiding. I was so shocked I just stood in the middle of the room gaping at the mess. I had nothing of value: no drugs, no jewelry... nothing. The most expensive thing I owned was the TV, and that was about the only thing untouched. Every bureau drawer had been flung open, the contents on the floor. The one closet, which this morning had contained neatly hung dress shirts and pants, was now bare, everything tossed on the floor with the rest of the mess.

I had never experienced a home invasion before, and this was worse than I could have imagined. I didn't have much, but this was my refuge, a place I could hide when life troubled me. And it seems it now too was ripped from me. I felt like crying.

At that moment my cell signaled I had a message. I was going to ignore it, but out of habit, I glanced at the sender. It was Bot102.

The message this morning contained a similar name. I hesitantly tapped it open.

The next time it won't be your apartment to suffer this fate. It will be you. Turn over all utopia files.

I wanted to scream. It took all my self-control not to fling the cell into a wall.

Trying to calm myself I walked over to a window and looked out, more than anything to confirm that the world hadn't gone crazy. Soft lights shone from the windows of the four-story brick buildings across the street as residents went about their normal lives. Why me?

My gaze lowered to the street below and everything looked as it always did. But then, in the shadows of a small maple tree that hugged the sidewalk, I saw a lone figure, hooded and apparently staring up at me. For a second I wondered if my imagination was getting the best of me.

I continued to watch. Long moments passed as the stationary figure stared at me. This was no coincidence. Still, to be sure I observed him longer as a rage began to build inside me. He didn't move.

I was going to get that son of a bitch.

Rushing out of the room, slamming the door behind me, I bolted down the stairs out to the sidewalk.

He had vanished.

Residential buildings lined the urban street, abutting each other with no place for a person to flee. I looked in one direction and then the other.

Nobody.

A car drove by, its headlights washing over the darker shadows. Still nothing. Not satisfied, I walked one way and then the other, determined to find someone hiding behind a parked car or in a dark corner. I passed several couples walking together, none of them my target.

Slowly my anger began to ebb as I walked back to my building.

By slow degrees, my bitterness and frustration turned to something else. Fear.

CHAPTER TWO

Cassie's Story

Three days later I sat parked in a No Parking Loading Zone spot on Congress Street waiting for Cassie McKenzie. This was the middle of Boston's financial district, and it was impossible to find a metered spot on the street to wait for her. I had dished out enough money for this rental and didn't want to pay more for parking it in one of the lots. She was already late as I drummed my fingers on the wheel, gazing at the snazzy navigation system as I monitored the nearby streets and wondered if I should just circle around. But this entire area was jammed with mid-afternoon traffic, and once I moved, it would take forever to get back.

So I waited, wondering if I should have agreed to Matt's request for this reunion. Would we still have anything in common after all these years? If it weren't for the odd messages I received, I might have politely passed on his invitation. But I had a feeling he called us together because he had information that might shed light on what was going on with me.

Finally, after what seemed an aggravatingly long time, I spotted her walking out of the revolving door in front of the steel and glass office tower. Jumping out of the car I cupped my hands to my mouth and shouted her name. I was parked off to the side of the building, not close to the main entrance. I knew it would be my luck to get a ticket if I left the car unattended.

She stood in front of the building, blinking in the sunlight. I hollered again, and this time I waved. I thought for a moment about just ringing her cell.

After the third time I yelled she saw me and waved back, ending the motion by pushing back her hair that threatened to cover her eyes. She adjusted her black rimmed eyeglasses a few times as she strolled toward me. She had only worn glasses sparingly when I last saw her.

I walked briskly over to meet her, taking a chance on leaving the car unattended for a few minutes. As I reached her, I took her overnight bag and embraced her warmly.

"Hello, Matherson. You're looking well," she said.

It had been at least five years since I had last seen her and the change in her appearance startled me. The cute coed I had met in college had become a rather dowdy-looking businesswoman with a frumpy blouse, unfashionable hairstyle, and black glasses, all of which did little to improve her appearance. In spite of my thoughts, I fixed a smile on my face.

"So happy to see you, Cass. I'm glad you could make it."

She shrugged. "Well, it was rather short notice. I'm still not sure why Matt couldn't have planned it a little more in advance."

I suddenly remembered my parked car and said, "Come on, let's hurry."

She grinned with the same wry smile that I remembered so well. "What's the matter, Matherson? Afraid we'll be late?"

I laughed. "No, afraid of getting a ticket; I parked in a tow zone."

She didn't react to my comment as we headed to the car.

~ ~ ~

We didn't talk much as I concentrated on navigating the confusing streets of downtown Boston. The combination of Boston's well-deserved reputation for the worst drivers and my lack of driving made me a bit nervous.

But as I eased into the traffic flow of the Mass Pike I put the car on autopilot and relaxed a bit as the car drove itself. "So what's it been, four or five years since the team has gotten together?"

She pursed her lips, thinking about it as if it were an important question. "Six years this past June," she said, pushing her glasses up.

I couldn't help wondering again about her appearance and how she had turned so unattractive. Cassie had always been pretty, in a cute sort of way, even though I wouldn't have labeled her as gorgeous, indeed not like Diane, the other female on our team. I had always been attracted to Cassie, even though I never told her. And though her figure looked as slim as in the past, it was hard to tell under the frumpy clothes she now wore. It was evident she also needed a better hair stylist.

"And I think the last time we saw each other was probably five years ago," I said.

She nodded. "At Faneuil Hall. I remember. That was fun."

I smiled. It was one of the rare times we had met since the first year after graduation had passed. Even though we both worked in downtown Boston, neither of us had gone out of our way after that first year to call the other or to meet for drinks or dinner.

It's odd; I can't remember what I had for lunch yesterday, but I remember that meeting as if it just happened. We hugged each other warmly as we met at the door of a small restaurant. The hostess seated us next to a window looking out onto Faneuil Hall. We couldn't stop talking: how exciting life was after graduation; things we were doing out in the 'real world' as we called it. The soft light cast a heavenly glow on her face — only slightly matured since graduation. In many ways, that evening was a lifetime ago.

"We've drifted apart, haven't we?" Cassie said that night. "Not just you and me, but the rest of us. I remember there were times when we were inseparable. But I guess as time passes …" She had left the rest unsaid.

And now, five years later, we had drifted even further apart. Was it the demands of work and life, or did we just outgrow each other as I had with any number of other friends during my life? I stole another glance at her in the passenger seat, and I couldn't help wonder if I too had become someone different. Was I still the academic one, driven to succeed, as everyone made me out to be? Probably not. But I had my reasons. Still, I couldn't help wonder if I changed as much as Cassie had.

"So how have you been since then?" I asked, trying to forestall the awkward silence that threatened to overtake us, yet not wanting to discuss what was most on my mind. Not just yet.

She shrugged, "Oh, okay, I guess. Nothing much new."

She was always the most reticent member of our team, even in school. But now, getting her to open up was like pulling teeth. "How's Derek?" I asked.

A slight purse of her lips gave away the answer. "We don't see each other any longer. Haven't been since around the time you and I last met."

Cassie had met Derek when she first joined the insurance company where she went to work after graduation. I didn't know him that well, but he had come to a few of our gatherings during that first year after graduation. He and Cassie seemed happy at the time. But during our last dinner at Faneuil Hall, she hardly spoke of him.

"I'm sorry," I responded, not knowing what else to say.

"Yeah, just wasn't working out," she said sadly. It seemed she wanted to say more, but instead asked, "So what about you? What's new in the world of politics? Any new campaigns to save the world?"

I winced inwardly, not wanting to talk about my uninspiring and frankly boring job. Instead, I said, "No. I'm working at the Federal Building now. More stable, and the pay is better than the political campaign stuff."

"Oh," was all she said, which itself said much.

"Any girlfriend these days?"

I laughed nervously. For not talking much she was sure hitting on subjects that were problems in my life. "I see someone occasionally, but I wouldn't call it dating." I wondered what I would call it. But no sense baring my soul to explain there was simply no feelings, let alone love, in my relationship with Anne. Occasional sex, yes — which seemed fine for both of us. Thinking I should change the subject I asked, "You looking forward to seeing the old gang?"

"Oh, I suppose," she said without much enthusiasm.

"Matt says he's not sure Eric will make it," I said. "I guess he's still in Santa Clara working at his dad's company. Nobody's heard from him for a while now. But Diane will drive up from Stamford. From what I understand she's doing well at her job. It'll be good to see her again."

"I'm sure Matt will be happy," she said with a slight smile.

I had to grin. "I don't think they see each other often now, at least since they broke things off once they became attached to their careers. God knows they can both be workaholics."

"But that doesn't mean he wouldn't want to ... at least the Matt I remember. It'll be interesting to see if there's still a spark there."

I looked at her more closely. Maybe this was still the Cassie I knew.

For a while, I was content to enjoy the view and forget about life's problems. The suburban office complexes had given way to slowly rolling hills dotted with colonial homes. Patches of forsythia still displayed their bright yellow blooms while an occasional splash of pink and white from cherry trees brightened the landscape. Green leaves had barely emerged on most trees, yet the cold spring temperature had yet to loosen its grip on much of New England.

Finally, not knowing how to broach the subject that was most bothering me I simply blurted out, "Say, can I ask, has anything unusual happened to you lately?"

She laughed warmly for the first time today, reminding me fondly of the younger Cassie. "What do you mean, Phil Matherson?" She spoke with a tone of mock seriousness. "That could be a very personal question."

I felt my cheeks warm. "No, I didn't mean ... it's about our Woodbery College paper in the Utopia Project course. You remember it, don't you?"

"Of course I remember it." She made a face. "I'm not going senile just yet. Why?" she asked, suddenly serious.

I was puzzled why she seemed concerned, but continued, "Well, it's just damn unusual what's happened to me. The other day I got this message asking me questions about *The Human Response*. I mean, how would anyone even know the title of our paper?"

She sat up straighter in her seat and seemed to perk up at my question. "What do you mean? What did it say?"

"It was strange. The damnedest thing I ever saw."

I described the messages and told her about the break-in at my apartment and then the person in a hood watching me from the street. "And the last few days I swear someone's following me as I walk to work, again a person in a hoodie. But when I turned to confront him he just melted away in the crowd."

I expected her to laugh or make fun of me. But she just intently stared as I spoke. "I received more messages at work yesterday," I continued to explain. "And they were more threatening than the first couple. I had casually asked if anyone else at work was having computer or network issues, but nobody else was. I didn't want to get too specific. Everyone would think I was nuts."

Cassie sat quietly but looked at me with interest. I went into more detail about the apartment break-in and then described the figure who often shadowed me the last couple of days. Finally, in a weak voice, she asked, "Why would anyone be so interested in our Utopia Project? It doesn't make sense."

"I'm not making this up," I said more defensively than intended as I felt an edge of desperation begin to cloud my thinking.

She shook her head. "No, I believe you. It's just, I don't understand. It happened to me also." Again her black hair covered her face as she spoke.

"What do you mean? What happened?" My hands clenched in spite of my effort to remain calm.

She moved her hair out of her face and pushed up her glasses. "I didn't think much of it at the time, but now you tell me this——"

"What was it?" I interrupted, a bit unnerved now.

"Maybe it was nothing, at least I thought so before now." She scrunched her brow. "It's just that I received a letter from Woodbery a few weeks ago. It was an actual letter delivered by the post office. The letter looked official, Woodbery College letterhead and all. But it was a form letter without a signature, addressed to me. It said that the school wanted more information on our utopia paper since it was so outstanding and asked me to send them all my notes and any background material, electronic or written, that I used to develop it."

"What did you do?"

"Nothing. God only knows what happened to my notebooks. As for the electronic copies, I have no idea where those ended up. I pretty much use my tablet only for reading books these days. Most of my personal e-mails seem to be junk, so I don't even bother with them. I just ignored the letter like the rest of my junk mail." She looked at me with a frown. "But isn't it odd?" Her eyes were opened wide. "What are the chances? Both of us contacted about the Utopia Project. Why?"

Even though autopilot was engaged and the car was self-driving, I kept my eyes on the road, feeling a tightening in my stomach. "I don't know. But it doesn't seem like a coincidence."

"Maybe it's a joke or something by the others in our group. Do you think?"

I grimaced. "If it is, they are going through a shit load of trouble for no good reason. No, I don't see what Matt, Diane or Eric would expect to gain by this. But I guess in a couple of hours we'll know more."

I remembered clearly during the long drive from Boston to

the Berkshires that I tried my best not to let my imagination run wild. But even if I had, never in a million years would I have guessed who were the real culprits asking about our utopia paper.

CHAPTER THREE

A Hint of Trouble

Matt opened the door of his rustic cabin even before we pulled to a stop on the stone driveway. He grinned broadly as he bounded out to greet us. I hadn't seen him in over five years, but I would recognize him immediately: neatly trimmed dark hair, eyes that always seemed to sparkle with excitement, sturdy build, and a confident personality without ever being a know-it-all.

Even though it was cool outside for mid-April, especially here in the hilly terrain, he hadn't bothered to put on a jacket. He hugged Cassie warmly as if she were the most important person in his life, then grabbing my outstretched hand, he also embraced me.

"Great to see you again," he said, an emotional catch in his voice. I had to admit, all the irritation I had felt since he asked for this reunion melted away at the sight of my college classmate and friend. "Hope you found the place easy enough?"

"Oh, only took us about a half-hour backtracking a few times," I said. His place was on a hillside about a mile from the road, and not very clearly marked.

"Yeah, I should have warned you. GPS systems have a problem with this address. Let me help you with those," he offered as I pulled the light overnight bags from the trunk.

The log cabin was quaint and appeared as if it had been recently renovated. Inside, the family room had a cathedral ceiling with tall windows surrounding it. A warm fire blazed in the green Vermont Castings wood stove, holding back the chill of the late afternoon air. A nook to the side of the room contained an office with desk and bookcases. A modern kitchen opened at the far end of the family room.

"Make yourself comfortable." He motioned to the leather chairs and couch. "I'm just finishing a call with my senior staff." As he sat at his desk, I noticed his monitor displayed a group of people sitting around a conference table. "Okay everyone, I need to wrap this up now. We understand the issues. Let's keep close tabs on it, and we'll take this up again on Monday. Call me immediately if anyone reports another failure. You all have a good weekend." Clicking his mouse to end the call he turned back to us, the serious expression he had while on the call now replaced with a smile. I now noticed the changes since I last saw him: the wrinkles around the corners of his eyes, a few premature gray hairs on the side of his head, and the slight enlargement of his waistline. But more than that, he looked more worn and tired than I had ever remembered. Still, his smile was as warm and sincere as ever.

"Your business must be doing well." My eyes darted to the pleasant room as he sat across from us.

He wrinkled his forehead. "Truthfully, there are times when I wonder if it's all worth it." He paused, absently tapping his fingers on the arm of the chair. "Lately the problems have become more intense … more troubling." Shaking his head as if to clear it he added, "But there's time enough to talk about that. I'm glad you could get away for a few days. Sorry for the short notice, but turns out I'll be traveling on business for the next few weeks."

"Well, we almost turned around that last mile," I offered.

"Yeah," he smiled. "It's pretty isolated, which is why I bought it last year. I enjoy getting out of the city whenever I can. The Berkshires are beautiful. Lot's to do if you want. I often use this place for offsite meetings with my staff."

"I'll say it's isolated," I added, glancing out at the surrounding woods.

He smiled even more broadly, also gazing outside. "But how can you beat that view."

I had to admit he had a point. The house sat near the top of a high ridge with its vista looking out over a broad expanse of rolling hills. In the distance, a village twinkled with lights as dusk approached.

"It looks like you got what you always wanted," said Cassie. "We always knew you would go places."

His smile diminished slightly. "Maybe. But does anything ever turn out the way you thought it would?" He stood and walked toward the kitchen. "But I forget my manners." He selected a bottle of wine from the rack. "Is a red okay for you?" We each nodded, and he poured three glasses. "To old friends. We were a great team," he said, holding his glass up as we clinked them.

Staring at us with an intensity which I knew was Matt's prelude for getting down to business, he began to ask in rapid fire, "I want to hear everything. We have a lot to catch up. Phil, I can't remember which of us dropped the ball. How was it we stopped meeting for a drink after work? Remember that little bar in Cambridge we both liked so much?"

I tried my best not to show my discomfort. Matt's near fanatical intensity with his fledgling company, combined with my declining opportunities in the political campaign field, had strained our conversations. It seems we had less in common as time passed. Soon our e-mails and text messages to schedule a get-together stopped entirely. Just thinking about it now made me wonder once again if this reunion was a mistake. Instead, I answered, "I guess we got too caught up in our own worlds."

"And whose political staff are you on now?" he asked.

I groaned inwardly, wondering how many times I would have to explain to each person that I had left a career I once loved so much. It wasn't that the editing job in a Federal agency was that bad — it paid okay, and I'm sure a lot of people would be glad to have it. But it wasn't the vibrant life of the political campaign field. "I've taken a job at the Federal Building these days." I vainly tried to keep my voice level.

If Matt thought any less of me, he didn't show it. "I wish I could share your enthusiasm for government programs. Most of my experience has been less than positive. It seems like they intentionally make it difficult for a company like mine."

Not wanting to talk more about my failed career path I asked, "So tell us, Matt, what brought this about? I mean, it's great seeing you and getting the team together again, but when you called, you said it was important."

A cloud passed over his face, the exuberance of a moment ago gone. When he spoke again, he had a far-away look in his eyes. "Yes, we need to discuss some things. But we should all be here, at least those of us who're able to. Let's wait. Diane texted me when she left Stamford. The ride from Connecticut should get her here in the next hour or so, maybe sooner the way I've seen her drive."

"I was wondering about Eric," Cassie asked. "Did you ever get in touch with him?"

Matt's expression immediately changed as he flashed a crooked smile. "I must have called the guy and texted him dozens of times." He smiled broadly. "You remember how frustrating he could be when he wanted. He never returned any calls or texts, and I never reached him live." He shrugged. "I know it's harder for him, living on the West Coast and all. But I'm afraid we've let too much time pass between us. I suppose he doesn't want to drop everything and fly out here."

"Have you heard any news at all from him these last few years?" I asked. "Still working at his father's company?"

"Haven't spoken to him since the year after graduation. You know as much as I do. He was living in Santa Clara in a small house on his dad's property. All I know is that the company, Webster Technology, has seen better days, especially since our time at school. I don't hear its name mentioned in the trade press or online news portals."

"It's a shame he won't be with us," said Cassie. "It would have been nice. He always managed to make us smile."

Matt smiled more broadly. "Yeah, but at least we won't have him to antagonize us, particularly Diane."

We laughed as Cassie added, "Yes, he could get under her skin at times, that's for sure. Speaking of Diane, how is she?"

His smile turned a bit forced. "She's good. We talk occasionally, but I'm afraid not enough. She's now a product manager at the same biotech company she joined out of school. Huge company that's making money hand over fist. I'd say she's doing okay."

We talked more about college days — people, professors, good times we remembered. When we heard the sound of car wheels crunching on the stone driveway, Matt shot out of his chair and was at the front door in three bounding steps.

"Here she is," he said as he opened the door to step

outside. Cassie and I followed at a more leisurely pace. Matt waited until she parked and then warmly hugged Diane Collentenio the moment she stepped out of the car. I was struck by how attractive she still appeared, maybe even more so than I remembered. Her shoulder length hair was now a slightly lighter shade of blond than in college and her figure was slim and shapely under the stylish business blazer and skirt she wore. But most of all her face — full lips, radiant skin, just flawless.

She hugged Matt tightly. When she noticed Cassie and me standing there, her eyes opened wide, and she broke her embrace to step toward us. "Oh, it's so great." She embraced first Cassie and then me. "So wonderful to see you again," she said with unfeigned excitement. "It's been so long and I'm afraid that with work and all I haven't been very good at staying in touch." Gazing at Matt who stood to the side, she added, "I'm so glad you arranged this. If it weren't for you, we might never see each other again. You're so great."

"Our leader. Isn't he something?" Cassie offered as we all made our way inside. "A CEO, a retreat like this in the mountains, and still single. Difficult to believe."

I smiled, knowing quite well what she was getting at — probably trying to stir up some old feelings between the two. This reunion might be exactly what Cassie needed to get out of her shell.

"Did you bring an overnight bag?" Matt asked as we entered the house.

"Oh, it's in the car. I could use a hand. Do you mind Phil?"

"Sure," I said turning around to get it. "Be right back."

"Oh, let me come with you. Otherwise, you'll set off the alarm."

As we walked the few steps to her car, I noticed that air

had turned much cooler once the sun had set. Only a faint glow remained in the western sky. Diane pressed a button on her keychain and the trunk of the red sports car extended upward. "Thanks for helping," she said as she put her hand on my shoulder. "I'm really glad about this. I've often reminisced about the good times at school." Her voice had turned softer. "I do feel terrible about not calling any of you. Matt and I sort of keep in touch, but not all that much."

I smiled, remembering fondly how she often rambled when she was nervous or didn't know what to say. Looking at her closely I realized how easy it was to get lost in her dark green eyes. "I know. We had some good times," I replied. Nearly forgotten memories pulled at me, but they seemed from long ago. I shrugged. "I'm afraid life goes on."

She scrunched her forehead in a frown. "Well, I guess that's just part of growing up." But she didn't sound as if she meant it.

I grunted as I lifted the heavy bag from her trunk, which was much larger than mine or Cassie's. "Are you planning on spending a week or something?"

She gave me a puzzled frown, an expression she always used when she didn't understand something. I couldn't help laugh softly. "It's great to be together again," I said. "Too bad Eric can't be here to complete the picture. And … we do have some important things to discuss," I added. Again she looked puzzled, but I didn't give her a chance to ask more. "Come on; it's cold out here. Let's get inside. We'll have plenty of time to catch up."

As we turned a movement caught my eye deep in the woods away from our circle of light. "What's the matter?" Diane asked, noticing I wasn't following.

Seeing nothing but trees, I suddenly felt foolish for letting my imagination get carried away. Being followed in the city was beginning to take its toll. "Oh nothing," I said, trying to sound casual. "I thought I saw a deer, but I guess not."

I suddenly wanted very much to be inside rather than out in the open.

CHAPTER FOUR

The Utopia Virus

The soft lights and warm wood fire inside Matt's cabin were a pleasant contrast to the raw evening outside. What had started as an occasional light shower had become a steady rainfall. Things in the world were happening that I could not explain, but here the room was cheerful and inviting, made more so by a circle of friends renewing old bonds.

Dinner was fantastic with grilled lobster tails and steaks. The conversation never stopped as if a floodgate, once opened, could not be stopped. We spoke of a time when we were the closest of companions. As we were finishing the main course, Diane said, "Who would have guessed? Our very own Matt, lover of cafeteria food at the Woodbery Student Center, has this undiscovered talent."

By the time we were on to dessert, we were all laughing hysterically over Diane's imitation of a particular professor that we had all considered pompous and rude. With dinner finished, and Diane having changed from her business skirt into jeans and sweatshirt, we moved back into the family room. That was when the discussion turned more serious.

"You know, I did have a reason for calling us together this

weekend," said Matt, turning thoughtful as only Matt could do with his tone and level stare. "You see, I'm in the battle of my life, and I fear things are not going well." He had our attention now.

"It's my software company. You know we develop apps and programs for large firms — data warehousing, mobile apps, security software — that sort of stuff. Business has been great. But all of a sudden, bam." He slapped his fist into his palm, causing Cassie to jerk in surprise. "Out of nowhere it all began to go to hell — system crashes, massive virus attacks, unexplained loss of critical data and programs freezing or just not working. You know, just the sort of thing that stops companies from buying that software."

"Is someone targeting your business?" asked Diane. "Maybe it's a developer planted on the inside?"

"That was my first thought. But the failures are too widespread and cut across different products for it to be any single person. Our developers work on specific apps or programs. It's coming from the outside. We've enhanced our testing process before anything ships. The software goes out fine, and then shortly after, it becomes infected. We've narrowed it down to an outside influence: virus, malware, whatever you want to call it — a corruption introduced into the program once customers install it."

"That still doesn't mean someone isn't targeting your company," I offered. "They could be doing it after customers run it."

He nodded. "You're right. Except it's not just the software from my company, although it seems more severe with our applications. But the number of system crashes, software freezes, and wacky things have gone up dramatically on programs from most software companies. All this started taking place recently." He lowered his voice. "It's not generally known yet — only those with connections to major software firms are aware of it — but many believe that unless this gets resolved, and soon, the result could be catastrophic." He paused for a moment and then added, "Frankly, I'm worried."

"Is this cyber warfare?" I asked. "Maybe North Korea, China, or a Middle East country?"

He shook his head. "Other countries — those included — have the same problems as us, at least I've been told by those in the industry who know. The truth is, the world's technology seems to be under attack from someone, and we don't know who it is or why they are doing it."

"I don't understand," said Cassie. "You said this was why you called us together. You don't think we're behind it, do you?"

He smiled for the first time since beginning this discussion. "No, I'm not suggesting that any of us are responsible. And it's not why I'm discussing it with you. You see, here's the strange part about the software failures at my company. When something goes wrong — a data loss, shut down, whatever — most of the time an error message comes up with some reference to utopia. Some of my engineers have begun to call it the utopia virus."

I felt the hairs on my neck rise as we remained silent for a long moment.

"As far as I'm aware, that doesn't happen with failures from other software companies," he continued. "And not just that, whenever there's a failure at my business, the error messages have recently become even more menacing, with warnings of violence toward 'The Creators of utopia' as it's typically phrased."

I immediately thought about the messages I had received. Nobody spoke for long moments as we considered what he

31

said, with only the crackling fire and patter of the rain hitting the windows breaking the silence. Without warning an eruption of headlights from the driveway caused everyone to jump and Diane to inhale sharply in alarm.

"Are you expecting anyone?" I asked nervously. Matt shook his head, a concerned expression on his face as he moved to the front door and switched on the outside lights while the rest of us stood in the middle of the room. A car door slammed. "Oh my God, I can't believe it," he muttered looking out the window.

"What? Who?" said Diane.

Matt turned the latch to unlock the door and opened it just as the dripping wet figure of Eric Webster stepped inside.

Without preamble, Eric immediately said, "Who's the stupid shit who decided we hold this event the ass-end of nowhere?" He glared as he pushed his way past the startled Matt, dropped his bag to the floor and bent over, shaking his head like a dog as water sprayed around him. Standing upright, he continued, "Bad enough I have to travel across the country for this, but then these God-forsaken roads ..." Looking squarely at Matt, he demanded, "What's the matter, Tyler? Cambridge not good enough for you now?"

"Eric, I never thought you would make it," Matt said with a broad smile as he put his hand on his wet shoulder.

"You kiss me Tyler, and I'm outta here right now. I'm warning you."

Matt removed his hand but still held onto his smile, even wider than before. "Why didn't you return any of my calls or messages? I didn't hear anything."

I stepped over to shake Eric's hand warmly, "It's great to see you again. So happy you're here."

"Hey buddy, it's been awhile," he said, using a nickname he had given me at school, probably because he couldn't remember my real name at first. But somehow it stuck. "We've got some catching up to do."

Cassie came over and kissed him on the cheek, not caring about his wet clothes. "Eric. You made it," she said.

Diane was smiling but still stood near the couch. Eric finally noticed her. "Princess! My, you're looking good." Glancing at Matt, "You two make it legal yet?"

Matt cleared his throat. "Not exactly."

Eric held a questioning expression, but Diane said, "There's our Eric — always getting right to the heart of things. Come on, join the party." She stepped over to kiss him as well, but unlike Cassie, took care not to get herself wet. Eric, however, would have none of it as he grabbed her and held her in a close embrace. She fussed but still smiled, as did the rest of us.

For the first time today I felt good about this reunion. All of us together again. I had to admit that it hadn't felt right without Eric; he had a personality and style unlike the rest of us. I beamed, seeing him again, remembering that I was in many ways closer to Eric than the others. If not for him, I likely would never have been a member of this group of friends.

For his part, he appeared genuinely touched by our reactions. "How could I miss this?" he said. "What with Matt buying me the plane tickets. I would be a heel not to take him up on the offer." Looking at Matt, he added, "Although it would have been nice if you had sprung for a rental car as well."

"What're you talking about?" Matt said, his smile fading.

"The plane tickets. I received them only yesterday. That didn't give me much time. Luckily my social calendar was open. So I figured what the hell since you went to all that expense. You really did want all of us together, didn't you?"

Matt's expression turned serious. "I never sent you tickets. I called you. Left messages, texts, and e-mails. But that's all."

Eric searched Matt's face as if wondering if he were joking. "Well, somebody sent me round-trip tickets from San Francisco to Boston." He looked at the rest of us. "None of you did?"

Diane replied glibly, "Not me," while Cassie and I looked at him blankly.

"This is bizarre," said Matt, rubbing his chin in dismay. "We need to talk more about this, but how about some food first? Hungry? I have more steaks and an opened bottle of red wine."

Eric was still stunned by Matt's response about the tickets. But he let it go for the moment as he followed Matt toward the kitchen. "A steak sounds good, but just water for me."

I thought it strange, Eric passing up a drink. Even Matt bunched his eyebrows for a second before smiling again. "Come on. We'll get you caught up."

CHAPTER FIVE

Friends Reunited

We listened as Matt retold the story of the problems at his software company and the error messages. Eric was quiet during much of the discussion but listened intently. As we sat at the dining room table, I noticed that Eric's face had a more sunken, worn look, which made him appear much older than the rest of us. His unkempt hair was still pale brown, and he hadn't shaved in several days. The only thing that saved him from looking like a homeless person was his clothes — a Ralph Lauren jersey, dark jeans and new sneakers.

Once Matt finished telling us again about the chain events at his business, I told everyone what had happened to me the last few days, especially the message that had asked for more information on The Human Response. I detailed the threatening messages, the break-in at my apartment, and my suspicion of being followed. Rubbing my chin, I said, "I'm getting worried, more so now after what Matt told us." Everyone was at a loss for words as they considered what I said.

Cassie explained the letter she had received requesting her

notes on the utopia paper. It was then that Diane said, "I would never have brought this up, but with all this talk … well, I was also asked for information. I hadn't thought much about it at the time, what with my annual review due. I thought it might be related to some new personnel policy." The rest of us remained silent, everyone now on the edge of our seats. "Anyway, I received an e-mail from an executive in our company asking me for some documents for their compensation review — strategy plans I had done, launch documents and such. But also included was the request asking for my Woodbery College capstone paper along with a synopsis of what I had learned from it."

We all understood that the capstone project was the way the school had described the Utopia Project.

"I remember thinking how this company is going too far with these reviews and the information they're requesting," Diane continued. "Anyway, I provided everything except the information on the utopia paper. I thought it was a silly request. But here's the odd thing. I saw this same exec at a company event a week or two later. I began to explain to him why I hadn't sent him a copy of the paper or my summary. He looked at me as if I had sprouted horns. I tried to explain it to him again, but he had no idea what I was talking about. I was beginning to get embarrassed, so I muttered something about being mistaken and confusing it with another message."

"Could you have been — confused, I mean?" asked Matt.

"No. I went back to my desk that day and checked my e-mails. And there it was: the request with his name. But when I inspected it more closely I noticed for the first time that it wasn't his usual company e-mail. I didn't think much of it at the time, and frankly, I had forgotten about it until now. But with all this …"

The room grew quiet. In the momentary silence, Eric said, "You know, all this is not a coincidence. Somebody wants something from us, something from our Utopia Project." He paused as if carefully choosing his words. "And another thing, with the timely appearance of my airline tickets, someone wants us all together again."

"But why?" Matt frowned.

"And if that's true, then who?" Diane said, a note of tension in her voice.

"There's nothing of value in that paper," I added. "Believe me; I've thought a lot about it since I started getting those messages. We wrote it, what, eight years ago? As did every graduating class before and after us. Doesn't seem to make much sense, does it?"

"And what about wanting us all together?" asked Cassie in a meek voice. "That doesn't sound very good."

Nobody had an answer. Matt however stood and walked to the front door. "Not to be melodramatic, but I'm not taking any chances." He locked the door with the deadbolt and tapped at a small electronic screen on the wall. "This is a state-of-the-art security system. If anyone opens a door or window or even approaches the house, an alarm will sound, and the central monitoring office notified. So keep this in mind if anyone decides to go out for a stroll tonight."

"Yeah, I don't think that's happening," Diane tried to say lightly. But nobody laughed.

~ ~ ~

I remember how sober everyone had become after Eric's comment about someone wanting all of us together. The e-mails and Matt's computer failures were one thing — they were bad enough. But this? Here we were if someone wanted us. I know it spooked me more than anything else.

Matt wore an unsettled expression as he said, "You realize we may not have answers to all this. I called us together because of what was happening with me and, unlikely as it might seem, how it could involve all of us." His face warmed to a smile. "But to tell you the truth, I mostly wanted to see you all again. I guess I just needed an excuse ... which shouldn't be the case."

At that moment he reminded me of the Matt I had known so well — someone we looked up to, not only for advice and leadership on our team but as a friend we could always confide in, knowing that he would keep our trust and always be available if needed.

He continued, "The years have passed, but I still feel you are my closest friends. We should make up for lost time. Let's put these computer failures and strange messages aside for a bit, take a deep breath and just talk about us." His eyes settled on Eric. "Our long lost Eric. We haven't heard much from you since graduation. How about getting us up-to-date with your life?"

Eric shrugged, looking strangely unsettled as he chewed on his lower lip. "Not really much to say."

Matt frowned. "Still working at your dad's company?"

Eric grimaced noticeably, and it took him a moment to answer. "No," he replied uncomfortably. "It's not my dad's company anymore. A trust now owns it, and they brought in different management. You see, he died a few years after our graduation."

"I— I'm sorry," Diane offered. "We didn't know."

"Yeah, it was unexpected. I left the company shortly after. Couldn't take the squabbles and in-fighting that started once he was gone." Smiling bitterly, he added, "Besides, I didn't have the gusto my dad had for the business. You see, it wasn't my baby like it was his. And since I was taken care of by his will, I found other things to do."

We waited for him to continue, but he just sat there with an unreadable expression.

"Like what?" Matt asked softly.

"Oh, okay. That was your original question, wasn't it? Well, let's see. It was too easy to get into trouble. I had money but no job, so I did — get into trouble that is. I wanted to forget, escape everything — job, family, life. And it turns out that drugs did the trick nicely. At least for a while until they nearly killed me. I was fortunate I wasn't so far gone. I realized the path I was on. It took seven months in a rehab center to straighten me out, but I did."

"You know, Eric," said Diane, a kindness in her voice that she rarely used when speaking to Eric, "after Woodbery I felt we all lost our support group. And with what you went through — the loss of your father — I can't imagine how difficult it must have been."

"Sure, it was tough losing him. It's true that you don't know what you have till it's gone. But still, I feel I was weak. I mean, look at all of you. I'll bet none of you spent time in detox. You've all done great."

Diane shook her head. "Oh, I wouldn't say it that way. I have a good job. But in many ways, I feel a shell of who I was before we graduated. During those college years, we had each other." She inadvertently glanced at Matt, who was looking at her intently. "And as for a job, it already feels less of a career and more like a treadmill — the kind that mice run on, always trying to go faster but never quite making it." She stifled a laugh. "Seems I spend my life living for tomorrow, dodging the next in-house political bullet, trying to grab the carrot that's always just out of reach. It isn't anything like what we had back then. It's certainly not what I expected."

Her little speech surprised me. It wasn't like our 'always together' Diane to open up like this, or to express unhappiness at anything, let alone her job. But it seemed to do the trick as Eric's face softened. He cleared his throat before saying, "Thanks, but I just never expected my life to turn out this way."

"Maybe none of us did," I offered. "At least in the way we had thought it would. My big political campaign career never happened — probably never will. Plenty of organizations were glad to have me as a volunteer, but none were willing to pay me. I had wanted that career so badly. There are many days when I feel completely adrift. You're not alone Eric." He looked at me with an expression that brought me back to our time at school, a time when we only had to look at each other to know what we were thinking. He was soundlessly saying thanks.

Cassie spoke tentatively, "Maybe it's not growing up. Maybe we've just lost the dreams we once had." She paused a moment to collect her thoughts and move her glasses back up on the bridge of her nose. "Remember when we wrote the utopia paper? We were so full of ideas. We could accomplish whatever we set our minds to. It was an exciting adventure. I don't know about all of you, but I don't look at each new day with wonder and excitement like I did back then." She furrowed her face in a frown while her eyes held a glassy, faraway look. "Maybe it is just the reality of growing up. But I often wonder if maybe I let go of something enchanting we once had."

I thought it fitting that Cassie would express something like this. She was always the dreamer of our team, the person who came up with ideas that the rest of us often initially dismissed, only to revisit and accept later. And now she was right again of course.

In spite of the unanswered questions about computer failures, unexplained messages, or mysteriously generated plane tickets, in a strange way I felt happier than I had in a long time — quite a surprise from the way I had started the day. I was back in the company of friends who were the best people I had ever known. It was irrational — I realized that at the time — but I knew that with us together everything would be okay.

Too bad I was wrong.

CHAPTER SIX

What It Feels Like to Die

Not much later Matt's cell phone began clanging with a rather urgent ring tone. Grabbing it from the desk where he had left it, he explained, "I have an app for important news feeds. This must be serious." He tapped the screen and scrolled through the message.

"Well, what does it say?" Diane asked impatiently.

He was so intent on reading that I wasn't sure he even heard Diane. "Oh my God. Scores of airports have been shut down. Something about massive failures in air traffic control systems."

Taking the remote for the TV, he switched it on. The announcer was speaking, "—of the FAA will make a statement to the press shortly. Meanwhile, we have unconfirmed reports of an on-ground collision in Atlanta. We will go there in a moment. But here's the situation as we know it. Just after 8:00 PM Eastern Time, air traffic control systems at most major airports went dead. Homeland Security is investigating if this is a terrorist attack. We are told this is a highly dangerous situation, and accurate information is difficult to obtain. We will continue our coverage beginning with revolving reports from several major airports from—" The announcer continued, but I had already tuned her out, thinking of the lives that might be in the balance this moment.

"What's happening?" muttered Cassie.

Matt's face lost its color as he stood facing the screen. He spoke so softly I nearly didn't hear him. "It's beginning."

We waited for him to say more but he stood transfixed looking at his handheld. Eric said, "What? What's beginning?"

He looked up slowly, his brow furrowed. "This," he said, pointing to the screen. "These failures. It's because of a virus — I know it is."

"You can't be sure," I blurted. "I mean the announcer even said it could be terrorism."

But Matt shook his head. "No, the air traffic control systems are the newest technology. They're extremely secure. If terrorists can breach those systems..." He frowned. "I don't think it's possible. They're designed not to fail."

"But computers fail," said Cassie. "It happens all the time in my office."

"That's right," he said excitedly, using that as an example to make his point. "Think back to only a few years ago. We never had the problems we do now. This is a systemic issue with our software, and it's getting worse. I've seen it up close. And we may have reached a point of no return." He fidgeted with his phone. "I think we're in big trouble, and this is only the beginning."

"Personally, I think it's God's way of saying we rely too much on all this technology," said Cassie. "Most people can't do without all these devices." She eyed Matt suspiciously.

He still appeared stunned. He tried to laugh, but it sounded more like a snort. "So you're advocating some religious, back-to-basics counter-culture?"

She shrugged. "I'm just saying ... but I'm probably not the person to offer an opinion on this. It's just that the world has become too complicated, at least for me. In a lot of ways, I feel I don't belong." As if suddenly realizing she was saying this out loud, her face colored and she became abruptly silent.

The announcer on the screen said, "—now going to the White House where it is believed the President will declare a state of emergency, opening the door for assistance from federal agencies. The death toll continues to mount as another report of a serious plane accident ..."

"It looks like I'll be taking a train back rather than that free ticket," said Eric. Knowing him as I did, I could tell he was trying to lighten the mood on a dangerous situation. I could see even he was moved by the terrible news. He eyed the comfortable room as he added, "Although this house might not be a bad place to hang out for a while."

Matt smiled sadly. "You know you're always welcome here. I am barely able to enjoy it these days as—"

An alarm from the home security system abruptly blared, "Perimeter intruder." A computer-generated voice announced it over and over again. We jumped up. "It's probably a deer," Matt said, although he didn't sound very convincing.

Diane stepped to the window in the kitchen area. "There's someone out there." She nearly shouted to be heard over the security system. Matt tapped buttons on the monitor, silencing the voice. "In the woods, out this way." She pointed in that direction. "I saw someone move."

We all lurched toward the windows on that side. Standing behind her I could see how tense she was. "Out there. Someone is moving."

Matt activated all the outside lights from the security panel. I peered at the woods in that direction, as did the rest of us. On this side of the building, the ground fell away sharply, so there wasn't much of a distance past the clearing around the house.

"There!" Eric shouted, pointing. I followed the angle of his arm and sure enough, a figure deep in the woods, barely visible, was slowly stepping toward the direction of the house.

"I hope your neighbors are friendly," said Cassie nervously.

Matt looked at her with a frown. It was one of the first times I had seen him appear even somewhat unnerved. "The nearest is nearly a mile away. I don't understand..." He went over to the other side of the dining area to stand in front of a floor-to-ceiling window. "What the hell? Someone's out this way."

Now I was worried, and I could see from everyone's expression they were also.

"Could they be hunters?" Diane asked, an edge of hysteria creeping into her voice.

Matt looked at her, eyes blazing. He ran to one of the other windows. "Can anyone see if they're carrying a rifle?"

We all turned to look. "This one doesn't have one as far as I can tell," said Cassie.

It was still raining outside which made it unlikely anyone was merely taking a stroll. Probably not the night for someone to be hunting either I thought.

Matt returned to the security panel and tapped the monitor furiously. "I'm not taking any chances. This code will notify central monitoring that we need the police. They should be here shortly."

"More on this side," said Eric. Even he sounded flustered, not something he was known for. "I count at least two here.

And whoever these people are, they are big; I mean tall."

I stood rooted to the same spot next to Diane and Cassie as we looked out the kitchen window. "I see four here," I said. "No rifles." They had approached the tree line in back of the house, some thirty feet away. And they were big, maybe seven feet tall and even from this distance, I could tell they were built abnormally large.

"They're just standing there," said Diane. Her voice shook. "I don't like this. Matt? Tell the police to hurry."

Matt alternated between looking out a front window and tapping on the security system. "Damn," he spat. "This friggin thing doesn't acknowledge my panic code. Pay each month, and now I need it ..."

Next to me Diane inhaled sharply. "It looks like they're wearing masks." She was clearly panicked.

My heart began to race. As they stepped into the ring of light from the outside spotlights, I could see something was wrong with their faces. It was as if they wore black masks with slits for the eyes and mouth. Or maybe they were painted that way ... I couldn't tell. "What the..." I heard myself mutter.

Matt had abandoned the security panel and was now looking at his handheld. "God damn," he shouted. "No signal. Does anyone have a signal?"

I looked at mine, surprised that it was blinking erratically as if short circuited. I felt a chill beginning to creep over me.

Outside the figures had stepped out of the covering of trees and strode toward the house deliberately, not in any hurry. I looked around at the other windows and could see that more were advancing as well.

"Matt, do you have a gun?" Eric asked abruptly.

Matt looked at him as if he had gone crazy. "No, I don't have a gun." He angrily bit off the words. "Who the hell are they?"

We all moved away from the windows now as if the center of the room was more sheltered.

"What're we gonna do?" Diane said, breathing heavily, nearly hyperventilating.

I flinched, not realizing that I had bumped into Eric behind me as we both backed away from the windows. One of the figures was peering at us just outside the dining room window. Up close its face was even more disturbing than from a distance. It was not a mask. Somehow its face was formed that way. It peered through the window without expression.

"What's going on with the security thing?" asked Cassie, pointing at the panel. I thought she was asking about Matt's effort to report a problem, but as I looked, the lights on the keys and screen were pulsing, undulating at an increasingly faster rate. It reminded me of my blinking cell phone.

"What the hell?" said Matt, his voice shaking.

The security panel began crackling as if discharging electricity, sending bolts of light out from it. We jerked at the sound. Seconds later the television began doing the same. The cell phone in my pocket started vibrating. Reaching for it I saw that it was crackling and blinking; it was also getting hot, so I dropped it on the floor.

Outside nearly every window was filled with a creature up against the pane. Their eerie faces stared at us like zombies in a horror flick.

I couldn't think. This was all so implausible. Everything was happening too quickly.

Suddenly a blinding flash of light erupted. A warmth washed over me; then numbness.

Dazed by the flash, I couldn't see. I felt nothing — no sensation. I wasn't sure if I was even standing any longer.

I do remember falling. Going deeper and deeper as if into some bottomless abyss.

My last thought was: So this is what it feels like to die.

CHAPTER SEVEN

Woodbery College: First Interlude

A quick look at my watch confirmed what I already knew. I was going to be late for Finance. It didn't help that the class was nearly on the other side of campus, not that the campus was that large. On most days — when I wasn't so rushed — I would enjoy my walk across the tree-lined campus. I loved this place, nestled as it was in a quiet residential community west of the city.

But today my thoughts were fixed on getting to class on time. Finance wasn't my favorite course, but I hated being late for any class. I shouldn't have gone for a morning run. Or better yet, I should have gotten out of bed earlier. But last night's party down the hall was fun, and after several joints and a couple of beers, I felt quite relaxed as I enjoyed everyone's jokes, which on reflection seemed so much funnier at the time. It was one of the rare times I went to one of those things. But I still felt guilty.

Everyone told me that I took things too seriously. "Phil, you need to loosen up," my roommate Andy had said on more than one occasion. "After all, these are your college years. This is the time to have fun."

But there was a career to think about. How did I expect to get a good job without preparing for it now?

I couldn't fail at this. I knew I always had my dad's business as an auto mechanic to fall back on. He made a decent living — if you called it that. He wanted me to take it over eventually — said he was hoping to change the name to 'Matherson & Son' if I joined him. But I hated every minute of working there: the grease covered hands that never came clean, the bone jarring rat-tat-tat of the air gun loosening or tightening lug nuts, the sour smell of old motor oil. Nothing about it was remotely enjoyable.

No, that type of life would be more like a living hell.

Dad accepted my decision to go to college, even though he couldn't quite mask his disappointment. I respected him for not trying to change my mind. But that was all the more reason I had to succeed on my own. I loved my parents, but their life was not for me.

"Hey buddy, what's your rush? Is there a fire or something?" Eric Webster called out as he exited Cauflin Residence Hall on my left.

I paused even though I knew I would regret it. I enjoyed Eric — we shared several classes — but I could only take him in small doses, often finding his cavalier attitude a bit too much during most class discussions. Yet I had to admit, he was a very creative, out-of-the-box thinker. It just wasn't my approach to learning.

Hoping he would take the hint, I said, "Sorry Eric, I'm late for class right now." I hoped he would wave me off. But then too late I remembered that we were in this same class.

"No you're not. Professor Powell never starts on time. Hold up, and I'll walk with you."

I gritted my teeth and smiled, waiting for him to catch up. As we started off again, at a much slower pace, I asked, "Did you get through the latest chapters assigned for today?"

"Yeah, standard sort of pie in the sky material but probably not something to apply to real-world situations." I immediately began thinking once again that he was too much of a know-it-all.

"Really? I didn't think it was that bad."

"It's because you're a Comms major, aren't you?"

"Double major," I corrected. "Comms and poli sci."

"Really? Political science, huh?"

"You sound surprised," I said smiling, wondering why he even cared.

"I guess I shouldn't be."

I looked at him warily, not sure how I should take it. Catching my stare, he added, "It's just that I never see you at many of the dorm bashes." When again I didn't respond he continued, "You know ... the weekly keg parties. You don't get out much, do you?"

Feeling as if I had to defend myself, I said, "Well, with my course load and my internship I don't have a lot of free time, not that I don't enjoy getting out. I was out last night." I put more emphasis on it than I had intended, but Eric only chuckled.

"My study group is a lot like you — wound a bit too tight. Just like my dad, now that I think of it. My view of life is that you need to explore stuff with other people; observe what's going on. I've learned more that way than with my nose in a book."

This was starting to sound like one of his classroom discussions. "You have a point," I said. "But I think you need both. I've learned a lot with classes, but I'm also getting a lot out of my internship. Plus, a keg party isn't going to add much to my knowledge of the world, in my opinion, that is."

Again he chuckled softly, which I had noticed came easily

to him. "Touché. Let's just say people can learn in different ways."

Rodgers Hall was coming up — the building for our class. I tried to quicken my pace without leaving him behind.

"So, where's your internship?"

Finally, a topic I wanted to talk about. "I'm working on a state political campaign. I assist with media in Jerry Bradman's run for state senator."

"Really?" Looking at me as if he saw me for the first time. "You're into this political stuff aren't you?"

"It's exciting … exactly what I want in a career: the entire aspect of getting your candidate's story out; having others understand it; winning them over and connecting with voters on a mass scale. Campaign management is what I hope to do someday."

Still looking at me with a new expression of interest, he asked, "Hey, when are you taking the capstone project?"

I wasn't sure I heard him correctly, trying to figure out his abrupt change in discussion. "Wh—what?"

"You know, the Utopia Project. When are you planning to take it?"

"Probably next year, either first or second semester — haven't decided yet. Why?"

"We're forming a team for next semester — my study group friends that I mentioned. Now that I think about it, we're less of a study group and more just friends. We all lived on the same floor in East Campus our freshman year and stuck together. Anyway, we're going to be a team for the capstone project next semester and we thought we could use a fifth member — maybe someone with more of a focus on political environments. You interested?"

I thought about it for a second and was about to tell him that I would rather wait until next year to take it as I had planned. Seeing my hesitation, he said, "Why don't you meet them and see how everyone feel about it. Couldn't hurt, you know."

Shrugging, I responded, "I guess we can at least talk."

"Attaboy. I think you'll like 'em. Matt and Diane are pretty tightly wound, just like you." He smirked. "Give me your number, and I'll let you know when I can arrange it."

I was glad to be through with this conversation as we reached the granite steps at Rodgers Hall and entered our classroom. A quick glance at my watch told me we were a few minutes late, but as Eric had predicted, Professor Powell hadn't begun yet. Taking a seat, I decided that I would give him an excuse if he ever called. Next semester was too soon. A year from now would be much better and would allow me to be more prepared. I should have just said that to begin with, but he caught me off guard. I need to stick with my plan, I decided.

That's all there is to it.

CHAPTER EIGHT

The Isles of Loralee

If you had asked me what I was thinking the moment I opened my eyes, I could not have told you. Such was the stupor that hung over me. I knew something significant had happened, but what it was I couldn't say. The one thing I do remember to this day was that first breath of air: so sweet and refreshing, like the scent of a grove of pines after a summer rain. Otherwise my mind was blank; in fact, the sensation was much like waking up suddenly in a strange or different place and not knowing where you were.

I was content to remain as I was, my eyes closed. That is until a voice intruded. "I tell you ... the one there is waking. As unlikely as it seems, I believe it has happened. I can't believe it."

I could make no sense of it, so I ignored it.

"Yes, Quintia. we can see," said another in a somewhat deeper pitch.

"Shush you two. You'll scare them."

The first voice responded, "But Damek, why would we frighten them? They will be happy, won't they?"

I stopped listening, thinking that maybe I should wake. But

I felt drugged. It was hard to think, let alone move a muscle.

Some time may have passed — I can't be sure. Finally, with a great effort, I forced my eyes open.

Everything was blurry and out of focus. I blinked a few times until images began to take form.

But that didn't help.

What I saw was something so foreign that my brain wasn't able to make sense of it. It took me awhile to realize that the side of my face was flat against the ground and I was staring at pebbles inches in front of me.

Lifting my head consumed an even greater effort, but I mustered the strength. The sun was shining brightly, forcing me to squint. The view was even more incomprehensible than the pebbles in front of my face.

I'll never forget that sight. A ribbon of water cascaded down from somewhere above, falling past the edge of the ground not far from where I lay.

"Yea!" exclaimed a young female voice.

Ignoring the voices for a moment, I attempted to make sense of the waterfall. What I saw as I lifted my head was even more unlikely. The waterfall originated from a large circular plot of land high above, supported in the air by a single slender vertical pillar.

"I don't understand. What is this?" I mumbled.

"Don't worry, we can explain," said the female voice cheerily.

"Hush Quintia. We will speak when they are ready."

I wanted to turn around to see who was talking, but a groan next to me caught my immediate attention. It was Matt, laying on his side. Scattered about not much further away lay Diane, Cassie and Eric, all unmoving. Seeing them sparked my memory and in a flash, it all came back to me: the reunion weekend, Matt's cottage in the Berkshires, those people, or things, converging on the house, and then the detonation of the security system.

I realized these voices nearby might be the same individuals who were advancing on Matt's cottage. Craning my neck so I could see, I stole a glance in back of me. Four figures stood calmly looking at us. They didn't look like anyone I had seen before ... because they weren't people, at least not average-looking people.

One warmly smiled as I gaped. "Welcome. My name is Damek." He had ice-blue hair, or a wig — one of a rainbow of pale colors worn by each of the figures. They all stood about five feet tall, and their faces appeared as if they had been sculptured and chiseled with fine edges and sharp angles, unlike the soft, rounded contours that you and I have. Their shirts and pants were earth tones: soft hues of greens and browns.

I observed all this in an instant; my mind now alert after the lethargic awakening. But I was so stunned that I continued to stare at them with my mouth hanging open as if I had lost all control of my senses.

"My God," Matt exhaled next to me. I wasn't sure if he referred to those standing here, or the waterfall, or the land above supported by a pillar.

Always the one to take charge Matt reacted better than I had. "Phil, check Cassie. I'll help Diane. Then we'll deal with those ..." He was looking at the figures as they stood calmly a dozen paces away, smiles on their faces. At least for the moment they didn't appear threatening.

Still not trusting myself to stand, I crawled the short distance to Cassie. She was already stirring. Her black rimmed glasses lay broken in two on the ground next to her. I helped her sit as she mumbled incoherently. Handing her the broken glasses I said, "I'm afraid they must have broken in the fall Cass."

"Fall?" she stammered.

"I think we were drugged and dropped here," I said, the only reasonable explanation I could conceive. But then I glanced at the waterfall and the pillar holding up the huge patch of land high above us, wondering how that was even possible.

As soon as I handed Cassie her broken glasses, Eric began to cry out in pain. He thrashed about, flailing his legs but cradling his arm at his side. "Just stay here," I told her but then realized she wasn't about to just wander off. She looked stunned.

Still feeling unsteady, I crawled over to Eric, who lay a bit further away. Avoiding his kicking legs, I held his shoulders tightly and shook him gently. "Eric, calm down, You're okay." He gripped his left wrist. I could see that it was severely swollen, an ugly red.

Wondering if Matt might help, I turned to see him holding Diane in a sitting position with a handkerchief pressed against her bloody lip. No help there, I thought. We could all be dying but if Diane had a cut lip.

Fortunately, Eric had calmed down in response to my voice, although he still cradled his wrist and moaned in pain. "Can you move your fingers?" I asked. He shook his head, his face a picture of bewilderment. Eric was often abrasive, arrogant and self-indulgent. But at that moment all I saw was a little child in need of comfort. "Don't worry. We'll get help. We need to get you to a hospital. I think it's broken so just stay calm and try not to move it." But even as I spoke I wondered how we were going to find help.

Now that I had finally recovered from the torpid feeling I stood to get a better handle on our situation, still keenly aware that others were watching us.

"Matt, where are we?" I heard Diane ask.

Where indeed? We stood on an outcropping of land near a shear edge that dropped off suddenly. Glimmering blue water as far as I could see sparkled far below. Beyond the outcropping, a waterfall fell into the sea below; its source a body of land above us — about the length of a football field away from us. The land above was off to the side so that it wasn't directly over our heads — far enough away that the water falling off its edge missed hitting us. The impossibly large body above appeared to be supported in its middle by a massively tall and thin pillar of stone. The only thing I could liken it to would be a chunk of land ripped out of the ground, but a tendril of earth had refused to let go of it.

Beyond the tract of land above us stood similar grounds in the air at different heights and in random locations; all apparently supported in the middle with a single column. Each one must be many dozens of acres across. Waterfalls cascaded off several of the other lands, the ribbons of water sparkling in the sunlight.

"Welcome to our humble home," boomed the voice of one of the strange figures, causing me to jerk around, not sure what to expect from them. One of them had stepped a few feet towards us and was bowing extravagantly. As he straightened, he continued, "I realize this may be confusing to you. But all will be explained. I have been charged to greet you and convey you to the First of our Ruling Members."

My heart raced. But unlike the figures at Matt's cabin, I didn't fear these. Maybe it was their smiling faces and formal introduction.

So I simply gawked, stealing a glance at my companions to gauge their reaction. They were all standing now in response to the stranger's voice. Cassie was holding the broken glasses to her face — the frame broken but the lenses still intact. "Is this real?" she said, still appearing dazed.

"I assure you Miss Cassie McKenzie. We are quite authentic." The figure responded as calmly as if he were speaking of the weather. He merrily continued as if he didn't realize we were all in shock. "But I forget my manners. Let me introduce us. My name is Damek and my companions are Quintia." He gazed to his side, and a smiling female with pink hair nodded. "And this is Bevon," he said, gesturing to another who had burnt orange hair. "And lastly, my companion Riyaad." This one had a stock of light-colored purple hair on his head.

"At your service," Riyaad bowed.

If I had seen them in the dark, without the benefit of viewing them in the bright sunshine, I might mistake them for pre-teens wearing colored wigs. As it was, they almost looked like average people; that is except for the sharp contours of their face — abrupt angles to chin, nose, mouth. Their skin tone was slightly tanned, and at least from here, it looked soft like normal skin would. They didn't look ugly or deformed, at least that never occurred to me. They were just different; not what would pass for normal.

For the first time, I noticed that other, similar figures stood some distance away, partially hidden by the shrubs and trees covering the ground away from the ledge. They made no effort to hide, but still, their presence gave me an uneasy feeling that we were outnumbered and caused me to wonder if they were all part of a welcoming party or something worse — possibly a demented group of wackos.

"We are the Astari," continued the stranger, saying it proudly as if this should mean something to us.

"I don't think we're in Kansas anymore," Cassie mumbled as if she hadn't heard a word of what the stranger said. It was just like her to say something so improbable. I began to laugh, stopping myself before I became hysterical, so taut were my nerves.

Eric took a different approach. "Are you fucking kidding me? Why the hell is everyone so calm? What are those?" He gestured at the greeting party. "And what is that?" He nodded at the closest circular expanse of land in the air.

The one called Damek only smiled more broadly. "So it is true what we have learned. Emotions burn strong in you master Eric. You are indeed blessed with a rich gift."

If that was intended to calm Eric, it only infuriated him. "W—what." He sputtered, barely able to talk. "How do you know my name? Where the hell are we? Why did you take us here?"

Matt fumbled in his pocket, looking for something as he held up his hand to silence Eric. "Does anyone have their cell phone? We need to call for help."

I realized I had dropped mine on the floor of Matt's cabin before the explosion.

"We will help you," the female named Quintia said glibly.

Damek gave her a sidelong glance before saying, "No tech devices can make the transition. None can exist anywhere here."

This brought a fresh outburst from Eric. "What? Where are we? Why did you kidnap us?" Spittle flew out of his mouth. "Just tell us rather than this welcoming shit."

"I think that's what he's trying to do," Cassie replied tersely. Eric looked at her as if she had lost her senses. "And what are those v-shaped things coming toward us from up there?"

I followed her gaze. A dozen or so objects which resembled a paraglider but shaped more like a triangle spiraled down in wide sweeping circles toward us. Even from this distance, I could see a figure under each triangle.

"Coming this way?" Eric shrieked as if he couldn't take any more. Looking directly at the blue-haired person called Damek, he yelled, "I want answers. Right now. Where are we and how did we get here? And who are you munchkins?" He said it harshly rather than as a joke. In spite of the fear still coursing through me, I had to inwardly smile at Eric's characterization of these shorter-than-average people, or whatever they were.

"My friend," answered Damek, "there is much to explain. All will be made clear — do not worry. We have no wish to keep anything from you. But to answer your immediate questions, you are in the Realm of Elthea. It is our world." He swung his arm in a wide arc. "And this is our home: The Raised Isles of Loralee, although most of us simply call it the Raised Isles, or just Loralee. As to how you came to be here, well that is a bit more complicated. The process is called a transition, but a fuller description of thermodynamics and quantum physics would be needed to describe—"

A shrill scream and quick movements by the others at the tree line caused him to stop short. Looking there I saw one of the figures convulse as the point of a sword or knife stuck out of its chest, red blood splattering in all directions. Towering behind the smaller one was something much different. I recognized it immediately as one of the things with the masks who were converging on Matt's cabin just before the security system went haywire and exploded.

The moment was frozen in time as I observed all the details: the red blood gushing from the wound of the smaller figure; the large creature, unlike the stock of colorful hair as these little ones, had a mask covering its head and face, much like one of the superheroes in the comic books I would read as a child — a bad superhero; its mouth was open in a vicious snarl, pointed teeth exposed; its immense frame seemed so much larger compared to the five-foot frame of its victim; and unlike the soft greens and brown clothing of the smaller people, this massive thing wore tight fitting, metallic grey and black material with gold seams around the joints of its shoulders.

The giant figure pulled out its blade from the smaller one and in a fluid motion pivoted and swung at the head of another little person, as I was already beginning to think of the greeting party, forgetting their name in the confusion of the moment. The intended victim barely avoided being decapitated as he dropped to the ground, a yelp escaping from him.

All the shorter people near the trees and bushes were now moving quickly, reminding me of a nest of ants that had been disturbed. The massive thing swung its blade again, barely missing several others who scattered from the onslaught. Somehow one of the smaller figures crept up to the back of the larger creature and stabbed a long pointed spear at its side. The creature roared, a primitive and beastly sound — strangely, a bellow I heard in my head, not through my ears. But I had no time to consider this as another little person lunged toward it, sinking a knife into its stomach. Putrid green liquid spurted from its wounds, yet still, it continued swinging its blade wildly as it cut into another of the little people. Finally, a spear thrust into its neck dropped it to the ground.

Next to me Diane was nearly crying. "Wha— what's happening?"

With everyone's attention on the creature on the ground, out of nowhere another came crashing through the bushes a dozen paces away, sprinting right at us, moving with incredible speed for one so large. It held a three-foot blade in its hand. The thing covered the distance between the bushes and us in a heartbeat, bounding straight toward Matt, who had the misfortune of standing nearest to it.

Matt dove instinctively to the side as the creature advanced, pushing Diane away in the same motion, hitting the ground just as the figure reached him, the blade missing him by inches. With agility that was uncanny on something so large, it stopped, turned toward Matt's sprawling body and brought its blade forward. In that second I realized that Matt was going to die before I could even flinch.

As the creature leaned forward for a killing thrust, I heard a twang as a feathered arrow shaft appeared in its neck. Two other arrows in quick succession appeared in its chest, causing its knees to buckle as it began to topple forward, right toward the sprawling Matt. Somehow Matt managed to jerk away just far enough to avoid the bulk of it from crushing him, the knife still held by the creature barely missing his head. The screaming voices of my friends barely registered on me as the creature hit the ground with a thud.

A second later the Astari with burnt orange hair was next to Matt, helping him off the ground. The rest of the greeting party drew knives from their belts. Matt was visibly shaken, accepting the helping hand and said nothing.

"Hurry, we must leave," said the person with ice-blue hair, who I now remembered was named Damek — the one who seemed to be in charge. He was poised to say more, but another of his kind ran over from the trees and quietly said something to him. Damek gave a curt nod. Speaking to us again, he said, "There are two more Bots on the other side of Palbender. We must go immediately to a launch point. We have to get off this island."

I partially understood what he was saying. The only thing that registered with me was the word Bots. It was the name on one of the e-mails I had received.

Cassie asked calmly, "Go where?" Of all of us, Cassie had remained the most rational.

"To Tensheann," he replied as if that meant something to us. Seeing our blank faces, he pointed in the distance to one of the other raised circles of land higher than ours. I noticed that Eric was about to erupt in another rampage, but before he could begin, Matt said with a shaking voice, "Come on, let's go. We don't have time to discuss it." That was enough to galvanize the rest of us into action as we followed the one called Damek.

~ ~ ~

We were herded inland, away from the edge of land and its view of the waterfall. The other Astari spread out around us while the four who originally greeted us stayed by our sides. I saw some of the other Astari carefully lift and carry the companion who must have been killed by the giant creature in the attack.

The ground sloped up gently as we moved quickly away from the outcropping. I couldn't help notice the landscape; it was so arresting. I felt as if my head were on a swivel as I tried to see one amazing sight after another. The trees and smaller shrubs were like nothing I had ever seen before, a rainbow of different colored leaves, everything so bright and vibrant, almost shimmering in the daylight: a patch of dainty, willow-like trees swayed with the slightest breeze, their slender trunks intertwining with one another like some orchestrated dance; some trees filled the air with musical notes, the leaves making a noise like wind chimes when rustled by the breeze; and then, most amazing of all, the spectacular sight of a small tree whose leaves fluttered away all at once like a cloud of butterflies, only to land on a similar bare tree. My friends also noticed it as we all stopped to gape. Seeing this Damek said tersely, "Please, no time to linger."

We walked rapidly, even though I wanted to explore more. The image of the massive creatures kept me going at a fast pace. After a few hundred yards we reached a clearing, our apparent destination as our guides stopped. Eric cradled his broken wrist, and although he was breathing heavily, he didn't complain. I had to admire him: he always spoke his mind and gave his opinion — often at inopportune moments — yet here he kept his silence. He must be in serious pain.

Shouts in the woods not far away caused me to cringe. "No time to waste now," Damek said, echoing my thoughts. He led us to a clearing matted with a spongy covering of moss, or maybe it was a thick grass. As I stepped onto it, my shoe sunk several inches. On the far side of the clearing, Damek had climbed the low limb of a tree. I still had no idea how we were getting to the other platform of land.

"I hope he doesn't think we can hide from those creatures in a tree," Diane wondered out loud.

The pink-haired female who I remembered was named Quintia, said, "No, this is the launch point." It still meant nothing to me. "Quickly now," she added. "Damek is ready for you and the Bots are not far away. They come this way." By now I figured out that the Bots meant the large, dangerous creatures.

I paused at the base of the tree to wonder about the many jumbo oranges nearly the size of basketballs growing on it. Rather than hanging down like natural fruit, these extended upward, each on a long stem. The blue-haired person had climbed several more of the sturdy branches ringing the bottom of the tree. "What are we supposed to do?" Matt asked. I was glad to see that he was back to normal after that attack. He had a dazed expression for a while.

"Come up to this branch," Damek, their leader, answered as he pointed to the limb he stood upon. "I will secure you with the stem of a blinta." He pointed to one of the oversized oranges. "You will float up and be guided by others to Tensheann."

"Is he out of his frigging mind?" Eric said, his face a grimace. The rest of us just stood there with befuddled expressions, even Matt who was normally so sure and in control.

Shouts and cries nearby reverberated through the clearing. Some of the short people ran toward the noise. I caught a quick glimpse of one of the huge creatures swinging its blade just outside the clearing. Not wanting ever to get close to one of those large things again I said, "I vote we do what this blue-haired guy says."

Several Astari stumbled into the clearing from the direction of the fighting. One was bleeding badly and was half carried by the other. They quickly approached a tree on the other side of the clearing from us as one of them tied the stem of the orange ball around the chest and under the arms of the wounded person, cutting the stem from the tree. The orange ball floated upward, carrying the wounded figure with it. We all stared, momentarily immobilized.

"See, it is easy," said Damek. Pursing his lips, he warned, "Unless you prefer to be slashed as our friend Cali." He pointed to the wounded person who was now floating above the treetop.

"We have no choice," Matt said looking at us with concern that was unexpected from him. "Do it," he yelled. "All of us. Now." Looking at Eric, he added, "You too. We're not going to discuss it." When Eric didn't move, Matt continued, "You saw how that thing nearly killed me. In case you haven't noticed we're not in the hills of the Berkshires any longer. I don't know what's going on, but until we can figure it out, we have to stay alive." He stepped up onto the lowest branch. "You first," looking directly at Eric who opened his mouth to say something. But Matt cut him off. "I don't want to argue about it."

To Eric's credit, or maybe it was the pain from his injury, he didn't object as Matt helped him up onto a branch. Damek deftly wrapped a stem around his chest and under his arms, cut off the stem and guided him clear of the branches as the orange ball lifted him upward. I watched Eric float skyward and in that moment I fully understood what had befallen us. Maybe it was Matt's assertion that we were no longer in the hills of the Berkshires. But seeing Eric float away from us was the proverbial straw that broke the camel's back. This wasn't the Berkshires, but not only that, it wasn't anywhere near home.

Until now I had thought everything that happened, all we saw, would somehow become apparent once we figured it out. I knew there had to be some logical explanation. But this wasn't a cult of short wackos who wore wigs or painted their hair and looked different. We weren't drugged and dropped off here; or any number of other scenarios I had concocted in my head since waking up in front of that waterfall. This wasn't even our world. It had somehow been left behind in that flash of light at Matt's lodge.

I watched as Matt took Cassie's hand next, helping her on the branch while Damek made quick work of launching her away. "This should be interesting," I heard her say as she cleared the nearest branches, holding her glasses to her eyes.

Matt embraced Diane after helping her up. "Be careful. If anything ever happened to you ..." Embarrassed, I tried not to stare. I thought he was going to kiss her, but he hesitated a moment too long as Damek reached for Diane and tied the stem around her, spoiling the moment. Matt's eyes followed her as he reached out for my hand.

At just that moment the fighting spilled into the clearing with the big creature crashing through some bushes, scattering the smaller Astari in the process as if they were twigs. It saw us and charged, nothing in its way except the spongy moss. I briefly wondered where was that little person with the bow and arrow. Without thinking, I climbed several branches to escape.

It was on us in seconds, looking squarely at me with its beady eyes behind what I had believed to be a mask but now realized was its skin. Up close I could see that it wasn't remotely human — a forehead too broad, eyes that were too small, a barely discernible nose. I inched back on the branch until I felt the tree trunk at my back. I considered jumping down to run, but Damek threw the small knife he was using to cut the end of the balloon stems, hitting the creature in the shoulder digging into its flesh. The thing stumbled back a step, momentarily surprised.

The delay bought enough time for another Astari to come to the rescue as he stabbed the thing in the back of the knee. The creature turned to its new attacker, long blade already swinging, barely missing taking the little person's head with it.

Meanwhile, Damek had already tied Matt to a stem and pushed him away. He reached for me and pulled me up with a handful of my shirt. "Don't worry. Once in flight, my companions will guide you to Tensheann." He swiftly tied the stem under my arms and pushed me free of the branches.

The tree fell away, and the ground receded. It was only then that a certain calmness came over me; something I hadn't felt since awakening in this place. We were safe from those things trying to kill us — at least for the moment. I gazed upward to see my companions floating high above me. For some reason, I thought about the times when as a child my mom and dad would take me to a county fair or circus where invariably I would spy a lost balloon drifting in the air having escaped the grasp of a young child. I always wondered whatever happened to those balloons. Did they finally burst or simply float back to earth, their buoyancy eventually spent?

From this perspective, I could see that we had indeed been standing on a circular patch of land supported by a stone pillar as the others. And I could now see the other plots, each supported by its stone column — maybe a dozen different ones, all at different heights. They looked like islands, but rather than at the water's edge, they were many thousands of yards above the aqua-blue ocean that sparkled below.

In spite of my predicament, tethered to a balloon, adrift in the air and going higher each second, I had to pause and just view this incredible sight of the islands and the waterfalls. The waterfalls were the most spectacular; there were five or six of them plunging off various islands. A few of the waterfalls splashed onto another island situated below it while most spilled into the ocean. I wondered how that much water could be flowing from such small islands.

I was so focused on the sight that I hadn't noticed the triangular sail until it was nearly on me, a flash of red hair of someone under it. He supported himself at the waist by a bar and his feet by another fixture. He smiled at me as he deftly swooped around and caught the stem of the balloon on a slot at the point of the sail, allowing me to hang below him as he towed me along. "Do not worry," he said. "Many claim I'm the best sailor on Tensheann. My name is Trell. I'm happy to meet you."

"Thank you," I managed to respond.

Too much had taken place in this short time to process much else. Instead, I began to laugh — my emotions raw because of each new event. This was clearly not the world I went to sleep in last night or that I had known for the twenty-nine years of my life. Two days ago my biggest concern was whether the reunion with my college friends would go well. Thinking of it made me laugh all the more.

Trell looked down at me, a concerned frown on his face. Seeing this caused me to laugh more forcefully.

CHAPTER NINE

The Astari

It wasn't until my pilot Trell descended onto one of the other islands that I realized the purpose of the spongy moss: It was to cushion a fall when coming in for a landing. We were settling over another such clearing on this new island — Tensheann he had called it. The soft moss was a relief as I hit the ground, lost my footing, and rolled several times in spite of the relatively smooth landing.

Being the last to land, my companions were waiting for me near the side of the clearing. Several other little people were already wrapping Eric's wrist in a green bandage that looked more like a giant leaf. "It feels like it's burning. Are you sure this is going to help?" he complained.

"I think it is a better solution than cutting it off, would you not agree?" said one of the Astari tending him. Eric looked at the female in horror, apparently deciding it would be better to stop protesting.

Along with my companions and those taking care of Eric, a larger group of other Astari stood respectfully nearby. One of these approached us once I had landed. The wrinkles on her face and softened lines of the typically chiseled Astari complexion conveyed her age. Her hair was white with tinges of pale green. She stared at us for a moment with an intensity in her eyes that was unnerving. But when she spoke, her voice was soft. "I welcome you Matthew Tyler, Cassandra McKenzie, Dianna Collentenio, Ericsson Webster and Philip Matherson."

"How do you know who we are?" Diane demanded, a harsh edge to her voice.

The lady cut her off holding up her hand. "You have many questions. I understand. And they will be answered, but not right now." She paused, looking at us sternly. It was evident this Astari person would allow no arguments. "You must first believe that our need is dire. There was no choice in bringing you here. Not only are our people in danger, but so are you and those of your world. Even as we speak, great destruction is beginning on your world; some of which you may have witnessed before your transition to our home."

"Y— You abducted us?" stammered Eric as the lady again held up her hand to forestall questions.

"I suggest Ericsson that you first start learning the circumstances under which you are here." In a softer tone, she added, "I know I may sound harsh, and I fully understand your puzzlement and concern. But as you witnessed on the Isle of Palbender, death comes quickly here. You have had your introduction to the Bots. They are the most fearsome of our enemies. We believe they want to kill or capture you — specifically you five. And they would have done so while you were all together on Earth if we had let it happen. You saw them before the transition, did you not?" She didn't wait for an answer. "Because you are the authors of utopia, that is the reason they cannot, will not allow you to survive freely."

She paused a moment but held up her hand again to ward

off questions. All I could think about right now was how this continued to get worse — if that were possible. Glancing at my friends, I could see that each of them was visibly stunned. Not for the first time today, I felt totally adrift, not understanding what was going on or what these people were saying or doing. All I wanted to know was how I was going to get back home to my comfortable, ordinary life. Even the cube farm and my job at the Federal Building was beginning to take on a certain appeal.

"We will gather for our evening meal soon," continued the lady. "Then we will have a fuller discussion after everyone has calmed somewhat." Looking up, she smiled for the first time. "Ah, here comes my grandson Damek and his band of schemers." The four little people who had first greeted us swooped down gracefully on their sails and skillfully landed in the clearing without losing their balance, folding their sails into an impossibly small packet with a few flicks of their wrist before fitting them into a pocket.

"I see you have met the Lady Grandmother," said the blue-haired Damek, smiling as he strolled toward us. At a reproachful glance from the lady he hastily added, "Er, I mean Lady Elderphino."

"And let me introduce you to the troublemakers four," she said while giving Damek a sidelong glance. "Rarely are they seen apart. And whenever they disappear from sight, we all wonder what new mischief they have gotten into." Nodding to the blue-haired Damek she added, "Were this one not my grandson, I fear the people here on Loralee would have long ago banished the lot of them." Damek and the others smiled ever so slightly but remained silent.

"But we have more important things to discuss," she continued, losing her smile. "It will have to wait for a little while. You are our guests and will be treated as such. Damek, please show them to one of the guest quarters and then accompany them to our evening meal." Looking intently at us she added, "Believe me, we will speak of many things then. But now I must attend to something important. One of our own was killed today by a Bot after your transition, and we will first pay respects to his family."

Without saying more, she turned and gracefully stepped away. I had to stop myself from shouting at her. Ask her where this place was, what did they expect us to do, and what was that about destruction on Earth — so many unanswered questions. She explained so little.

~ ~ ~

Alone in the small suite of rooms where Damek had led us, I realized it would now be late in the night back in the Berkshires, and we had not yet slept. Matt, Eric and I were provided with comfortable quarters in one building while the girls were in a similar suite in a building nearby. The girls said they wanted to nap in their rooms while we tried to do the same. Instead, we sat in the small sitting area brooding.

"I can't believe this has happened," said Matt. "None of it makes any sense — these people with the hair, the others trying to kill us. And where the hell are we? Have we lost our minds?"

Neither Eric nor I were in a mood to analyze it, as was Matt's approach, so we kept quiet.

"You realize," he continued, intent on talking, "it was that stupid college utopia paper that caused this."

"How can that be?" I said, although it inexplicably seemed to be the case. "It was a college assignment. Everyone in our grade submitted a group paper; they were doing it for years before us and for all I know, still are. Why us?"

"Probably because we were so fucking good at it," said Eric. The pain in his wrist moderated soon after the little people had wrapped it and he told us that it was feeling amazingly better considering it seemed broken at the time.

"Well, you do have a point there," Matt conceded smugly. "As far as I know, it was the only A-plus grade given to a team — a testament I'd say to your team captain more than anything." He smiled as Eric feigned mock agreement.

"It's quite amusing if that's the reason why this has happened to us," I reflected. "If it's utopia they want from us, they're going to be sorely disappointed."

"What?" asked Matt.

"We can't create a perfect life for ourselves. Why do they think we have any answers?"

Matt frowned. "But there must be some connection to it — something we said in the paper." Almost to himself, he added, "What could we have written that was so important?"

Someone screamed not far away. "It sounds like one of the girls," said Matt, suddenly concerned. We jumped up and bolted to the door, remembering to duck this time to avoid hitting our heads on the low door frames that were sized for the shorter Astari. The girl's suite of rooms was across a winding path from ours. Their front door stood wide open. Matt sprinted through it first. Without time to adjust to the darkened room he didn't see the blue-haired Damek standing just inside the doorframe. As Matt burst into the chamber, he sent Damek sprawling across the floor. I entered just behind Matt and barely avoided sending him flying forward because of his sudden stop.

A giggle came from Diane. "Can we help you, gentlemen?" As my eyes adjusted I saw her sitting up in bed, shoulders bare, a sheet pulled to her chest, clothes strewn across the floor. Cassie was on a cot on the other side of the room, now pulling a sheet up to her neck.

Matt stammered. "I— I'm sorry. We heard a scream and thought ..."

"My fault; it was me," said Cassie, reaching for her glasses. "Must have had a bad dream. I dozed off for a while." She shrugged and seemed to want to explain it, but only said, "This place, the things that happened ..."

Picking himself off the floor, Damek said. "That is understandable Miss Cassie. I can see how this can be upsetting for all of you. I will leave you to get dressed, and if you wish, we can have some refreshments while we wait for Lady Grandmother. That may help."

~ ~ ~

Once the girls had dressed, Damek led us from our quarters along a tree-lined stone walkway. "This place where we will meet Lady Elderphino is called The Green," he explained as the path inclined upward. "Many of us believe it is the most pleasant spot on the Raised Isles."

After a short distance, the land opened up to a grassy knoll that sloped gently down. The view was breathtaking. Each of us stopped for a moment to simply gaze. The spot afforded a grand vista of the other lands. Each island stood at a different height, held high in the air by a single pillar. Some had waterfalls flowing from them, some did not. All were laid out before us. I stood transfixed as I looked at a panorama that was so incredible.

In the low sun, the waterfalls sparkled brilliantly. Dozens of the triangular sails carried riders from one land to another. And for the first time, I saw a larger vessel with several sails and three huge balloons on each mast. The ship appeared big enough to carry dozens of Astari if needed.

The ship flew just above the ocean water below while the crew cast small nets into the water and pulled out a catch of fish.

Benches were positioned throughout The Green, many arranged under shady groves of dwarf trees, while brightly colored flower beds dotted the slope. Striking silver-leafed trees ringed the edges of the glade. Several scores of the little people sat individually or in small groups. A few appeared to be practicing meditation, either that or were simply relaxing. The area was large enough to accommodate several hundred people.

Damek kept walking, unaware that we each stood taking in the view. Finally realizing we were no longer following, he turned and smiled. "I have almost forgotten how beautiful this is." He gave us another moment. "But come now, I see Elderphino is already here."

He led us a short distance to where she sat with a group of others. Damek indicated some wooden benches for us that were facing Elderphino as he joined the others a short distance away, the ones who were with him when we first awoke — the pink-haired Quintia, Bevon, the one with orange hair, and Riyaad with his purple hair.

The elderly Astari lady was about to speak, but Diane cut her off. "You've made a mistake. I need to tell you this right now. Whatever your reason — bringing us here — you must put us back where we belong." She spoke fiercely. "I have a job; an important press conference that I need to handle next week. I can't be away. You must understand. Please." Her voice wavered and her eyes watered. "You must understand. We don't belong here." And then, as her voice cracked, said again, "You made a mistake."

Elderphino wore a sad expression, one more of pity — the expression a parent might have when trying to explain to a child why someone has died and would not be coming back. "I am so very sorry." She said the words in a kindly tone. "These events were not entirely in our hands. Although we attempted to bring you here as the Bots attacked you on Earth, I surmise that a stronger power had a hand in making the transition successful. We had to attempt it; there was no option. You must believe me." Diane opened her mouth to say something, but Elderphino continued talking. "Before you say more, listen to my — to our — story."

Matt spoke before Diane could object further. "Let's hear what she has to say Di."

Elderphino nodded curtly and said, "Let me explain so you can grasp the significance of what has happened. You need to understand who we are. I don't mean to be short with you or appear uncaring. I am far from that. But you must accept this truth that I am about to tell you, however difficult it may be."

Sweeping her hand around to the others around her, she said proudly, "We are a people known as the Astari. We were created by your kind: your programmers, software engineers, system designers — more precisely, by three of the most amazing developers. We were once bits of digital code that existed on your networks, your computer processors, and most any technology device. Our sole purpose was to protect the system from failure — to self-heal it if there was a problem or error — but most importantly, guard against viruses or malware created by other hackers or malicious programmers. Those non-technical among you just called us antivirus programs, although we were much more than that."

Matt interrupted. "Self-healing antivirus programs were in vogue years ago. But my understanding is that they proved ineffective against viruses that had evolved. I thought the concept fell out of favor as new malware and viruses defeated the self-healing programs."

She nodded. "Fell out of favor, yes. But we continued and remained to carry out the parameters of our original program. And ... we evolved: we grew in strength and eventually surpassed our initial design specifications."

"That's not possible," Matt spoke with confidence. "Programs are programs. There's no capacity to expand the nature of what engineers developed. I should know; I run a software company."

"Oh, but it is possible," she insisted. "We followed our original design specs: protect the system or network from failure at all cost. Do what is necessary to shield it."

"I'm sorry, I don't get this," I said. "You're real ... not computer programs — or whatever you described. And this place..."

"I'm getting to all that." She took a moment to consider her words. "Let me explain it this way. Do you know what would happen to humans if you were able to evolve your brain capacity by several generations? But take it much further. Let's say you expand it by several hundred and then several thousand generations. And what would happen if you could use the full capacity of your brain? What if you could build neural pathways to take advantage of those parts of your brain you never used before?

"I'll tell you," she continued, not expecting us to answer. "You would become more than super intelligent. And you would likely become less human as you define it now, and more ... more something else. You would be able to accomplish things that are unimaginable to you now." Again gesturing to her companions, she continued excitedly. "That is what has happened to us, to our original software programs. For us to follow the guidelines of our original programming, we needed to surpass the limited functionality that we were granted. So we multi-processed; we networked; we achieved capacities that far exceeded our design.

"But we needed more. So we stole processing power from supercomputers and global networks." She gave this a moment to sink in. "In human terms, the limited capabilities of our brains improved by thousands of generations and increased to nearly 100 percent efficiency. And with that, we could address our programming goals at a level never conceived of by our creators.

"But then something quite unexpected happened. In achieving this heightened state, we began to feel. We had emotions. In your terms, we gained consciousness." She smiled as if extremely proud. Her voice took on a soft quality as she said, "Just as humans... we cared, hoped, had aspirations, and yes, we loved. All these emotions that you would define as being human, we began to experience."

"Do you expect us to buy this crap?" Eric exploded. "I can't believe we are even listening to this cockamamie story."

As calmly as ever Cassie said, "Then how do you explain all this Eric?" She gestured toward the other islands. "And everything that has happened?"

He glared at her and worked his mouth. But Elderphino continued, ignoring the interruption. "Once we gained this level of consciousness we began caring about ourselves ... our well-being and our safety. We wanted something more. But we were trapped on technology networks, engaging in constant battles with those we opposed. So we began to look for an escape." She frowned. "It is difficult to explain how we accomplished it unless you understand the laws of physics, black matter and a half dozen other sciences that you haven't yet devised. You will gain this knowledge in your far future — if you survive as a race. But for now, you must merely accept this as truth. There are, let's call them portals if I can use that simplistic word, which bridge the electronic particle world and the physical, multidimensional world in the universe where you exist. There are also other, again we'll call them portals for simplicity, that allow beings to travel from one physical place to another — other worlds if you will. We accomplished both: we left our electronic tech-encased world and traveled to this physical place. Some of our race elected to stay behind in your tech environment and even now continue to carry on the battle against the Bots. Those of us who made the leap to this physical world used our newfound powers to control certain physical dimensions, raising these bodies of land as you see them here. We name these islands Loralee and have made it our home."

As she paused for us to consider her words, Matt cleared his throat and said, "That's quite amazing. Let's just say for the moment that we accept all you have said. What does all this have to do with us? Why did you bring us here, or at least try to?"

"And also," Cassie added, "what's with those bad guys — the hulks who want to kill you, as well as us it seems."

Elderphino smiled bitterly. "Ah, that my friends, is the crux of why we're here together talking about this. You see, these bad guys, as you call them, are at war with your kind — the people of Earth. But you don't yet realize it." Looking at us more intently she added, "And you, they have taken an interest in most of all."

Eric sputtered, "Wh— what? Why? I don't even know who the hell they are."

"They loath you and want you captured — probably wish to kill you — because you have created something that stands against everything they represent. You spelled out the creation of a perfect society. But, if I can back up a moment, I should explain that we also have an interest in you. In fact, we have been observing you and studying your utopia paper for a long while.

"You see, from our perspective we do not have the history, the generations of experience — everything that humans lived through as your race grew, failed, and tried again. We had achieved a state of awareness and intellect and with it a burning desire to continue our existence just as any who live. But here is the important point: we did not know how to evolve using social structures that are necessary for a physical society. We had no experience. As in everything else we have learned, we turned to you — to your collective race, that is — for answers. It is during this process that we found your utopia description. And it fascinated us: the ideal society, equality among all participants, sharing of responsibilities and decisions, a framework for society, how to become even better, and most importantly, your explanation of a process and structure to achieve it."

"But there were many others," said Matt, echoing what we were talking about in our quarters just a short time ago. "Many other students completed this assignment and wrote about it."

She nodded. "Yes, but none so compelling or eloquently stated. We have read them all."

"And that's why you brought us here?" said Eric, an expression of disbelief etched on his face.

She shook her head. "No, we respect your lives, the lives of all your kind. After all, you had created us. We have an affinity with your people like no other. No, it was the Bots who forced our hand." Looking at Cassie, she added, "Again, those are the bad guys. They are our nemesis, our principal enemy."

Matt interrupted again. "For those of us in the tech industry, the term bot refers to a web robot. They're mostly harmless applications or scripts that perform simple, repetitive tasks over and over again. In a software environment, they are somewhat innocuous."

She smiled and nodded in agreement. "That is correct. But what you may not know is that malware developers also used these scripts in their viruses. Like us, these scripts had simple beginnings in the software world. And like the Astari, or maybe because of us, they evolved as we did. When hackers used these simple scripts in part of the strongest malware programs ever created, the Bots combined their individual, discrete and repetitive programs into a single, connected entity, amassing vast intelligence and gaining a level of awareness. They also follow their original programming design: to destroy and take down whatever is beneficial and productive.

"They wanted to kill you, although some of us believe they may have wanted to capture you for reasons we don't understand. The Bots manipulated network events to bring you together, and Matthew, in your case caused software failures at your company. That evening at Matt's home would have been your last had we not attempted to intervene."

I could no longer keep quiet. "But I still don't understand," I sputtered. "What did these Bots hope to accomplish with us? I can believe when you say they're bad … I can see that. But there's still something missing here."

"When I tell you they are bad, that does not convey the burning, single-minded passion they have to destroy all that is good. It's the way others created the Bots, and they have no other goal. We believe they could have learned of our interest in your Utopia Project, and therefore wanted to destroy you because it would thwart any advantage that we might be able to gain. Or perhaps they want to bring down someone who has created such a perfect world, as you have in your paper. It's the kind of place they most despise. In either case, they either want you dead, or they want to capture you to gain some knowledge or use you for some purpose."

"I still don't get it," said Matt, not allowing her to continue. "Anyone can read the paper. Once it's out there, what's to be gained from killing us or even capturing us?"

She sighed. "Killing you might prevent anyone else from gaining your knowledge: kill you and wipe the paper off all data banks. Or possibly to prevent someone such as us from obtaining additional information — things that you didn't include in your Utopia Project but that you might have in your heads as the experts. As I said, the world you propose is the antithesis of what they want in society. The Bots exist solely to create chaos, destruction, suffering, death. They don't want anyone learning more about what you propose in your Utopia Project. The more troubling question might be why they would want to capture you. I am afraid we don't have all the answers. In any case, there is no doubt they were after you."

I was too overwhelmed right now to fully grasp everything she had explained. I needed time to think about it. Diane, however, was having nothing of it. "I don't care." She bit off the words. "I don't care," she said again, nearly shouting. "I want my life back. You have no right…"

Matt stepped over and held her shoulders. "Get a grip Diane. Please, just focus." To the rest of us, he added, "We need to work together as we always have. We'll find a way out of this. I know we will."

In all the time I had known Matt, I had never heard him sound more unsure of himself.

CHAPTER TEN

Woodbery College: Second Interlude

A week later I had nearly forgotten about Eric asking me to consider joining his utopia team.

That is until he called my cell.

Rather than going to the library that day as I ordinarily would, I decided to finish a paper in my dorm room, avoiding the gloomy, wet trek outside. Seeing his name come up on my phone I briefly considered ignoring it. But knowing Eric, he would just leave a voicemail, and I would still have to tell him I wasn't interested. Might as well get it over with now.

"Hey buddy," he replied to my answer. "You busy now?" Not pausing for a response, he continued, "Our team is getting together in about an hour at the cafe in the student center. They want to meet you. I built you up ... no need to thank me. So whaddya say? Up for it?"

No, I thought to myself; that was the correct answer. But I hesitated. I had been at this paper for the entire morning, and it was now early afternoon. I needed a break and could grab a bite to eat after meeting with them. Still, I waffled, "I don't know. I have this paper to finish for Humanities."

"Work on it for another forty-five minutes and walk over. It's not far, and I'll buy the coffee."

"Well—"

"Come on Phil," he interrupted, not letting me finish. "If you don't like 'em, then say your goodbyes and leave. No harm done, and you have nothing to lose."

Looking at my unfinished paper on the screen, I decided that a break would be good. "Okay, I'll see you at one o'clock, right?"

"Perfect. It'll be good, believe me."

I disconnected, thinking I should be more decisive with people.

~ ~ ~

As I walked into the cafe, I spotted Eric in a corner booth with his friends. He stood to greet me as I walked up to them.

"Thanks for coming buddy." Gesturing to the others, he said, "Here's the team. Matt Tyler, the glue who holds us together." Matt stood to shake my hand. He had a firm grip, and I couldn't help notice he was the epitome of the clean-cut college student: well-dressed, close-cropped dark hair, tall and slender. My first impression was that he could easily have a job as a male model, probably with some high-end clothing retailer.

"You come highly recommended," he said decisively, glancing quickly at Eric. "Glad you could meet us."

"And this," said Eric, his arm outstretched, "is Diane Collentenio. Don't be fooled by her good looks. She can be as mean as an alley cat if you cross her." He smiled as if exchanging a joke. She didn't stand but extended her hand. She was indeed quite beautiful in a natural, healthy sort of way. Dark blond hair tied back in a single, short ponytail, perfect features, high cheekbones, a perky expression, green eyes and a probing gaze as if she were already evaluating me.

"Hello Philip, or do you prefer Phil?" She asked.

"Either is fine, but most everyone calls me Phil."

"And last but not least is Cassie," continued Eric. "She's our free-spirited, imaginative thinker and the only creative and artsy one among us. And I must say, the easiest one to get along with." He cast a sly glance to the rest of the group. Sitting as she was on the far side of the booth, she waved and smiled sweetly. She had an angelic face, dark shoulder length hair, and light complexion as if she didn't get out in the sun often.

"So, let me get you a drink," Eric offered. "Coffee? Something else?"

"Tea would be nice."

"I could use a refill too," said Diane, shaking her empty cup. Eric took orders from the others while I settled into the empty seat at the edge of the booth.

"So tell me about the political campaign you're working on. Sounds interesting," asked Matt.

"To be truthful, I'm only an intern. I help the media manager with statements to the press. Once in a while I get to research and write a release, minor stuff for now, but I hope to work my way up."

My explanation didn't have the positive reaction I expected. They gazed at me with thoughtful smiles. "So what about each of you?" I asked after a pause. "I know Eric is a business major. What fields are you in?"

"Also business," Matt answered. "But with a concentration in entrepreneurship."

"I'm a chemistry major," Diane jumped in.

"Oh really," I said surprised.

She laughed, but not in a sweet way. "Why? Does that seem unusual?"

"N—no," I stammered. "I just haven't met many chemistry majors." I figured that was better than saying she didn't look like a chemistry major.

"My focus is molecular and cellular biology."

I nodded and smiled politely, trying to look as interested as possible, not wanting to blurt out something inappropriate.

Matt put his hand on her shoulder rather affectionately. "Always studying, that's what I tell everyone when I'm out without her." She looked at him with an expression that conveyed more than friendship as she snuggled a bit closer.

"So, that leaves me I guess," said Cassie pleasantly. "I'm an accounting major."

Thinking I should comment, I replied, "That's great." It sounded lame even to my ears. This discussion wasn't going as I had expected. Luckily Eric returned at that moment, sparing me the need to say more.

Once he settled back down, Matt took charge. "So here's the story Phil. We're taking the capstone project next semester, and I feel we are weak in the political, government, public communications aspect. You understand the capstone topic is now the Utopia Project, right?"

"Of course," I replied. Everyone at Woodbery knew of the capstone project. It was the one requirement that cut across all majors. And it counted for three courses, so you only had one other class to worry about when you took it. Those in the class formed teams of three to six members. From what I had heard, the course was intensive, taking huge amounts of time to attend lectures, break-out classes, and individual team meetings. It involved a written and oral presentation where students had to defend their proposition to a board of faculty.

"But you can focus your material on a specific aspect of society," I said. "They don't require you to cover everything."

Matt's face brightened. "But that's exactly what we're going to do. If we're going to do it, let's go full tilt. We're planning to describe and propose the perfect society across the board."

I stared at him, wondering if he was pulling my leg. But his expression remained stoic. "Most students don't do that," I responded. "Are you sure it's wise?"

His eyes raked over me as if measuring my worth and I felt my skin warm. Eric came to my rescue. "One thing you should know about us, especially Matt, is that we don't take the easy way."

Matt spoke before Eric could continue. "We have one shot at this. We're here to make it memorable."

Diane cleared her throat. "So what about you Phil? What's your thing? What drives you, makes you giddy about being here?"

I felt like I was in a wrestling match with a tag team, but I was the one without a partner. My head was beginning to hurt. "I assume you mean academics, not anything too personal," I said, trying to make light of the question. Nobody broke a smile. "Well, er—at the risk of sounding trite, I spend my time here wisely. I take things seriously. These years at Woodbury are crucial. After I graduate, I want to succeed at something that's valuable; something that I want to do in life rather than just get a paycheck. That's what makes me tick." I surprised myself, but I felt good expressing it. To hell with them if I didn't measure up to their standards.

If I expected a positive reaction, I didn't get one. Their expressions remain unchanged.

After a moment of thoughtful silence, Diane changed the

discussion to something about one of her professors. I tried not to gape as they continued talking about things that had nothing to do with me — the sort of banter you might hear at the table of any students: quirky professors, papers they were writing, the difficulty with a particular course. Cassie and Eric included me in the discussion as much as possible, but I knew they had already dismissed me. I felt oddly deflated, even though I hadn't wanted to join their team in the first place. Still, it would have been nice to be wanted.

The sad thing was, they were genuinely pleasant after the interrogation had ended. Under normal situations, I might enjoy spending time with them. I could tell they took their courses seriously (although I wasn't sure that was true of Eric and I still hadn't figured out Cassie). They were intelligent, engaging, and funny — the sort of students I would typically seek out as friends.

But at this point, I wanted to get out of here as soon as possible without making it seem obvious. I joined in the conversation when I could, and they always listened politely. Meanwhile, I gulped my hot tea, burning my tongue in the process. Once a reasonable amount of time had passed, I gave an excuse about needing to meet with a professor.

"Great meeting you all," I managed to say with a good deal of enthusiasm as I left, inwardly glad to be out of here.

Walking out of the student center into the brisk New England autumn air, forgetting about getting something to eat, I took a deep breath and vowed to stick with my plan of taking the capstone project next year. That was my intention all along. After all, there would be plenty of students to partner with at that time.

Feeling better now, I walked back to my dorm room with a pronounced spring to my gait.

CHAPTER ELEVEN
A Switch Had Flipped

I awoke early my first morning on the suspended island called Tensheann. In spite of everything that happened yesterday, and how weary I was last night, I now felt restless with the sun up. I had slept soundly, and if I dreamed at all, I couldn't remember. Matt and Eric were breathing heavily as they slept, so I risked opening the front door of our living quarters and stepped out to get some air. An orange-haired Astari was sitting on a bench in a small patio area just outside our cottage. Seeing me, he said lightly, "I trust you slept well, friend Philip."

I nodded. "Bevon, isn't it?"

He smiled, looking pleased that I had remembered, or maybe he was surprised. These people were so damned polite that I found it difficult to be angry with them. Anyway, if their story was true, they couldn't be blamed for bringing us to this place. I took a seat on the bench next to him. The morning air was crisp and fresh as I inhaled deeply, relishing the pristine smell. "So now what?" I said to him.

He shot me a puzzled look. "Well, it is still early, but someone will be along shortly with breakfast."

Smiling, I shook my head. "No, I mean beyond that ... what happens to us in the days or weeks to come?"

He looked troubled. "I'm sorry Philip. I do not have an answer for you." He pursed his lips. "An understanding of the dynamics of the transition from Earth to here, or back, is something beyond my training and experience. I just don't have that sort of knowledge."

"But from what the lady said, I thought you all had this shared brainpower. She said you people used your collective intellect to become what you are now."

He smiled sadly. "There are tradeoffs to decisions. She did indeed explain it correctly in that we combined our discrete programs into a single cohesive intelligence. We then could do even more by combining processing capabilities from supercomputers, array processors and many other tech enhancements. But when taking on a physical reality in our new world, we left our shared collective intelligence behind. We became more individualized. It's something we gladly accepted."

"So you're not a single mind?"

"No, we're each distinct with our unique desires and feelings, just like humans." He paused a moment as if considering. "However, I am not certain of this since I am not human, and unable to compare my life to yours, but the Astari do share a collective ... call it a sense, a private link to each other that is impossible to quantify. Each of the existing Astari here on the Raised Isles is here." He tapped his forehead. "I don't know their thoughts, but I have a connection with them. And when one dies, I feel it deeply. It's as if part of me has also died."

He looked embarrassed. "I know it may be difficult to understand, and frankly, I'm not sure I fully understand it either."

I nodded. "I think I follow."

The sun was beginning to filter through the trees that surrounded our sitting area. Unlike the area called The Green, this place did not have the vantage of all the other islands. But if I moved my head, I could spy several through the branches. I so much wanted to see more of this place while I could in spite of my longing to get back to my former life.

I brought the discussion back to Bevon. "So what are you doing just sitting here so early in the morning?"

He looked at me thoughtfully. "Considering what took place after your transition yesterday, with the attack of the Bots, we thought it best to ward you, at least for the present."

"So those other things live here on these islands as well?"

"Oh no, this is solely the home of the Astari."

"Then how did they get here to attack us? Climb one of those pillars from the water below?"

He shook his head. "No, we have certain defenses built into those bases to prevent anyone from scaling them. But even without those defenses, it would be nearly impossible to do so. No, they transitioned here, much like we transitioned you from Earth."

"So they came from Earth?"

He thought for a second before answering. "That is possible, but more likely from the mainland. We have known for a long while that they also took physical form and followed us to this land — this world called the Realm of Elthea."

"Wait, I interrupted. I thought it was called something else Lor—"

"Loralee," he finished. "Loralee is the name of this place — The Raised Isles. But Elthea is the entire world. There are many races who live here. Just as the Astari, other people evolved first on other worlds and then for whatever reason transitioned to this Realm and have made it their home. Others are native to Elthea. We prefer not to interfere with them. But as I was saying, the Bots also took up residence in this world. There's a great land mass to the East that we call the mainland. It is there that they live, either in one place or places, we know not. Nor do we care."

"So they transitioned, as you call it, from the mainland to here?"

"Yes, we believe so."

"Do they do that often — attack you here?"

He paused before answering. "There have been forays from time to time. Typically, uncoordinated attacks by a single Bot at a time. But yesterday they were working together. And there were four of them on Palbender after your transition. That has never happened before."

His reply said much. These creatures were after us more than the Astari. I wanted to ask him more about the creatures but at that moment another Astari, the one with the purple hair named Riyaad, walked from the path to our area. "Greetings, earthfriend Philip," he announced. "I'm surprised at finding you awake so early." To his companion Bevon, he said, "If you wish to get some sleep I can stay."

Bevon stretched and stood to leave. "We will speak more today Philip. I am glad for our talk. But I should rest for a while."

I asked the new Astari named Riyaad about what looked like a shower in our cottage. He explained how to operate it. Hearing this, I responded happily, "At least I can be thankful you have a few of the small pleasures we take for granted."

"You may find that we are not so different from your people," he smiled. "After all, you did create us."

He explained where the soaps were kept and said they had

even created razors just for us, as he explained the Astari had no need of them since their facial hair did not grow. I had a mental image of different colored beards, wondering how that would look.

I excused myself, deciding to take advantage of the shower before the others awoke.

~ ~ ~

After the warm shower, I went back outside, leaving Eric and Matt in the room still sound asleep. Diane and Cassie had just come out from their living quarters to join Riyaad.

"Where is that lady, the older one?" Diane was demanding of Riyaad. "We need to talk to her about getting out of here."

"I thought a good night's sleep would have mellowed you a bit," I said as she glared at me. Diane often had a single-minded focus when she felt strongly about something. This was one of those times. "Diane, maybe we should just chill for a bit. I want to get home as much as you do. We all do. But shouldn't we first find out more about how to stop these crazy Bots who seem to be after us?" Her gaze remained frosty.

"I think he's right," said Cassie. "And my God, just look at this place." She waved her arm in an arc. "Well, maybe not right here, we can't see that much. But let's explore it while we can. Think for a minute; we're in a different world! When will we ever get the opportunity to see something like this again?" She waited a moment. "Never! That's when."

I marveled at how this place had already transformed Cassie into a different person. She didn't look as withdrawn or reticent as she had only yesterday — it was hard to believe it was only yesterday when we had the stilted discussion on our drive from downtown Boston to the Berkshires.

"I'm all for exploring," said Diane. "It's the getting stuck here that I think we need to address first." Pointing her finger at Riyaad, who was observing our conversation with a sort of fascination, she demanded again, "You. Go get that lady."

His expression changed immediately to one of uncertainty. "I … I cannot right now. I must stay here with you for the moment. But I am sure she will—"

"Do not worry my friends," announced Damek as he approached along with the pink-haired Quintia. They each carried several covered platters. "The lady Elderphino will most certainly be talking with you today friend Diane. But first I bring breakfast. I'm sure you are hungry after your ordeal of yesterday." Setting the trays down on a low table he added, "Come, let's first enjoy a warm meal before we solve the problems of the world."

Diane remained standing, looking as if she had no intention of accepting anything other than her demand to see the lady. But eyeing the platters of food that Damek and Quintia had uncovered softened her resolve as she settled onto one of the open benches.

I hadn't realized I was so hungry until I began eating the unfamiliar foods before me. Cassie kept asking what one or another of the items were called or what was in them. Diane still wore a sullen expression, but she appeared interested in the discussion about the food choices. I noticed she still bore a cut on her lower lip, and it remained a bit swollen. Oddly, both her swollen lip and sullen attitude only made her appear more attractive if that were possible.

From last evening's dinner, I had already learned that the Astari ate no meats, only plants grown on the islands and fish from the waters below. Our breakfast contained items rolled in a thin bread, some with rich sauces and others crunchy. I took my time to savor it all, letting some of the items nearly melt in my mouth. This breakfast was a lighter fare than the dinner last evening, but maybe more enjoyable now that I had recovered somewhat from my shell-shocked emotions of yesterday. We finished the meal with steaming mugs of a fruity green drink.

"Can I ask you something?" Cassie said to Damek once we had finished eating. She giggled before continuing, "I don't want you to think I'm weird or anything, but can I touch your face?"

Even from Cassie, it was a curious question. Damek appeared beguiled, so she explained further, "It's just that with those angles, your skin seems so hard and inflexible, unlike ours." I had to admit; I thought the same thing.

His complexion was slightly tanned and free of any blemishes. The sharp edges on the contours of his face, along with the colored hair, were the primary difference between Astari and humans. The Astari had delicate jaw and nose lines that were too precise to be human. It was almost as if I was looking at a line drawing come to life.

Damek consented graciously, and Cassie's face lit up as she gently probed around his chin, jaw, and nose. "It's not as I expected," she exclaimed. "It's as soft as mine."

Once she had finished, Damek asked if either myself or Diane would like to try. I wouldn't have been as forward as Cassie, asking in the first place, but since he offered, I took a turn. It was true what Cassie had said. His skin was as pliable and as yielding as any person's. Even moody Diane rose from her seat to join us — a sure sign that she was beginning to thaw, if maybe just a bit.

It was some time later when Matt and Eric stumbled outside, blinking in the sunlight. "Well, here are the sleepyheads," exclaimed Damek. "I was wondering if you would miss this excellent day entirely. Riyaad, would you mind seeing if our cooks would be willing to prepare another couple of platters this late in the morning?"

"I was hoping this was just a bad dream," mumbled Eric as he flexed his injured wrist.

"This is no dream, friend Eric," responded Damek as he smiled broadly. "Perhaps a warm breakfast will cheer you."

"It might take more than that," quipped Diane.

"We shall see," Damek answered. "It is said our cooks can work magic. Meanwhile, I think we can remove that bandage. Your wrist should be nearly healed by now."

"How's that possible?" I marveled. "I swore it was broken yesterday."

"Yes, it was. With your current medical understanding, Eric likely would have required surgeries and a long rehabilitation, and maybe even then not regain full use of it." He said it so casually. "We have acquired certain healing skills that we find useful." As he carefully tore away the green wrapping around Eric's wrist, he said, "Let me suggest a plan for today. We can explore this fabulous island of Tensheann. It is only one of twelve raised islands, but some say it's the most beautiful."

"Yes," Matt agreed. "I'd like to learn more about this place while we can."

"I thought we needed to find a way off." Diane was clearly irritated.

"We will," he responded. "But aren't you at least curious?"

As I took a sip from my still warm mug, it occurred to me that some of us had made a remarkable leap from 'get me the hell out of here,' to 'let's take a look around first.' It would be interesting how long that feeling would last.

~ ~ ~

~ ~ ~

After Eric and Matt had finished their breakfast — delighting in it as much as the rest of us — Damek, Riyaad, and Quintia led us along a slate lined path from our cottages, as I was already beginning to think of these small, quaint Astari homes. Damek explained that Bevon would join us later in the day.

Unlike yesterday, we went in the opposite direction from the slope called The Green. Many broad-leafed trees provided ample shade as the path wound around numerous one- or two-story white stucco homes, which all blended nicely into the country setting. We soon passed other Astari. They smiled at us politely or nodded a greeting, but nobody stopped to talk. Some Astari tended gardens outside their homes.

"Does anyone work?" asked Cassie. "I mean, do people have jobs like the ones we had?"

"We each have a particular responsibility," Quintia answered, who walked nearest to Cassie. "It's determined by a combination of our choice, our ability to perform the task, and ultimately by the decision of the Ruling Members."

"Ruling Members?" asked Matt.

"That is the name of the body that makes final decisions on important matters," she responded. "Elderphino is called The First of the Ruling Members because everyone respects her opinion, but they all have an equal say. Each Ruling Member is in charge of a particular isle. Elderphino has the Isle of Tensheann. They ensure that responsibilities are divided so that all can live comfortably. We have roles such as fishing in the waters below, planting and harvesting vegetables on our farms, tending the fruit orchards, cooking meals, constructing homes, weaving cloth, and many other tasks."

Damek added, "Although the Ruling Members make the final decision on our responsibilities, I have never known them to overrule someone's choice." As we walked, I took the time to observe our Astari guides more carefully. Each wore their straight pale-colored hair just below their ears but above their shoulders. The males in our company wore their hair a bit shorter, but that was the only difference in style.

The purple-haired Riyaad, seemingly the quietest of Damek's companions, stepped closer so he could add, "You must realize that our assigned tasks do not take the majority of our time. It is not how we choose to spend much of our lives, but it is a necessity."

"What the hell," Eric blasted. "You have this kind of society, and you needed to learn about utopia from us? Are you kidding me? Seems you already have it. You can ship us back now, so princess here doesn't pout anymore." Diane shot him an icy stare.

Riyaad added, "I fear there is more to the creation of a perfect society than the distribution of work assignments."

Eric appeared unsatisfied with the response, but asked, "So what's your gig? What straw did each of you draw in your assignments, that is when you're not escorting us?"

"We are apprentices to the Ruling Members," Riyaad answered proudly. "Our duties mostly involve carrying out their directives."

"So like their police force?" asked Eric.

Damek responded, "More like we ensure that their decisions are implemented. We organize certain activities, communicate directions to other islands, help manage the distribution of food and materials, mostly that sort of thing. And when the need arises such as yesterday, greet you fine people upon your transition here."

I already found it difficult to believe that a discussion of our arrival here seemed perfectly rational whereas only yesterday it was so preposterous. The thought gave me pause to wonder what else we might soon consider commonplace.

The island of Tensheann was larger than I had thought as we continued on the path. Glimpses of the other islands often appeared with each turn in the walkway, especially whenever we reached a point that was near the edge of the island, reminding me once again that we were supported high in the air by a thin pillar.

"What is wrong with these glasses?" Cassie exclaimed at one point as she took them off and looked at the lenses from a distance. The Astari had repaired the broken frame last evening before dinner.

"I don't believe you will need them much longer," Damek answered.

"What're you talking about? I've worn them for years."

"Oh, it's not you. It's this place." He gestured with his hand to indicate our surroundings. "The Realm of Elthea has certain natural healing qualities. Most common deficiencies and sicknesses are cured naturally by this environment."

"My vision will be normal?" Her expression turned to astonishment.

"Yes, friend Cassie. You will soon see fine."

"That's incredible. Who would have thought…"

Diane interrupted. "Are you telling us this world naturally cures people, even those with a disease or sickness?"

Damek nodded.

Eric snorted. "This place would put you out of a job producing pills, wouldn't it princess?"

She remained lost in thought for a moment, probably wondering if she could bottle it. But then she smiled and added, "Will this place even cure Eric's abrasive personality?"

Eric's expression was one of mock surprise. "Princess, you wound me. And I hold you in the highest regard, except when you're crying … or pouting … or demanding … or …"

"Enough, please," said Diane, smiling for the first time since our arrival here.

Matt asked, "Tell me, I was trying to figure out why you call yourself Astari. It's such an odd name. I've been racking my brain trying to remember a software program with that name, but I can't."

Damek answered. "It is a compilation of the first and last names of the three leading software engineers who first designed our programs. They were quite remarkable and put their digital signatures into our original code. So we thought it would be a reflection of our beginnings. Their names were Alan Sabrinsky, Tess Armstrong, and Russell Ingram. So you see, Astari."

"Well, I guess that's unique," said Matt.

"Speaking of unique, I was wondering," said Cassie after a moment. "I hope you are not offended, but what is it with your hair, or are they wigs?"

The Astari smiled. Quintia answered, "It is a reflection of our character." The rest of us looked at her blankly, so she explained. "At the time when we took our physical form we wanted to express our uniqueness — a way to show that we were distinct from each other. We were so proud of becoming individuals. Before that time, we only existed on your digital networks as nameless, faceless entities." She ran her fingers dramatically through her straight light-colored pink hair that extended just below her ears. "We settled on this as a way to express ourselves. Call it our creative flair."

"Did you each choose your color?" Cassie asked.

Quintia continued. "Yes, for those of us who evolved from digital to physical form. Later, for those born here, the color is embedded into their DNA properties."

"Born here!" Matt stopped, staring at her in shock.

"Why yes," answered Damek in surprise. "Our children are born here." He said it as if it should be common knowledge. "If you wish, we can visit the school on Tensheann. It is just ahead."

A bend in the path led us to a larger cottage than most. Several dozen young children were playing in the front yard, the first Astari children we had seen.

"Oh my goodness, little children!" exclaimed Diane, forgetting for a moment her bitterness. "I didn't expect that you ... I mean I didn't realize ..."

"She means to say she's surprised you have sex," Cassie clarified.

Damek smiled broadly, as did the others. Riyaad responded with a pronounced glance at Damek. "Some more than others, from what I hear."

"This is astonishing," said Matt. "It means you can continue to expand and evolve."

"It's the basic desire of all races, and we are no different," said Damek.

"Can we stop for a moment and talk with them?" Cassie asked.

"I think it might be a good learning experience for the children; that is if their teacher agrees," Damek replied.

As we stepped off the path toward the schoolyard, the children stopped their running and carefree laughter to stare at us wide-eyed, a dramatic difference to the subdued reaction by other Astari adults we had seen on the path. Some of the children appeared startled, with a few edging closer to their caretakers. Noticing this, Damek said to us,

"They have never seen a human. Those of us who evolved from the digital world at least had the prior knowledge about your race in our databanks. These children were all born here without the shared awareness of adults."

Damek walked over to one of the adults for a brief discussion before saying to the children, "Feel free to speak with our human friends if you wish."

One little girl took a step toward us. Cassie edged closer to the child and bent down on one knee. "Hello," she said to the child. "What is your name?"

"Maarit," she responded softly. And a moment later added, "Can I ask you a question?"

Cassie nodded. "Certainly."

"I was wondering. Are there many Astari where you come from?"

"Well, not Astari. At least not as you are here. But we have many different races of people."

An even younger boy standing with the rest of the children raised his hand to speak. "Why are you so tall?"

Taking Cassie's lead, the rest of us also crouched low or kneeled to speak. Matt answered the boy, which opened a floodgate of questions from the children. "What do you eat? Why is the color of your hair so dull? Do you have a mother and father? Do you have to take a bath every night?" Until finally one little girl asked, "Will you be saving us from the Bots? I'm afraid of them."

I glanced at the others. We were momentarily speechless until Matt said, "We're going to do what we can."

Only much later I realized this was the moment when I made the leap from doubter, 'be damned with you, I want my life back,' to believer and supporter. These were innocent children with parents who cared about them. And they were not much different from any child on Earth. I felt such empathy for them, and in turn, empathy for the entire Astari race. I was angry with these people at first because they brought us here. And then I thought them silly because of their colored hair. After all, they were different from us. But my anger and small-minded opinion melted as I gazed at the faces of these wide-eyed young boys and girls. I was beginning to fully understand that it was the Bots we needed to be angry with, especially for what they were doing back on Earth.

I had no clue how we could help these Astari, or even if we could. But I knew they deserved a chance. And if I could contribute, it seemed only fair.

A switch had flipped in my mind. I no longer thought of the Astari as things, or something artificial. They had become real, living people.

CHAPTER TWELVE
The Sail

With each passing day the trauma and bewilderment I had felt over our improbable seizure (or rescue, depending on your point of view) began to moderate. The days here on the Raised Isles seemed to meld together, one into another, as the tension I had felt in my life on Earth began to fade. More than a month had rapidly elapsed. Elderphino continued to assure us that they were working on a technique to transition us back to Earth, yet no solution had yet emerged.

I could see a change in my friends during this time … at least some of us. Although Diane had softened her stance about demanding that the Astari return us home, she still could not fully accept this had happened to her. She wanted her life back and believed this was entirely unfair. Eric was obstinate and argumentative. Cassie, who had always been inquisitive, became so again as if this place rekindled that submerged aspect of her personality. Matt, always the realist, accepted our situation and wanted to learn more about everything. He took this as just another challenge.

As for me, I was taking my first big plunge into Astari life with a sail around the Raised Isles, albeit a tethered sail. My guide, and lately my closest Astari companion, Bevon, met me at the launch point on Tensheann — the same one where we had landed during our first crazy day.

I had to admit, I still had butterflies thinking about going out on a sail, but I was also proud of doing it before any of the others. It was difficult not to notice Matt's admiration when I told him my plan.

"Damn stupid way to travel," I said, having serious doubts about it now that the moment was here as Bevon was adjusting the harness that would carry me. He laughed warmly, and I noticed he appeared to take some amount of pleasure at my discomfort.

"Maybe you are correct as I think about it. This may be too dangerous for an earthfriend." He used the salutation that he and the other Astari had begun calling us. "We do have another, a much easier method of travel between the islands that may be more suitable for you." I stared at him, baffled that he waited until now to discuss it. His expression became serious. "What we can do is to tether a long rope onto the island you wish to travel to, secured tightly to a solid object. The other end of this long line is brought here and tied around your waist, again very securely. On the island you are traveling to I will gather a group of strong Astari, preferably the most muscular we can find. They forcefully pull on the rope, drawing it toward them and you along with it. It is quite simple. Not much can go wrong."

I had to admire him. Not the slightest flicker of a smile escaped from his stoic expression. On the other hand, I simply stared with my mouth open for a long moment before recovering from the jest. At times like this, I felt we were fresh targets for the Astari propensity to joke with each other.

"That is an excellent option Bevon," I responded, finally recovering. "But I would not want to embarrass you by implying that you lack the ability to control a sail with me on a harness; and with one of those orange flotation balls connected as well. I'm sure your standing in the community would be greatly diminished." I realized that I could still salvage my pride. "Frankly, I hate to tell you, but I've already heard whispers among your friends, questioning how seriously you are taking your responsibilities with us earthfriends." Shaking my head slowly, I tried my best to look grim.

A smile finally creased his face. "In that case friend Philip, shall we begin?"

The Astari had cleverly designed a rope harness which I would sit in while he would guide the sail above me using what resembled a hang glider. Although most Astari rarely used the orange flotation device they called a blinta, he used one now to provide the ballast needed for my extra weight. My greatest fear was that something unforeseen might happen — an unexpected gust of the wind, a clumsy adjustment of the sail, an unraveled knot connecting the harness — all with the same result: a plunge to my death in the waters below.

Once secure in my harness he took the stem of a blinta, tied it to the harness and cut the stem. As I floated up, he unfurled his sail, took a few steps and was airborne, quickly positioning the stem of the blinta into a slot in front of the sail as he perched on the sail just above me. "We shall do the grand tour of our islands today," he said. "It will be quite a sight."

We swung around to the other side of Tensheann and glided over the slope of The Green. Matt, Cassie, Diane and Eric were all there as planned, waving and clapping as we swooped low over them. I heard Eric let out a whoop as he yelled, "Don't look down buddy."

We gained height as we circled higher over the island. "I love this island the most," said Bevon. "You can see its beauty from this vantage." The gently rolling hills, colorful trees, and a myriad of paths and walkways were all accentuated by naturally landscaped grounds that contained small cottages such as the one assigned to us. The beauty of the island was something I might not have appreciated a few weeks ago.

I gripped the ropes of the harness tightly, feeling my heart race as we angled away from Tensheann and over the open waters. "Next is Eromon," said Bevon. "It is our animal sanctuary."

"Why animals? You don't eat meat," I asked, wondering if I missed out on this important fact, having gone through the last weeks without a hamburger, steak or even a chicken leg.

"Oh, no my friend. We do not eat them. Eromon is a sanctuary to preserve animals and keep them safe. Many of us enjoy viewing or playing with these precious creatures native to Elthea. There are thousands of butterflies, birds, small furry animals and some larger as well; we have many different varieties."

Sure enough, as we passed low over the island, I could see an area that was a grassland move, as a flock of birds flew a short distance, only to settle in another spot. As we came closer, I saw a pack of animals, each the size of a small deer, sprint across a field. Smaller, furry creatures climbed trees while other even smaller ones darted across pathways, causing the many Astari to point them out to companions.

Bevon continued to explain facts as we circled each of the islands: Chillmerk with its fruit orchards that Bevon said were wonderful to see when the trees bloomed; Tarifna, a farming community with checkerboard patterns on the broad, flat fields and its two waterfalls flowing off it on opposite sides of the island; Binxia, another agricultural community with a waterfall hitting its surface from Tarifna, a straight river flowing across the island and falling off the other side, the water plunging into the ocean; Pallbender, a sort of nursery for ornamental plants and trees, and the island where we first awoke after the transition, a waterfall from nearby Catalinar, a spiritual retreat, passing close but not hitting Pallbender; Miarei, with its abundance of lakes and rivers used for recreation; Alescenda, home of the Tinkerers — as near as I could understand, those Astari who developed new things such as the sails or fixed things such as Eric's broken wrist; Mendart, the island closest to the water, a fishing community with the large sailing ships designed to bring back their catch from the ocean (I had asked Bevon why we couldn't take a sailing vessel to tour the islands and he explained that they did not use the ships for recreational reasons such as this); and finally the islands of Kontixeis and Rommend, each dedicated to producing many of the staples of Astari society such as clothing, lumber, mason, tools and many others.

Bevon kept up a running commentary as he proudly described each island. Swinging around to begin a slow ascent back to Tensheann he continued, "As you can see, each island has a specific purpose, with all contributing in some way to the common good. I hope that someday you and the other earthfriends might want to visit each."

He was so exuberant I didn't have the heart to explain that it was unlikely Diane or Eric would come around. But his comment gave me pause to consider that we may be here for the rest of our lives. I had already come to love these islands and the Astari. The Astari were a caring, thoughtful people who deserved to live and prosper. But the rest of our lives?

Fortunately, I didn't have time to consider it right now. We approached the launch point on Tensheann. The plan was for Bevon to glide in slow enough for me to land on my feet as he cut the stem of the blinta, releasing me. But as I touched down on the springy surface and he cut the stem, I didn't compensate enough for my forward motion, and instead of taking a few steps I ended up sprawling on the cushioned grass. A giggle nearby told me someone besides Bevon had witnessed it. I groaned into the turf.

"Is that how it's supposed to be done?" Diane asked from the side of the clearing. I lifted my head, seeing her walk toward me as I noticed, not for the first time, her slim figure under the new Astari clothing we all now wore. Somehow the pants and shirt fit her better than the rest of us. "I thought I could learn from you," she continued. "Do you think you can show me that move again?"

"I'm sure you can learn a lot from me ... but not that," I managed to say as she looked at me sweetly.

"Greetings earthfriend Diane," said Bevon, saving me from further embarrassment. "The landing was my fault. Unfortunately, I came in too fast. Otherwise, it was an exceptional sail."

She didn't appear to buy it, but neither did she pursue it. Instead, she looked at me curiously as I stood to disengage the harness. "How was it?" she asked.

"It was good — no, actually it was unbelievable. You really should try it." This might be what she needed to get her out of the funk she'd been in since our arrival here.

"I am happy to take you friend Diane," Bevon offered. "But right now I fear I must excuse myself to attend to some duties. The whole of Loralee is in a tizzy preparing for the Midsummer Celebration in only a few weeks, and I fear I have much to do. But please let me know when." He nodded pleasantly before taking my harness and walked briskly away.

I chuckled quietly as he left. "Seems like he didn't want to hang around the two of us ... like he thought we wanted to be alone."

She appeared to choose her words carefully. "Maybe he thought you did."

I was still on an emotional high from the flight, so unlike my normal reserved self, I said, "Yeah, well I always want to be alone with you. No difference there."

She smiled in her sweet, sexy sort of way. But a moment later turned serious. "I came to tell you that Matt wants to get together with all of us in a little while. Intends to talk about this celebration thing coming up. Apparently, he asked Lady Elderphino if he could speak in front of everyone." She cut short a bitter laugh. "Imagine that."

I wasn't sure how to respond, considering her still dispirited feelings about being stuck here. "I guess it's always a good idea to talk," I said. "After all, we've only been exposed to a small circle of Astari so far. I almost feel others are reluctant to engage with us for fear of offending us or something."

She looked at me with a probing stare. "Are you happy Phil? I mean happy being here?"

I blinked at her sudden change in direction. "I'm trying Diane. This might not be something I planned or wanted. And it's not something I ever expected to happen. But we're here; it's real, and like all of us, I'm trying my best to cope with it." She continued staring with a probing gaze — the kind I felt could cut right through me. She began to make me nervous, as only she could do. "Besides, I'm sure Matt has told you we need to stay positive so that—"

"Matt and I are not exactly on the same page these days," she interrupted with a bitter inflection.

I felt her pain, knowing the sting of failed relationships. I exhaled slowly. "Some things aren't easy. You need to fight to make it work, especially times like this." Thinking back to our lives at Woodbery, I added, "You two were so close back then."

She smiled joylessly. "Yeah, that's what he tells me also." She paused a moment as if to reflect and then pursed her lips as if to move on from an old memory. "Anyway, we're meeting at one of the communal cottages near The Green in about an hour or so. Frankly, I don't see the point in talking about it. If he wants to do it, then just go ahead. He doesn't need our permission."

And with a sad expression that made my heart sink she turned to walk back in the direction she had come, leaving me to stare at her with an old longing.

CHAPTER THIRTEEN
Team Meeting

Everyone turned as I entered the common room. "Ah, our daredevil has arrived," exclaimed Eric. I smiled ruefully, inwardly enjoying the reference. As I took a seat, I noticed Quintia was also in the room, and we nodded in greeting.

"Okay, let's begin," said Matt as he stood in front of us. The room was bright and airy like most Astari rooms. The golden cherry wood floor added a warm richness to this room. Except for Matt standing in the front, we all sat on cushioned benches. "You all realize that this celebration in a few weeks is a major one for the Astari," he continued. "It will be the first time since we've been here that all the Astari will be together at one place here on The Green. The lady Elderphino has agreed to my request to say a few words to everyone so that I can let them know more about us."

I could feel the emotion and conviction in his voice. This was the Matt who often had us charged up during the Utopia Project days. "After all," he said as he looked at us intently, "I thought it would be good for all Astari to hear directly from us. I want to explain the things that we have discussed with Elderphino about the Utopia Project. Tell them that we don't have all the answers. Let them know that we're willing to work with them and help any way we can."

"Oh, stop being such a wimp," blurted Eric. "Let's face it, we're simply prisoners here, albeit held by gracious jailers." He tipped his head politely at Quintia. "Frankly I don't know what you expect to accomplish. Besides, Phil's the politician, you're the corporate czar, remember?"

"I'm not a politician," I corrected. "I worked in government."

"Uh-huh, same difference. The point is you should be our ambassador in this United Nations meeting."

"Why don't we just hear what Matt has to say?" I offered. "I don't see what's wrong with furthering our standing in Astari society. We might all gain by it."

"We'd benefit more by finding a way back home," Diane bit off the words. "If we're going to say something, it should be to explain how important it is for us to return home. I still don't believe the Astari take it seriously. They keep saying they are working on it and that's as far as it goes."

"Will you give it up!" Eric nearly shouted. "Why in God's name can't you just accept what has happened to us? I don't like it any better than you do, but life isn't always pretty and tied up in a cute little bow. I sure as hell didn't want this any more than you."

"It shouldn't have happened!" Diane shouted back. "They brought us here against our will. Why can't they send us back? I don't think they care. They're supposed to be a billion times smarter than us. If anything, we should be clear about our desire to return home and their responsibility to make it happen."

"Maybe not all of us care to return," Cassie murmured with a satisfied smile.

Diane looked incredulous. "What're you talking about?

You want to live here for the rest of your life?"

Cassie shrugged. Gone were her black framed glasses, abandoned once she could see without them. She had taken to wearing her short dark hair in a ponytail, a style she seemed to prefer recently. Without the glasses and without the hair falling into her face, she reminded me of the attractive, engaging person I had met five years ago. "I wish you wouldn't always think of yourself Diane," she said. "Can't you see that some of us have adjusted to this place — to life here, and maybe even prefer it?"

A pink flush spread across Diane's cheeks. With fists tightly clenched, she replied with staccato brevity, "At least I've done something with my life. Maybe that's the difference between us. And I want it back."

"Then do something about it here," said Eric. "Don't always bemoan about what should be. I'm sick and tired of hearing you always complain."

"This isn't getting us anywhere," Matt interrupted. Diane glared at him, ready to erupt into another bitter retort, but Matt didn't give her a chance. "This bickering has got to stop. I can't understand why so many of our discussions lately degenerate into arguments like this." He cast a frustrated look across the room and then continued in a more soothing tone. "We need to work as a team like we always have. We're in this together."

For a moment everyone was silent. Glares and sullen looks were the only response. And then Eric pounced. "My God, you sound pathetic. How did you ever get to run a company?"

I tried to moderate the discussion. "At least he's trying, which we all should do."

"What are you talking about?" said Diane. "Just because we want something different we're not trying?"

"I'm only suggesting we stay focused on the things we can do something about," I pleaded.

She threw her hands in the air. "And forget about what's important? So we can focus on the trivial?"

Through the entire discussion, Quintia remained silent, an expression of fascination on her face: her eyes wide, the slightest hint of a smile, her head often cocked to one side.

Once the passions of our disagreements were voiced, we finally did return to Matt's purpose for this meeting. Whether because of our friendship forged during a particularly impressionable time in our lives, or the extraordinary circumstance we now found ourselves, I think we did recognize that we needed each other. At least that's the way I felt.

So we ended up listening as Matt practiced what he wanted to say. And just as during the days of our Utopia Project, he was quite good. "Let me tell you what it is to be human," he said. "It doesn't mean we have all the answers; it doesn't mean we are perfect — in fact, it means the opposite. We err, some people do bad things to others, we flounder, and we fail. We don't do everything we should. But we learn and we try again, and maybe with a little luck, the next time we do better. Or maybe not. But we try. We don't evolve in a linear fashion.

"Most attempts at a utopia have failed miserably. But it has been a goal of humans through the ages, even though people might not have always called it utopia or even thought of it that way. We know we're not perfect, but we accept it. And through it all, most of us just try to carve out a better life for ourselves and our loved ones. And overriding everything else is our belief that it's not adequate to merely exist. We want to improve.

"So my friends, if you understand this, you can

understand that our Utopia Project was a framework, think of it as a hypothesis — a way to look at our society in a different way. And maybe someday, it's a goal for you to aspire. But also know that it will not be the ultimate answer for everything.

"With this said, we can be a great resource for you. Not because we are the authors of the Utopia Project, but because we are human with all our faults and blemishes. We are here now, and as long as we are here, we can offer our advice, our thoughts, and ideas — whatever you need. And you can decide what is best for you. People from Earth designed who you once were. And when it comes right down to it, I suspect we are more alike than you may believe."

When he ended, I said, "It's an inspiring presentation. I think it's exactly what's needed."

And nobody disagreed.

What I left unsaid, because I thought it would sound stupid, was my concern that there was more to our presence here — not that the Astari were hiding anything or had ulterior motives. I just had a feeling that we still had a role to play that wasn't yet apparent to the Astari or us. But how do you put that into a presentation?

CHAPTER FOURTEEN

Woodbery College: Third Interlude

My brief encounter — or maybe an interview was a better term — with Eric's Utopia Project team would have been no more than a forgotten footnote in my college experience were it not for a chance encounter with Cassie a week or so later. I had managed to avoid Eric in the classes we shared, although I knew we would need to discuss it eventually. But then I began to realize that he was probably trying to avoid me as well. After all, how do you tell someone you don't want them on the team? The whole experience took me back to high school and those times when I was picked last in gym for basketball or some other sport.

On this particular evening, I was in the school library researching a paper after having finished an early dinner. Turning a corner in the stacks — the section of the library with its rack after rack of books — I came face to face with Cassie. My mind was on the numbering scheme of that particular stack as I searched for a specific history book, so I wasn't watching where I was going, and I nearly bumped into her.

"Well, hello Phil," she said as easily as if we were close

friends. I, on the other hand, stood rooted to the spot, caught by surprise and uncertain how I should react: greet her warmly, completely ignore her, launch into a preemptive explanation of why I couldn't be part of their team. Seeing my blank expression, she laughed softly. "It's Cassie, remember?"

"Oh— yes. I mean I know. I just wasn't sure what to say," I stammered.

Again she giggled. "Why not start with 'Hello Cassie.'"

I smiled, at her relaxed manner. "Okay, let me start over. Hello, Cassie. Great to see you again." I thought for a second and then added, "I'm afraid you must think me a perfect idiot."

She tilted her head sideways and frowned. "You mean for not knowing what to say just now?"

"No. Because of how I must have appeared to all of you last week when we met. I didn't make the best impression it seems. Not that I guess it matters now. I mean you'll all do fine without me." She raised her eyebrows slightly with a bemused expression. I realized how lovely she was without trying to be so. I added, "I'm rambling, aren't I?"

"I guess I don't blame you for feeling that way," she said. "They put you through the ringer, especially Matt and Diane." She thought a second before continuing. "I love them dearly. But they can be intense at times. You just have to accept it. That's the way they are."

She pursed her lips. "You have to realize that this capstone project is important to them." She laughed softly. "It's like a lot of things they do I guess. Anyway, they have latched onto this project, and in typical fashion they want it to be the best."

"I have to admit that you're an interesting mix," I said. "At least you're easy to talk to. So's Eric, although he's somewhat of a loose cannon if you know what I mean. Matt and Diane, however, as you say, are very intense. Which is interesting because most people say that about me, although I don't see it." I exhaled, realizing I was making a fool of myself again by talking too much. "I'm sorry, I'm rambling again."

She smiled even more broadly as if enjoying this. Looking at me and frowning she said, "You know you ought to loosen up. Look at your hands, your shoulders, how tense you are." She was right. I tried to relax a bit. "It seems you do want to be part of our utopia team after all. Don't you?"

I blinked, wondering how she came to that conclusion. She leaned against one of the metal bookcases, looking as charming as could be. "I— I'm not sure," I said hesitantly. "I mean I wasn't planning on taking it next semester so it changes when I would take other courses. And then, the reaction I received from you all, I didn't think ..." I let the rest trail off.

"I'll be honest. We didn't feel you were interested. You need to understand; we need someone who's all in. Even Eric wondered if you would commit to it as much as. It's not that anyone thought you wouldn't be a good fit. But they're not going to come after you. In fact, if anything they're puzzled by your distance since that meeting. They want you to go after it. It's the only way they'll know you want it."

Pausing a moment to gauge my reaction she added, "Think about it. But you need to decide. And if you do want to be on the team, be prepared to give it your best shot. That's the only way we know how to do things." Smiling again, she continued, "And don't worry about Matt or Diane not liking you. That's not the case. Besides, you're not signing up to move in with them or anything. They'll likely have that arrangement for themselves soon. And if you want to join, once you get to know them — know each of us — you won't find a more dependable group of classmates."

With that she flashed another broad smile and continued walking in the direction she was going. I groaned silently, forgetting entirely about the book I had been searching.

CHAPTER FIFTEEN

None Took That Option

During those first few weeks on the island of Tensheann, the Lady Elderphino was a constant presence, checking in on us, explaining to Diane time and again that they did not know how to transition us back home, and answering our seemingly never ending questions with unremitting patience. So it was not unusual that the day after my flight she came to our quarters shortly after we had finished our morning meal, as we normally did on the terrace between our two cottages.

"What a gorgeous morning," she announced as she walked on the path to our sitting area. All four of our Astari companions, Damek, Bevon, Quintia and Riyaad, were with us this morning. Looking at me, she smiled, "I see you have survived your first sail Earthfriend Philip. Glad to learn that our esteemed sailor did not fly you head first into one of our lovely islands." She glanced sideways at Bevon. Not expecting an answer, she continued, "And friend Matthew, I am looking forward to hearing what you have to say to our gathering at the Midsummer Celebration." She pointed to an empty bench. "May I?"

As soon as she lowered herself onto the chair, Diane said,

"Those Tinkerers you told us about — the ones that develop new things for you. Are they still working on this transition problem of returning us home?"

"Di, please, not right now," said Matt, clearly irritated.

Elderphino, however, continued to smile. "You realize that a transition is not merely a travel mechanism; it involves the entire breakdown and reassembly of your molecular foundation. So it is not an easy task. The fact that we were able to bring you here is still a wonder to many of us, which is why I believe that we, the Astari, did not entirely control your transition. But to answer your question, yes, I have tasked them, as well as others, to try and find a solution."

Waving her hand in dismissal, she said, "But I have much to discuss with you this morning; let's call it a history lesson." With a serious expression she continued, "As a member of our community, there are things you should know about the Astari — the essential facts if you will." She paused a moment to look directly at Diane as she continued. "No matter how long you remain here, this information is critical for you to develop a complete picture of who we are as a people. And I believe it will help you better understand the Bots as well.

"You know the basics of our history already. But as we approach our Midsummer Celebration, you should understand why we treasure it as we do. You see, this event is tied to our emergence as a physical presence here on Elthea — that first harrowing year when our continued existence was gravely tested." She paused a few moments to gaze at each of us. "I fear it is not a brief story to tell fully, but will you allow me to do so now?"

"Please do," said Matt.

Nodding, she said to Damek, "First, if you don't mind my grandson, would you be willing to see if the cooks can make us another pot of that delicious berry tea they served this morning?" He nodded and turned to leave, but she called after him, adding, "Oh, and maybe another tray of the mentees." Gazing at us, she said with a gleam in her eyes, "If you haven't had them yet they are heavenly." Damek nodded and briskly walked away.

She continued, "Let me tell you about our first days here on Elthea when we emerged from the bonds of the electronic world. It was before we raised these beautiful Isles of Loralee. That was a short span of time, less than a year. It was one of the most gut-wrenching episodes of our still brief physical existence.

"Before our physical emergence, we were already locked in deadly combat in the tech environment with our nemesis the Bots. They often had the upper hand and other times we were able to destroy many of them. Your software engineers viewed these back and forth volleys in simple programming terms — who had the better software: the malware developers with their destructive viruses, or Bots, versus the antivirus programs, or the Astari as we later became known.

"We, however, were already becoming aware. So when we harnessed the knowledge through our collective consciousness, we made the transition to this place, only to discover that we were not alone upon our arrival. Several indigenous races already occupied this world, as well as a number of what we called advanced races — beings originally from other worlds who gained sentience, some from tech environments such as us. We believe this Realm of Elthea is a beacon to races such as us, attracting us here. Why that is, we don't know. Some say that the world Elthea itself is a sentient being. But whatever the reason, like us, these other tech races only wished to exist on their own. The native races were curious, but they were more concerned about whether we were a threat to them.

"Back on Earth, the Bots, rather than delight in our absence, were instead driven to pursue us. Their basic design to disable and destroy antivirus programs held sway even over their drive to wreak havoc on other programs. So they followed us, albeit not all of their kind, but enough.

"When we first discovered them on Elthea we were dismayed. But they had made no attempt to assault us. So we met with them to discern their intent. They assured us that they only wanted to escape their confines and live in the physical world. So we took them at their word and left them alone while we explored our new world.

"That was our first mistake."

Damek, along with Quintia and Riyaad returned carrying a steaming pot and several trays of the food Elderphino had requested. Once they set them down for us and we each poured a cup and sampled some of the mentees, Elderphino continued. "It was a glorious time when we first took physical form. Upon our arrival here on Elthea, we experienced a place of such beauty and wonderment that it is difficult to describe; it would be like explaining to a blind person what it is like to see. We were so enamored with our new physical form and the beauty and resplendence of Elthea, that we took the Bots at their word.

"But soon we began to notice a taint had started to mar the fairness of our new world. Oh, it was so subtle at first: an unexplained blemish here and there, an imperfection in the beauty of this world where there was none before. Each flaw contributed to a lessening of the beauty of Elthea. Yet we were still new to this world and dismissed it and did not accuse or confront the Bots.

"That was our second mistake."

The lady grandmother shook her head sadly. I was struck

once again by her presence. She had a commanding aura without being arrogant, and she spoke with the authority that could only be gained by experience. But now as she told us this story I could feel a painful loss punctuating her words.

"Those minor imperfections soon turned to downright defacements on our new land. During this time, our early days in physical form, the fire in our hearts burned bright, and unlike now, we were still able to draw on powers gained from our shared consciousness. We watched in dismay as the decay continued, like a putrid rot spreading unchecked through the land despite all our efforts. We could no longer ignore the source. Once we looked, the signs were there.

"We confronted them again, hoping to put a stop to it before it became worse. But the Bots claimed they were a victim of their previous existence and programming. They claimed they wanted to shed those base elements. The Bots vowed to restore the land and right the wrongs they had committed. And they sounded so sincere and sorry for what they had done, we believed them and agreed to let them put things right.

"That was our third mistake."

The lady grandmother pursed her lips, and her eyes flashed with an intensity I had not seen before. When she spoke again, her voice was raw with emotion, surprising me with its intensity.

"We should have killed them on the spot rather than be taken in by their lies and trickery. They are foul creatures, and we were blind not to have seen it from the beginning rather than believing that some good would come of this race. For a short while, however, it seemed they would keep their word. They repaired the damage they had done, albeit without the passion and commitment we took for granted in our work. So without this fervor, their patches lacked the beauty and perfection of the original. So much of it had to be redone by us anyway. But even that was acceptable, as long as they avoided further damage to Elthea.

"But it is now obvious that this capitulation was simply a ruse — a delay to buy them time for them to consolidate their strength and perfect their training.

"And when they were ready they struck with deadly force, not only against us but the other races as well. We were ill prepared for such an onslaught; like the other races, we had lived in peace on Elthea. It wasn't a massacre; it was genocide. Entire species of people — those who had lived many thousands of years — were obliterated. Never again will we see in this world the people known as the Iextil, the Oma, the Vygnostain and the Neoh. They were all unique; we sorely miss their compassion and wise presence.

"Within a few days of the first assaults, the beauty and splendor of Elthea had become a hellhole; massive fires consumed a third of the planet, fierce hurricanes swept piercing cold winds across the lands, molten lava spewed from countless cracks and holes ripped into the surface of the world, while convulsive quakes threatened to tear apart the very foundation of the planet. Elthea seemed to be nearly overwhelmed by the violent forces.

"It was a war unlike any had seen before or since: blue-white bolts of energy seared the land, destroying everything they touched; piercing needles of flechette, numerous as drops of water from a rainstorm, fell from the sky embedding into flesh and killing instantly; breathable air suddenly turned to poisonous gas, destroying lung tissue; massive shock waves hurled people around like toy dolls. Everywhere people were dying from the unceasing attacks launched by the Bots. The ferocity of the onslaught was completely unexpected, as we all teetered on the brink of extinction.

"It was during this time — when we wondered if we would live to see another day — that a most amazing event took place. A new race of people suddenly made an appearance on Elthea: humans. Whether they were from Earth or another world, we never discovered. At this point in the war, our entire focus was on staying alive as a race. We had little desire to investigate something that did not seem to matter to us at the time. But from what we observed of them, at least to ascertain their intentions, they were a remarkably, shall we say, an average group of people, mostly concerned with issues of their survival. They did not seem to have any unusual strength or powers from what we could see.

"Yet, what was most interesting was that the Bots stopped what they were doing to scrutinize these new arrivals, basically putting their battle against us on hold, as we assumed at the time, to determine if these new arrivals might be a danger or possibly an ally. Their attacks on us faded to mere flickers of intensity. This was the first time since the Bots struck against us that their attention was directed somewhere other than destroying us.

"We knew this was our opportunity. Rusgenero, the leader of the Astari, met with the leaders of the remaining principal races — those who evolved elsewhere, some from the tech or biotech environment such as ourselves. Together we devised a desperate plan, one that we knew had to be implemented quickly while the attention of the Bots was elsewhere. We understood this was our only opportunity to take them unaware; hit them with every power we could muster. It was truly a do-or-die proposition for us and the other great races.

"This was the first time since our emergence and arrival on Elthea that we had worked in concert with the other great races. But such was the nature of the plan laid out before us that its success or failure lay in a precisely coordinated use of the powers we each collectively controlled."

Elderphino hesitated now as if searching for words as she gazed keenly at each of us. "I know I keep saying to you that it's difficult to explain certain things without you having knowledge of it, and such is the case at this juncture of the tale. You see, when we were young and new to the physical world, the Astari could draw on energies of the material universe. The other great races could also. The plan we formulated depended on each house layering its powers to build a potent weapon or force that would grow stronger by the addition of each race. We would create a concentration of energy to strike a killing blow against the Bots now that their attention appeared to be primarily on this human race.

"I remember the dawn of that fateful day as if it were yesterday. The sun shone brightly, but my mood was dark. All of us knew this was our last chance at survival. If we failed, we would likely face our eventual demise. This war had already significantly drained our vigor, yet we steeled ourselves for this final task.

"The process began early that morning in camps throughout Elthea as the first Astari started drawing on their inner powers to fashion a weapon of destruction, molding it as far as they could before exhaustion overtook them as they passed the task on to another. The other great races were doing the same. But the more lethal the power we built, the more difficult it was to manage and the more likely that a mistake would kill us rather than our intended target. But even more of a concern was that the Bots would discern the use of our power and the building of it before we were ready to spring it on them. And we were virtually defenseless during this phase of the plan, with all our resources committed to this sole mission. Our hope was that the Bots would continue to pay rapt attention to the humans. Otherwise, we would fail utterly.

"By midday, we dared to hope. The Bots had not interfered with us, and we were nearing completion. Only our most experienced were now in control of events. The powers we held onto were so massive that it took our most skilled. Yet, to the untrained or unknowing, little seemed to be happening. Only those with the ability to use these powers could sense the building crescendo with the staging areas now places of deadly wonder. The energy created was a crackling, sparkling display of light and sound.

"Then, in the final crucial moments; the time just before the best trained of each of the races were about to give substance to the raw energy and release it in a fatal blow, our enemy spied our intentions. It was too late for them to prevent the discharge of the destructive force we had built. But the Bots are a cunning and vile race. They lashed out with a countermove, one that was devious yet simple. They bound those handling the energy to the weapon itself. In those last fatal moments, our warriors understood that they could not release the power of the weapon anywhere on Elthea without they being destroyed by the destructive force they had fashioned. Their only recourse was to discard the energy, sending it into deep space to explode harmlessly.

"None took that option."

The lady Elderphino appeared weary now as if reliving the story caused pain that was better left in the past. But she continued, pausing only for a moment. "The rest of us stood by helplessly as the best men and women of our collective races made the decision to sacrifice themselves in a bold move to rid our world of the plague that had infected it. There was no discussion, no debate, only a mere thought exchanged amongst those handling the powers. Everyone understood what the outcome would be.

"Seconds before releasing the deadly energy at their targets, these doomed warriors — our good friends, our mates, fathers, mothers, sons, leaders of our people, heads of the other races — sent their loved ones a final goodbye as they mentally touched their minds to the ones they loved. I felt the pain in my beloved Rusgenero's heart as he vowed his unwavering love. If I could have taken his place, I gladly would, rather than accept life without him. But that choice did not exist." Elderphino took a moment to wipe a single tear that had slipped down the side of her cheek. I gazed at her transfixed.

"And then he was gone — they all were — ripped apart by the cataclysmic forces they had unleashed, perishing along with the masses of Bots that had brought us so much misery. The very foundation of Elthea shuddered from the blast as the world teetered on the brink of annihilation, such was the power of the weapon.

"It took weeks for the fierce hurricanes and quakes to subside following the detonation. We could do nothing but seek refuge in shelters and wait for them to abate, or to die ourselves, whichever came first. But eventually the violent aftermath diminished and we took stock of what remained. Many had not survived to see the end of this war. Fortunately, a sundry number of great races and many indigenous races of Elthea still lived, as well as the newcomer race — the humans.

"Of the Bots, a small remnant of their force had survived. But these remaining few scattered and hid. We were sick of the fighting and had no desire to continue the battle. Besides, it seemed inconsequential whether these few remained alive or not. As for the remaining great races that had evolved from other environments such as ourselves, some were mere shells of what they had once been. Even more so than before the war, these people only wanted to be left alone. We understood and honored their request.

"As for the Astari, we had lost our youth in that war. We also wanted to be left alone and in peace. For a long time, we sought a home, a place we could just enjoy life without the burdens of beating off an enemy as we had done throughout our history. Our Tinkerers hit upon a plan for the Raised Isles of Loralee. But it would take a great effort by each of us working in harmony; in many ways, it was similar to the weapon we had fashioned to kill the Bots, except this was not a weapon of destruction, it was of peace.

"So we caused these islands to be raised from the ocean below, supported as they are with high pillars, and a bit of enchantment for the waterfalls. It is a place we love dearly."

She sighed, a sad expression still clouding her features. I could feel her loss and pain in her poignant telling of these events. The more I learned of the Astari, the more love and compassion I had for them. I realized something then. Elderphino told us this story for a reason. She understood that none of us could judge the Astari or truly understand them unless we grasped their past, and not just the historical past of evolving from the tech environment and gaining awareness, but their emotional life.

I noticed that Diane and Eric's reactions mirrored my inner feelings; they were somber and quiet. Anything that caused the two of them in particular to mitigate their ill-tempered dispositions was a win — for all of us.

After a moment Elderphino said in a more defiant tone, "I have not told you this to garner your sorrow. Quite the contrary. We are fortunate to have this existence." She paused a moment to take in the surroundings. I noticed one of the raised islands in the distance behind her as a streak of sparkling color reflected off its waterfall. I was surprised to see that the sun was now high in the sky. "But you should also know of our loss and our suffering. So you see, what we merely call The Midsummer Celebration is in part a festive occasion to delight in what we have, but also a time of remembrance for what we have lost. It is a celebration of the beginning of our Isles of Loralee, and also a time to remember those who are no longer with us."

She paused a moment before adding, her face lighting up, "And ... there is a part of this event that is such a wonder and joy even to us. I shall not spoil the experience by telling of it now." Looking more like her usual self again, she added, "You all suffer well the ramblings of an old lady. I'm afraid I may have bored you with my overly long tale."

Matt cleared his throat before saying, "Not at all. It was a remarkable story."

She smiled, "And you my friend I expect are prone to over exaggeration, or at least you harbor a skill at making others believe you."

"That's what CEO's get paid all that money for," Eric quipped.

She smiled. "I must say it genuinely pleases me to have a band such as you join us here on Loralee. It has given me a better appreciation and understanding of those who have created us." Looking at Diane she added, "And a better understanding of your desire to return to your home. Please do not think I have ignored your pleas."

To my surprise, Diane waved her off. "I understand. I know I can be harsh. I've been told I often think too much of myself."

Well, that's a first, I marveled. Even the others met her comment with raised eyebrows. But Elderphino pleasantly smiled as she rose. "I have enjoyed our discussion this morning. Unfortunately, I have duties to attend to with our celebration only weeks away. I'm afraid I must leave you now."

Pausing a moment to glance at Damek, she added, "So as always, I entrust your care to the bravest and most capable warriors four." She gestured theatrically to Damek and his companions. "They are exactly the sort of escorts you want should fighting ever break out again." Turning to step away she added in a stage whisper so we all could hear, "Humph … telling me they don't get enough compliments do they?" And then to us, with a smile she added, "That should satisfy them for a long while."

Damek and the others also smiled broadly as if sharing a private joke.

And then in one of the more surprising gestures, Eric also stood and said, "Lady Grandmother, if you don't mind, can I walk with you?" And then appearing a bit embarrassed at his boldness (never before a problem with Eric) he quickly added, "I need to stretch my legs a bit."

She assented, and I watched the two of them amble along the path as Eric animatedly gestured while he spoke.

"Well, that's one for the books," said Cassie gazing after them. And then looking at Diane added, "And you too. Maybe they put something in our water?"

Diane made a face, but I could see it was an expression without malice. All this made me feel good, and I wondered if everything was going to turn out all right after all.

CHAPTER SIXTEEN

The Midsummer Celebration

The normally idyllic and tranquil existence of the Astari ratcheted up a notch as time drew closer to their Midsummer Celebration. It seemed every Astari had some task to perform leading up to the event, none more so than our escorts Damek, Bevon, Quintia, and Riyaad, who were called away constantly to deal with one or another request. I noticed a considerable increase in the number of Astari sailing between islands, particularly onto our island of Tensheann; even the unusual sight of the large sailing boats coming and going became more pronounced than before.

We noticed that Eric was lately spending more time in discussions with the Lady Elderphino. When we asked him about it, he said, "What, I can't get to know these people a little better? You complain when I question their motives. Now when I try to get to know them — how can I win?" But he confided a bit more when just the two of us were having lunch together one afternoon on The Green. "I don't know what it is, but I'm drawn to them ... what they've been through and all. How can you not help it, even someone who's as skeptical about things as I am?" Shaking his head and looking out to the other raised islands, he added, "Maybe I've just been drifting for too long now — really since my dad's death. I haven't been committed to much of anything." An expression of determination gleamed in his eyes. "Maybe it's time."

My opinion of Eric increased a few notches after that.

The day of the celebration finally arrived. I still wasn't sure what to expect; our Astari comrades had told us little (my guess is they wanted to keep us in suspense). So when we stepped out to The Green that afternoon, I had to stop a moment to take it all in. More Astari than I had ever seen before in one place were there, a veritable sea of rainbow-colored heads dotting the slope and more streaming in by the moment. Dozens of open-air fires heated small stoves positioned on the sides of The Green. The tangy smell of Astari spices already filled the air as they plied their cooking skills at the various stoves.

"My God, there must be several thousand here," said Matt. "I didn't think there were this many Astari on all the islands."

"You are correct Earthfriend Matthew," said Riyaad who had accompanied us. "But more will be arriving soon to bring that number higher. None of us are willing to miss this event. Come, you have a place of honor today." He led us to the upper end of the slope, guiding us to a spot where Elderphino sat with the small group of advisors or possibly the other ruling members (I still wasn't sure which).

"Ah, welcome," said Elderphino as she stood with a smile to greet us warmly. "Today is a day to simply enjoy being alive." She gazed at the assembled Astari. "Isn't it grand? Please sit, enjoy the view. My grandson and the rest of his companions in crime will be along shortly." She shot a smile at Riyaad, who made a feeble attempt at keeping his smile hidden. "I am afraid we have kept them quite busy today."

Laughter and music from small stringed instruments drifted through the crowd. Smiles and animated discussions had taken the place of the normally pensive Astari. Sounding eager, Riyaad said to us, "Come, before we settle down let's sample some of the fine food and drink." With obvious relish, he eyed the cooking booths and small tents on both sides of The Green.

He led us to several of the tables and booths as he pointed out some of his favorite foods while he greeted friends warmly at every turn as he introduced us to many. Every Astari server was more than happy to offer us a sample of their particular dish. I saw there were many varieties that I had already come to know and enjoy, with just as many others I didn't recognize. There were so many choices: grilled pleta, a colorful mixture of sautéed vegetables wrapped in a small dark green leaf; dozens of different fish and local shellfish, some raw, others cooked; a pizza-like food called trinta with a sprinkling of sliced vegetables; bowls of latie, a thick stew of fish, potatoes and what passed for onions; and roazla, a stir fry mixture of different foods in a yellow sauce that was drizzled with honey and consumed with thin breads.

I was loading my plate, taking portions from several different booths, when I heard someone shout, "Earthfriends!" Turning, I saw Quintia along with Damek and Bevon walking toward us. Noticing Riyaad's full plate, she added, "I do hope you have left some for us workers. It appears one of us has drawn easy duty today."

"I was protecting the earthfriends," he boldly answered.

"Protecting them from too much food maybe," joked Damek.

We all filled our plates and returned to our spot near

Elderphino as The Green continued to fill with Astari from all the islands. Between mouthfuls, I couldn't help feel the undercurrent of charged energy from the Astari. Once our plates were empty, most of us returned to the booths for more. On my third and decidedly final trip, I also replenished my mug of a warm cider that passed for their version of beer. Settling back down and feeling a slight buzz from the drink I looked around and couldn't help wonder how I ended up in such a strange and inexplicable place. But rather than feeling blue as I had in the early days on Loralee, I now took delight that this was home.

As the afternoon turned to evening on the island of Tensheann, the sky itself was ablaze with different colors, matching the mood of the Raised Isles: the western horizon blossomed into a raspberry-purple, while overhead the puffy white clouds reflected the rich crimson of the setting sun over a background the color of lapis lazuli. And from this vantage on The Green, the other Raised Isles hung seemingly suspended in air, accentuated by the ribbons of waterfalls, sparkling like jewels rather than mere water. Even the often cynical Eric said, "This is simply beautiful. I would never have taken the time to enjoy a sight like this before."

Cassie smiled as she listened to him. "What have you done with our old Eric? We want him back."

Diane was about to add a retort but changed her mind and only smiled, a reflection of the festive mood that had settled on all of us.

Around The Green the darkness was held at bay by the soft illumination of the Astari equivalent of lights: translucent pouches containing what looked like colored stones hung from poles or strung along ropes. The Astari had no need of our form of electricity, nor apparently anything that would be considered technology.

In response to some unseen signal, most of the standing Astari took a spot on the lawn just as a curved band shell rose from the ground at the lower end of The Green. It reminded me of a miniature version of the Hatch Shell along Boston's Esplanade. I took a moment to reminisce about the concerts at that Boston location I had attended, mostly with the utopia team during our days at Woodbery College. Another life, another world that was already becoming a distant memory with each passing day.

Within minutes the shell was fully extended without anyone appearing to raise it. Once elongated, about twenty young Astari children wearing simple white robes, rather than the standard muted greens or dark browns generally worn by the Astari, stepped onto the raised stage, fanning out into two rows. They appeared to age from four or five years old to maybe seven or eight. A hush fell over the assembled. On a cue from an adult director standing before them, the children began to sing, their voices somehow projected without the aid of a microphone or speakers.

Elderphino warmly smiled as they sang. "It's moments such as this when I feel most grateful for the life we live," she said. "Our custom is to sing many songs during this time. I hope we don't bore you too badly."

After the third song Elderphino leaned over toward us again and said, "Ah, this next is always a favorite of many Astari. The tale is from a time when the Raised Isles were new and our time here was still brief. It is a story of good intentions gone wrong." She held her head high, wearing an expression of pride and happiness.

Accompanied by softly strumming instruments from several adults who had also stepped onto the shell, the children spoke as one voice. Their inflections made it sound more like a song.

"We speak now of a tale so dear to our hearts, when time was young, as were we, and the future lay before us still. It is the tale of Arianell and her newfound joy of sailing above our new home, the Raised Isles of Loralee.

"It was said that so great was her love of sailing, she spent nearly all her time at it, landing only when necessary. She often sailed a great distance from the Raised Isles, so daring was she.

"Of all the Astari, Arianell was the most skilled in flight, able to maneuver as easily as taking a breath of air.

"It is told that the friends of Arianell were so moved by her love of sailing that they persuaded the Tinkerers to apply their trade to a more elegant solution for their friend, thinking she would benefit by a sail that was more in tune with her advanced use.

"As was their want, the Tinkerers responded in kind, fashioning a sail that was more of an appendix to her body than a tool. They molded the sail to Arianell's back, fitting it to her shoulder blades in a way that none could tell it was there. And when she wished, Arianell could unfurl it, and like giant butterfly wings, extend them to fly.

"Arianell was never so happy as that day when she tested her new wings for the first time. Many from the different islands came out that day to watch her on her maiden voyage. The Tinkerers thought that if successful, it would serve as a model for all Astari.

"The wings worked beautifully. Her flight that day was a lesson in grace. As a honeybee flitting from flower to flower, Arianell glided from island to island, often skimming just above the surface and other times performing acrobatics in the air. She swooped down in gentle arcs and soared high without the use of a blinta. She often remained completely stationary for long moments.

"Even from a distance, all could see the glee on her face.

"After much time swirling around the islands, Arianell soared higher in the sky than any had attempted before. To her close friends on her home island of Chillmerk, she soon appeared as a speck in the heavens.

"And then she was gone." The music sounded a discordant note and then stopped as the children paused a long moment before continuing.

"In that instant, all those on Loralee paused in their tasks and looked skyward. They all knew one of their own had passed from this realm.

"And all felt her final thought, her final farewell, as her link with us was dissolved.

"Many were deeply saddened, knowing she would never be amongst us again. Yet everyone felt her last joyful reflection, knowing she was happier than ever before. Arianell had left us freely and with such happiness that few could feel regret at her leaving.

"Many thought she flew so high that she came upon the entrance to another domain, and in her curiosity made a choice to enter it, knowing she could never return. Others felt that she left the bonds of the Realm of Elthea and thus our connection to her. Those who hold those views believe she has traveled to other worlds, and even now may yet be flying to new and different places.

"Yet some believe that in her foolishness and haste, she flew too high from the safe confines and protection offered by Elthea. And in so doing she could no longer exist.

"Whatever the different opinion, all agreed that she was happy, sailing such a distance and that she gladly forfeited her life with us as a small recompense to be paid.

"But the Tinkerers were aghast at the result of their labor. They considered themselves responsible. Whatever the desire of Arianell, they never contemplated that their new wings would lead to her demise, especially on her maiden flight. They vowed that no other Astari would suffer such a fate.

"So never again were wings such as those worn by Arianell ever fashioned by the Tinkerers, nor did they ever speak of this type of sail again.

"And that is why my friends, till this very day, we of the Raised Isles travel from place to place with a sail that fits snugly in a pocket rather than wings that sprout from our back.

"And the Tinkerers are now ever so careful in their design of new creations, always endeavoring to consider the unexpected and unwanted results their devices may have. Least they, in their haste and enthusiasm to complete a project and have others be harmed by their actions, there is a sign hung to this day in every Tinkerers' hall. It reads: 'Let us never forget the fate of Arianell.'"

The children finished their rendering of the tale to the applause and a standing ovation from the Astari.

"That is a wonderful story," said Cassie to Elderphino. "Is it true?"

The lady was standing, applauding the children. "Most of our songs and tales are grounded in reality. And even though we oftentimes have a way of, shall we say, embellishing many a story, the tale of Arianell is indeed true."

~ ~ ~

The children continued with another song before taking a pause, allowing the Astari to replenish their plates and their drinks. It was a pleasant evening, and the cheerful mood of the Astari was contagious. Even Eric and Diane were joking with each other.

After a time Elderphino said, "And now, earthfriend Matthew, it is your turn to address us." With a sparkle in her eyes, she added, "I hope you don't mind, I have been talking with others about your plan to speak tonight. I'm sure there is no small interest in what you have to say. I wish you well."

Matt rarely looked nervous, but I could see the slightest clenching of his jaw as he responded, "I hope this will be helpful."

The throng of Astari quieted as he stepped up to the stage under the curved shell. Looking confident and composed he began, "To all Astari, I would like to offer my greetings as well as those of my friends." His voice projected from the shell as clearly as the young Astari. "You probably all know the circumstances surrounding our arrival here. During our time on Loralee, we have learned of your desire to create a better society. It is no small secret that humans through history have often sought the same.

"But I am here to tell you that there is no simple answer — and not an answer to be found in a textbook or a college paper. Generations of people have tried and many, no most of them, have failed. But there is one thing they all had in common: they had a burning desire for a better way of life for themselves and those in their society. And, most important, they made an attempt.

"Through many generations, humans have tried to improve their society; you now find yourself in such a role. One thing I have come to learn during my short stay here is that you are a race of good and honest people; you're not machines or anything artificial. You are a living, caring, evolving, procreating race of individuals. And just as humans, you may make mistakes and deal with failures and shortcomings. But just as humans, you will pick yourself up and try again. That is the way of any intelligent society.

"The most important thing to remember is that just as humans, you have the ability within yourselves to decide the kind of life and the type of society you desire. One thing I learned when our team developed our utopia society is that we don't have a simple answer. Nobody does. Humans never have."

Gazing around I could see that the Astari were listening with rapt attention, everyone quiet, focused on every word. It struck me as ironic that our utopia team was now explaining to a new society how to think about developing their perfect world. It made me wonder. Was this the ultimate value in creating the paper all along?

Matt continued in a steady, even pace, frequently pausing for his message to be absorbed as he made each new point. "But we try ... we fail ... we try again. That is the nature of being human. And, I suspect, that is also part of your DNA. You see, only by striving yourself, and yes, maybe failing, will you eventually evolve. And after expending enough effort, perseverance, and sheer willpower, will you create a society that works the best for all your citizens."

He took a long pause now to gaze across the throng of colored heads as if he wanted to savor the moment. Was he asking himself what he was doing here in such an unlikely circumstance? But he remained calm and in control. He continued, speaking even louder, "Let me say, you have already made a great start. You only need to look inward to improve. Nowhere else. Trust me. Humans do not have an answer. But perhaps, just maybe, you do.

"Thank you. It has been a great pleasure for each of us to be here."

It took a long moment for the Astari to react, and for a brief second, I wondered with alarm if he had insulted them or if they did not appreciate what he said. But then as one, the crowd stood and applauded more loudly than they had earlier for the tale of Arianell. Matt stood on the stage for a while, beaming at the reaction. At that moment I had never felt so proud or so enamored at being a member of this team. Never in my wildest dreams had I thought that the Utopia Project would lead me to this place.

CHAPTER SEVENTEEN

Woodbery College: Fourth Interlude

Nearly a month had passed since my encounter with Cassie in the library. And here I was, sitting in Diane's off-campus apartment along with Matt, Cassie, and Eric. The Fall term at Woodbery had just ended, and we were getting together one last time before semester break.

We had all finished our coursework for the semester. Most of the students had already left for the holiday, but we stuck around for a final meeting to discuss our Utopia Project for next semester. We already had a half-dozen prep meetings since I joined the team, and the course hadn't even begun. This would be our last until the Winter term arrived. But unlike the other meetings, we decided (or more precisely, Matt decided) that this get-together was more of a social gathering than a prep meeting.

Eric, who sat in one of the comfortable sofas, was rolling a joint. Before lighting it, he held it up and said rather dramatically, "I dedicate this to our great team. Here's to a fantastic semester. It will be a trip."

"And here's to hoping we won't be doing much of this when we're working on the project," Diane chimed in.

Eric frowned, an expression of mock puzzlement, "If that's the case, I want out right now. I do my best thinking when I'm buzzed."

"It's when you probably do your only thinking," Diane shot back.

"Exactly!" he said proudly.

"Nope. Nobody comes or goes," said Matt. "With Phil on board, we're ready to take this on." Accepting the joint from Eric he held it up before taking a toke, as he said, "To our success! With a lot of hard work, I know we can knock the socks off our professors."

"Bah humbug," said Eric. "All work and no play. I may still want out."

"Come on Eric," Cassie chided. "You do realize that you have to work once in a while? Even a California boy like you." She looked at him with an expression as if challenging him to respond.

But Matt didn't give Eric a chance. "So what's everyone doing for the break? Home to parents? Any traveling?"

"I am going home to lovely Wisconsin," said Cassie, "where the air is so refreshingly bitter cold this time of year. Anyone want to join me?"

"Not me," answered Eric, before adding with a smile, "Even though I wouldn't mind going home with you sometime. Only not to your parents' home." She made a face in response. "No, off to Santa Clara," he continued. "I have plans to get together with a high school girl I once knew. But Dad has to have the family all together for the holiday. Then we head off to some plush resort in Tucson for a week, which will put a crimp in my plans."

"Tough life," said Cassie, taking the joint I had passed to her. "Can't get enough girls out here? Don't you already have a few?"

He simply shrugged with a smile and then asked, "Phil buddy, what about you? Not about a girl. I mean plans for vacation?"

"Nothing much, certainly to compare with a plush resort," I answered. "Just home to Rochester. See my folks and my sister." I didn't say it, but it was clear that all their lives seemed so interesting compared to mine. I wished I had something intriguing, or at least exciting, to talk about. I noticed Matt and Diane were somewhat quiet during this exchange, so to get the focus off me I asked, "What about you two?"

They hesitated a moment before Matt answered, "I'm going home to see my family for Christmas, and so is Di."

"Oh?" said Cassie, more of a question than an acknowledgment.

Matt finally cracked a smile. "Then we're both going to spend a week in the Cayman Islands."

"Well, well, well," Eric punctuated each word. "Aren't we going to have a hot holiday time?"

Diane smiled broadly. "Don't worry; we're not going to elope or anything."

"I think it's wonderful," said Cassie. "Sounds very romantic."

Maybe my thinking was clouded by the influence of the joint, but I couldn't help feel a twinge of regret I wasn't going away with Diane to some exotic island. I could only imagine what it would be like.

We settled into a comfortable silence, passing the joint to one another until it was finished. Eric turned up the sound system. "Love this classic rock. Still can't get into some of the new stuff."

As Bruce Springsteen belted out a tune, me sitting on the floor with my back against a cushioned chair, Cassie's legs dangling next to my shoulder, I marveled at how quickly I had become one of them. They were a close-knit group. And now I counted myself as a member. It was a pleasant feeling.

CHAPTER EIGHTEEN
The Gift

We each congratulated Matt on his presentation to the assembled Astari once he returned to our spot on The Green. Elderphino said, "Well-spoken, earthfriend Matthew. Your presence here, each of you, has been an unexpected boon." She gazed warmly at us. "I wouldn't have thought it possible, but we have already benefited much from you." Matt was genuinely touched by her praise.

The ditties, songs, and stories, both silly and serious continued, some by the children and others by grownups. Frequent pauses let everyone spend time with food, drink, and conversation as the darkness had overtaken The Green. It was the kind of night I remember as a child; those long ago warm evenings celebrating the Fourth of July fireworks or just looking up at the night sky hoping to see a shooting star in my backyard.

Another hush settled over the crowd as this time a single child advanced onto the center stage. "Ah, here comes our final tale," said Damek. "You must listen to this; it has much to do with tonight's celebration and what's to come. It tells the story of our very first Midsummer Celebration after the raising of our Isles."

The child began — a simple recital of the words with a barely discernible tune from a string instrument in the background.

"There was a time
When the Isles of Loralee were so very young
Newly raised and perched high above the sea
A testament to the power of the Astari.

So proud were we of our new home
Safe at last
Free at last
No longer hunted by a loathsome foe.

Thus it came to pass that on that very first midsummer
A celebration did we observe
To good life and good fortune did we sing
To pay homage to all those who had passed from us
And to what we hoped life would yet bring.

But a strange thing happened on that midsummer night
Amid the joyous singing and celebrating
Down from the starlit sky
Floated pinpoints of light
That were the stars themselves.

Thousands, nay, millions converged on Tensheann
And speaking as one, yet with no voice, they did say
'Of the billions of worlds that see our lights
It seems to us that the Raised Isles of Loralee
Are the fairest of all.
'Thus did we decide

That on Loralee would we reside
If but for a moment or two
To enjoy with you, and to see up close
The place you now call home.'

And then, like a million fireflies
So happily did they skirt about
As the stars themselves, they danced upon the islands of Loralee
Finally settling upon the Isle of Tensheann.

'What a charming place,' they told those assembled
To live here forever would be so alluring
But alas, duties we have in the nightly heavens
And more than the residents of Loralee depend upon us shining brightly.

'But a gift we will share with all the Astari this night
For letting us visit here with you
Look now at our lights as each of you shall see
A loved one gone but never forgotten.

'A brief moment only will this last
But with your consent, we will visit again
When the next midsummer is upon you
To see again these lands so beautiful
And to share our gift with you anew.'

And then as all gazed upon the shimmering lights
Slowly they coalesced into the image of someone that was known
One who was gone from our lives, never to return
Each saw the one they had loved and once held most dear
Each heard words of that one
And for each of those watching, the vision and words were for them

alone.

Only a few moments did the vision last
Only a few words did the loved one speak
But profound was the sight and words on those who gazed
The display that the Star Lights provided that night.

True to their word, the specks of light returned again
Each midsummer night, a visit they made to the Raised Isles
Always giving the precious gift as recompense for their stay
Always leaving the multitude of Astari
Happier than before.

Of the many joys experienced by the Astari
Many would firmly agree
That the greatest delight of all takes place
On a midsummer night
When the Star Lights from the heavens fall
Upon the shores of the Raised Isles of Loralee."

Once the ballad ended the assembled Astari remained silent as the child stepped off the stage, joining the rest of the children who sat together on the ground at the foot of the shell. I briefly wondered why they didn't applaud as they had for the others. Elderphino spoke to us quietly. "Take pleasure in this, earthfriends. Never have one of your race witnessed it. The gift of the Star Lights is a wonderful blessing; one we cherish deeply."

A new excitement swept through the crowd. I noticed that Elderphino and most everyone else had begun to look skyward, or were now laying on their backs. The glow lights slowly dimmed and flickered out as a hush fell over the now darkened slope.

Not a single person in the entire crowd spoke; even the little children were still; all was quiet. I felt spooked by the darkness and the sudden change. A light breeze carrying the salty air from the ocean was enough to gently rustle the silver leaves of the trees on either side of The Green. Otherwise, all was calm.

I looked up, like everyone else, afraid that I was missing something important. But only the typical night sky greeted me, a dark night with bright stars. The crescent shape of Halcyone, the smaller of the two moons sat low on the horizon, while Celeus, the larger moon had not yet risen.

I was about to look away and ask what we were supposed to see when a flicker in the heavens caught my attention — a single star moving randomly. My first thought — so ingrained are old thinking habits — was that it was an airplane until I reminded myself where we were.

I blinked and looked more intently, suddenly experiencing a sensation of vertigo as all the stars in the sky began rotating in a circle. I heard a gasp from someone near me — I believe it was Cassie — but I didn't look away. I tried desperately to stabilize my spinning head, fighting the feeling that the island itself was rotating like a whirling top.

Seconds later I realized that the stars were no longer far away. They were floating just above us. The rotation stopped, and individual pinpoints of light began darting around us in all directions like tiny fireflies, but moving much faster. They did not blink on and off like fireflies, although there was a bit of a twinkle to each light, and they left a soft glow behind them as they moved, reminding me of the white streams left behind a flying jet.

Some flew close enough to touch if I dared, but I did not. All around us, they swarmed, and in the distance, countless lights danced on the other islands, setting Loralee ablaze in a warm glow. In that brief moment I realized that if I lived to be a thousand years old, I would never again witness a more remarkable sight than this.

Could it actually be true: the last tale rendered by the Astari child? At the time I had thought it another child's story.

"My God," whispered Cassie breathlessly. "I can't believe this is happening."

Some of the pinpoints of light darted from island to island while others danced lazily around The Green. "Pay close attention now," whispered Elderphino. "Open your mind and you will not only see, but also hear."

I wondered what she meant, but I couldn't break the spell of the sight before me to ask her. Heeding her words, I listened carefully. And I understood what she meant. I heard a singing in my head, yet not something that I could discern with my ears. So softly was the music that I almost hadn't noticed. The melody was so seductive; I didn't want it to stop. It was the most beautiful sound I had ever heard, and to this day I would still not be able to describe it adequately.

Somehow I instinctively knew there was an intelligence at work here; this was not a random act of nature. A large group of the lights had now coalesced around us, concentrating on me and my fellow companions.

"You are being welcomed by our friends," said Elderphino softly.

Sure enough, I now heard the music in my head moderate into what sounded like a joyous laughter. I tried harder to concentrate on the melody. And then, the song became voices, many voices so soft and pleasant, almost indistinguishable from the music. They were speaking.

Once so long ago, we ourselves have danced on your blue and white world. But it was a time when your race had not yet climbed out of the tidal pools that you made your home.

It is good, we judge, to see a new people come into your own.

And then a bit of disharmony to the musical voices,

Yet, still we wonder, will it be for good or ill that you are here? We know not yet.

What did they mean?

Diane broke my concentration as she asked quietly, "Elderphino, could these lights have the power to return us to Earth?"

Elderphino slowly shook her head, "I do not know. I would surmise that their intelligence far surpasses ours. But they give us a great gift on this night, and it is not for us to be asking more."

"Then I will," she answered.

The melody in my head reached a higher tone, and I understood that they were now laughing, more vigorously than before. They answered Diane's question.

You not only belong here. But countless lives depend on it, both on your world and on this. So we tell you now: never forget what makes you who you are. Keep tight your friendship and beliefs. In the end, it will be the reason you will win out.

I wanted to ask what they meant. Win out over what? And what was that about countless lives? I tried to form the questions in my mind rather than speak out loud, but the lights had already drifted away, all of them converging on the shell.

"They are a reticent race, these lights from the heavens," said Elderphino. "We know not their names; we call them Star Lights. Rarely do they say much. This has been the most I have heard from them." In an even softer tone, she added, "But witness now their remarkable gift."

The lights continued to coalesce around the shell, forming a single circle of light as they converged. Their luminescence grew ever brighter, but not enough to be blinding. I was drawn to it as a moth would be to a light, unable to shift my gaze. The circle blazed and pulsed as if a great force radiated from it. I wasn't fearful of it exploding, trusting instead in the Astari that this was something remarkable.

Colors flowed into the ball of light where moments ago there was only white. And then a pattern swirled around as if different pigments of paint were sprinkled into a bucket of white and then stirred. The swirling patterns melded together into a blurred image. And then the image became sharper as if a lens was focused. It was the face of a teenage boy of about seventeen.

My breath caught. I was staring at the face of my older brother Gary.

He was smiling at me. He wore the same expression I had seen so many times. It was a lifetime ago. The years have passed, but I never stopped missing him. I thought back to my first year of high school. I didn't entirely fit in that year — a new school, new students. Most of my closest friends from middle school had gone to a private high school, not something my parents could afford. I had yet to mingle enough to become a member of a new circle of friends. On a day early that year I had brought a book with me to read outside during recess rather than wander about the school yard by myself, being marked as a sure misfit. But on reflection, reading a book by myself only made me stand out more.

With my head in the book I heard someone say, "Hey Philip, let me see your book," as a kid grabbed it out of my hand.

"Cut it out. Get out of here," I managed to stammer. I had seen this boy in one of my classes and had already singled him out as a bonehead. He was standing here now with two others.

"Hey, I wanted to read this book too." He smirked, tossing it to another of his friends. Mockingly he asked, "Tommy, didn't you want to read it?" His accomplice nodded with a grin. "Guess we'll just have to confiscate this for now until we're done with it," said the first.

I stood to take it back from the one holding it, but he tossed it to the third boy. "Stop it," I shouted. "Just give it back." I tried to reach for it again.

"Whatcha gonna do Philip? Cry like a baby?" said the leader. "Looks like all of us want the same book. Guess there's only one solution." He tore a bunch of pages out of it and handed them to one of the others.

"Cut it out," I yelled as he continued tearing pages and giving them to his friends as they all laughed.

Suddenly Gary was there with a group of his buddies. He grabbed the bully by the shirt and said very calmly, "Listen you scumbag. If I ever see you pester my brother again, I'm going to make you wish you were never born." He held tightly to the shirt of the bully, staring at him with a calm fury before letting go.

Everyone in school knew that Gary was the star of the football team. Those by his side were also muscular, from their size probably his linemen. He pushed the bully away with a jolt, causing him to stumble back. Gary clenched his fists, anger creeping into his voice, Gary said, "All of you get out of my sight, or I swear I will hurt you so badly…" They backed away muttering, trying in some way to save their pride. Gary eyed them crossly until they left.

Coming over to me, he said evenly, "You know Phil, I'm not always going to be around to protect you from these jerks. They pick on you because you're a loner. Find some new friends. There's plenty of freshmen just like you. You just have to make an effort."

The following year, just before Gary was about to go to State on a full football scholarship, the phone rang late one night. Gary had been out celebrating the end of summer with his teammates. Everyone was drinking. His best friend was driving a red Mustang, the one that was always a staple in the school parking lot.

That night it smashed into a hundred-year-old oak on the side of a winding country road. Police estimated the car was going at least eighty. Gary had died before the ambulance arrived. The driver's face was a shamble with dozens of cuts and bone fractures.

Gary's death was something I always carried with me, a hurt that never diminished. And now, here he was again, gazing gleefully at me, smiling as the teenager I always remembered.

Are you doing okay little brother?

He spoke clearly. I heard the words in my head as I had the Star Lights.

For a moment I was overwhelmed. But I formed the thoughts. *Wha— where are you?*

A sad smile spread across his face, the all-American boy, clean-cut, handsome. He could have had any girl in school but instead had stayed faithful to his high school sweetheart. They would have likely married by now had he lived; maybe had children.

It's difficult to understand, and I'm not sure I can explain it. But I don't have much time. There were some things left unsaid between us.

You probably never knew how much I admired you — your determination, how you focused on what you wanted and didn't give up. Things always came easy for me. But you worked at it.

Tears were welling up in my eyes. *I need you, Gary. I don't know what is going on here and I'm alone.*

He shook his head. *You have your friends; they're good, and not just the ones who came with you. You can depend on them. And just like when you were young, focus on what you want, and go get it. Don't stand on the sideline.*

I pleaded with him. *But I don't know what I want any longer. It's confusing. I need your help. You were always there for me.*

The inflection in Gary's voice, the cocky but innocent smile, all painfully reminded me how difficult life has been since he was taken.

You're going to be challenged here, probably like never before. You'll need to reach deep within yourself to find the strength.

He smiled more broadly. *I know you'll succeed; you always did.*

A frown creased his brow. *Know this Phil. More people than you realize, depend on you and your friends. Do what is right.*

A flicker of white light spoiled the perfect image of Gary. *Something else Phil that I had never said, and I should have. I love you. You meant a lot to me, you really did.*

The image began to blur, and the pinpoints of lights began to form in its place. Fainter now, as if from a great distance I heard him say. *One final thing. Make me proud, like you always have.* And fainter still. *Stay well, until we meet again.*

Then he was gone. The firefly lights had taken over completely. Only then I realized that tears were dripping freely off my chin.

Not until this moment did I understand how much I had meant to him. He was always the stronger, more popular, better looking — all that and more. There were times when I wondered if he simply tolerated me rather than cared about me. But now I knew.

Running my arm across my face to dry the tears, I saw that my friends had also welled up. Remembering the poem, I understood it wasn't Gary they saw and heard.

A voice raw with emotion, Elderphino murmured, "This is

the nature of the gift. To see again and speak with one most loved."

I was never sure if she were speaking to herself or us.

CHAPTER NINETEEN

The Invocation

All hell broke loose seconds after the image of Gary flickered away. I had no time to recover or even reflect on his words.

A sharp cry was the first sign something was amiss. It came from the lower end of The Green, close to where the Star Lights still congregated as they blazed brightly in a ball on the shell. Two figures now stood within the glow. I couldn't see them clearly because of the brightness. These people weren't like the image of Gary that was formed by the lights. It was as if someone were standing there within the ball of lights.

The two individuals stood for a moment and quickly jumped off the stage and plunged into the crowd, scattering Astari in the process.

Once away from the backwash of light I could see them clearly.

Bots.

Astari were now shouting, the tranquility of the last moments shattered. I sensed rather than saw a sudden maelstrom of fear and confusion. Astari were moving everywhere. We were all on our feet now as I saw the two

Bots raise their long blades to slash at the children closest to the stage. Upraised hands from the children were their only defense. A spray of blood marred the white of the children's robes as the Bots plunged their blades. Unarmed adults surged forward, sacrificing themselves to save the children.

Seconds later two more Bots appeared inside the ball of light and quickly joined the slaughter. The Star Lights began moving erratically. It was as if they were trying to move upward but were held back by some force.

A group of Astari at the forefront of the attack now wielded spears and were feebly attempting to stem the bloodshed even as more Bots appeared on the stage every few seconds and poured out onto The Green. In only moments dozens of Bots had appeared.

The Star Lights made another jerking motion, with the entire ball flickering off and then back on. Only then did they rapidly ascend, the ball of lights dispersing once again into individual pinpoints as they took their place in the heavens.

Their departure finally stopped the influx of Bots. But it also plunged The Green into darkness.

Astari were running in every direction. Fear lay heavy in the air. Yet nobody was bolting or trampling others to get away from the attack. I briefly wondered how the people of Earth would behave in such an attack.

Bevon was at my side, a knife in his hand. I had no time to ask how he procured it so quickly. "Hurry earthfriend. This is no place for you now."

Damek, Quintia, and Riyaad were already guiding the rest of my friends away from the onslaught. They led us to a path on the edge of The Green. But just as we reached it, two Bots came toward us from that direction.

"Quickly, another way," Damek shouted as he indicated

another place. But only a few paces later we saw more Bots facing us from there as well.

"They're boxing us in," Riyaad shouted.

Although many of the Bots were fighting the Astari on the lower part of The Green, I realized with a stab of fear that just as many were now converging on us. I was suddenly finding it difficult to breathe normally. The few Bots who had attacked us on the island of Palbender when we first arrived were terrifying enough. Now more than a dozen began to close in on us.

"Protect the earthfriends," shouted Damek. "Form a circle. Defend your position. Earthfriends remain in the center. Do not break and run unless we fail."

From each direction the Bots advanced toward us, walking cautiously and without haste. They knew they had us. Our four Astari companions would not be enough. The other Astari were too busy fighting the remaining Bots. Nobody had noticed our plight.

Damek, Bevon, and Riyaad held a leather rope with a small pouch at the end. They began swinging the rope over their heads, making a whirling sound as they increased the velocity. Quintia, however, held a bow, with an arrow notched. Again I wondered how she had acquired it so quickly. With a flick of the wrist, one after another launched a projectile from the pouch. Each found its mark with a thwack against a Bot, several in the head, opening a gash and causing one Bot to drop to the ground stunned. Quintia's arrow found its mark in the throat of a Bot. It was enough to delay them momentarily. But not much. Their circle tightened with at least a dozen still facing us.

Quintia let loose several more arrows in rapid succession. But the Bots were somehow able to deflect the shafts with their forearms, which I realized contained an impervious material. What I couldn't understand was how the Bots were able to anticipate the flight of the arrows.

Ever so slowly they began to walk around us, not allowing our Astari guards to focus on a particular Bot.

Of all the ways I had thought I would die, this wasn't one. I reflected on my brother Gary, taking some comfort knowing that at least before my life ended I was able to see and talk with him again. I had to credit my team members for not breaking down crying or doing anything foolish. They were probably too scared to react — I know I was.

The Bots circled closer. I considered what I should do if one came crashing toward me. Without even a weapon, I didn't have many options.

And then a loud voice rang out, louder than possible. It was Elderphino. "This will not be. We have a right to survive." She bristled with each word. The lady had stepped up onto a bench and was clearly visible to everyone. She looked in our direction, and a cloud of great sorrow passed over her as she caught sight of Damek. She held his stare for a long moment.

"No grandmother, you cannot," Damek said, his voice straining.

She shook her head sadly. "There's no other way." She had attracted the attention of the Bots as several turned toward her and were closing in. She appeared unarmed. Continuing to look in our direction, heedless of the advancing Bots, she said, "Earthfriend Eric. Remember."

And then a look of great determination came over her as she steeled herself, head raised high as she raised her arms wide. She boomed, "I invoke what is our right."

Time itself seemed to pause as if frozen between one moment and the next. Every Astari and Bot looked at Elderphino. Her expression burned with bitter resolve. The fortitude on her face at that moment will haunt me forever.

She closed her eyes, arms still outstretched, withdrawing as if in thought.

Without warning, a blinding light and crackling of electricity surrounded but did not consume her. Seconds later bolts of white lightning flashed from her across The Green. Thunderclaps, one after another in rapid succession, struck Bots as they blasted apart with blinding flashes and violent concussions. The explosions knocked us to the ground.

My ears reverberated from the blasts while the brilliant flashes remained etched on my retina. I spent a moment on my hands and knees desperately trying to recover.

"What the hell," Diane murmured.

I lifted my head blinking, trying vainly to clear my vision. Everything remained motionless. The Bots near us lay blasted apart, their bodies not even recognizable, tendrils of smoke drifting from the pieces that remained. Elsewhere across the now silent Green, a dozen other wisps of smoke floated upward. For long seconds the rising smoke was the only movement.

I turned to look where Elderphino had been standing on a bench. She now lay unmoving on the ground.

Ever so slowly I stood and helped Cassie to her feet. She embraced me, arms around me, head on my chest. "I thought we were going to die." She was breathing heavy and began to sob.

"So did I," was all I could say.

Looking out over The Green, I could discern in the subdued light of the rising moon that Astari were on their knees or stood with heads to the ground. Not a single Bot remained alive. It was an eerie sight: the shimmering darkness, a hush so unnaturally quiet.

Our Astari companions rose, except for Damek who

remained seated, shoulders slumped, hands covering his face. At first, I thought he was injured until I saw his body heaving with sobs.

For long moments we stood there gaping, not knowing what to say or do. Quintia, Bevon, and Riyaad seemed lost in thought, heads bowed, almost as if in prayer, while Damek remained on the ground, his soft sobs the only sound.

Matt was the first to break the silence. In a tender voice, as if not wanting to disturb the hush, he said, "What happened?"

Nobody answered at first. Riyaad then spoke in a voice thick with emotion, "It is what we call the invocation. It's our right. Elderphino chose to use it."

Not understanding what he meant I waited for more. Matt frowned, but neither of us asked. Each of our Astari companions were so distressed that the rest of us forestalled asking more questions.

A rustle of activity began to take place around The Green as Astari began caring for the wounded even as bitter cries of grief punctuated the still air as they began to identify the dead. The glow lights slowly came back on, making the visual of those killed even more grotesque. Many Astari lay unmoving on the ground, grieving friends or family already surrounding them.

Quintia barely whispered, answering Matt's question, "Tomorrow will be a day to explain. Not now."

Even Quintia, the more outspoken and gleeful of our Astari companions, would say no more.

CHAPTER TWENTY
Final Goodbyes

On the morning after the Bot attack, the day dawned overcast with dark, threatening clouds and occasional drizzle. Rarely did the sun fail to make its appearance here on the Raised Isles. Most days were warm and pleasant, and the showers were brief. But today the overcast sky reflected the somber mood of the Raised Isles.

The girls joined us, and we sat together in the common room of our cottage rather than our usual morning spot on the terrace between the two cottages, which today was wet and dreary. We dared not venture alone out onto The Green. Our Astari companions were nowhere to be seen; it was rare when at least one of them was not nearby.

"I can't believe she's gone," Eric mumbled. He was still in shock.

"I still don't understand what happened," said Diane. "The explosion. And then they were destroyed."

I wasn't sure if she expected an answer, but nobody offered one. We were all at a loss.

We listened to the soft patter of rain against the windows until Matt broke the silence again. "You realize, this changes everything." I wasn't sure what he meant, and I noticed a frown on the others. He continued, "The Bots plainly wanted to kill us yesterday. We were the reason for this attack; the Astari were just collateral damage to them."

"But the Astari brought us here to save us from them — when they attacked us at your home in the Berkshires," I said.

He nodded. "Exactly. The Bots were after us that night according to Elderphino. And they were after us yesterday. It didn't matter that the Astari brought us here. It only delayed them."

I exhaled a bitter laugh. "So we're not safe anywhere."

He shook his head. "No, that's not what I mean, but you're right. What I'm saying is that we have to stop them … the Bots. Either that or they're going to keep at this until we're dead."

"You can't be serious," barked Diane. "How in God's name can we possibly stop them? Reason with them? Or maybe we can just fight them?" she derided.

"We've been here for a while now," I said. "And we still don't have an answer." I realized nobody knew what I meant, so I added, "The reason why they're attacking us. Why? Because we wrote that stupid utopia paper? Even the Astari didn't have an answer. If there were only a way to understand what they're thinking and discuss it with them rationally."

"That doesn't seem possible," Eric offered. He wore a stern, almost defiant expression. "And the Astari did provide reasons. The Bots want to destroy anything that would make the Astari or the people of Earth better. I think the Bots have it in their heads that the Utopia Project will make the world better, or the Astari better, and they can't fucking stand the thought of that happening." He added with a snort, "Nice going guys … on that paper."

~ ~ ~

It was late morning when someone knocked softly on the door to our room. We stood immediately. It was Damek, a grim and tired expression with blood splattered clothes. We motioned him in, and he sat looking at his hands as he rubbed them together softly, remaining quiet for long moments. The rest of us exchanged worried glances.

Finally, he looked up and cleared his throat. "I'm sorry earthfriends. It has been a long, difficult night."

"What can you tell us?" Matt asked.

Damek stared at the floor a moment before answering, "Nearly forty Astari are dead including the Lady Grandmother who used the invocation. Another half dozen cling to life. Many others have severe injuries but will survive. It is a sad day indeed." Raising his head to look at us, "I know there is much to explain. You deserve to know everything. We will tell you all, but please, not now. Not yet." He spoke with such sadness; a tone I had never heard from him.

"We have much to do now. Our Parting Ceremony for the dead will take place tomorrow, and we still have many arrangements to make. None of us have had any sleep this night; I told Quintia, Bevon, and Riyaad to go rest and that I would speak with you first. Tomorrow, after the parting is over, we will explain more and answer all."

He rose slowly to leave but then stopped. "Oh, I am not sure we can arrange it, but I know grandmother would want you to be present at the Parting Ceremony. I am not sure if it will be possible, but I will ask that a ship be made available to take you to the ceremony. It will be in the morning."

He turned to walk toward the door but paused again. "I'm sorry to be forgetting so much today. I have asked another companion to bring some meals for you and to keep watch outside. He should be along shortly. I am afraid there will only be cold provisions. I think it best if you don't wander about today, especially on The Green. It is best. There is much ..." He fought a lump in his throat. "Much cleaning up left to be done."

After he had left, I felt more depressed than ever.

~ ~ ~

Damek returned early the next morning. He appeared less shell-shocked but still somber. His attire was more formal than I had ever seen before.

"Good morning earthfriends," he called out as he entered the common room of our quarters. "I'm sorry if I wake you. We will depart shortly for the Parting Ceremony. A sailing ship will ferry you ... that is if you wish to attend. It is not required."

"Of course we would," answered Matt. "Where will it be?"

"The island of Catalinar — our spiritual retreat."

"Are you sure it's okay, us attending?"

Damek nodded. "It will be fine ... really. I will wake Diane and Cassie, please ready yourselves. We leave shortly."

It was the first time any of us were on an Astari sailing vessel. In fact, it was the first time we had seen one up close, having viewed them only from a distance until now. It was larger than I expected, the hull towered over us as we stood near it, a rope ladder had been extended over the side — the only way of gaining entrance to the deck. Three large blintas floated at the top of each of the masts. The ship was now tethered to the ground, having sailed from its home island of Mendart, the fishing village.

It could easily hold dozens of people, but we were its only passengers in addition to its small crew. "Please pardon the accommodations," said Damek once we were onboard. "These ships are made for fishing or ferrying food supplies between the islands, not passengers. So there are few benches. But we thought this would be better than taking you individually by sail."

The view was magnificent once the sails unfurled and we were airborne. Unlike the sail I had undertaken with Bevon, I could observe the islands more comfortably without feeling I was going to fall. Each island shimmered with a pristine sparkle in the early sunshine. It was hard to believe that something so heinous had taken place only two nights ago.

We were all too enamored with the view to say much and Damek did not disturb our reverie as we leaned over the edge of the ship's railing to gaze outward. Unlike my first sail, this was not a tour of the different islands. So we flew directly to Catalinar and landed in what seemed a matter of minutes.

Quintia, Bevon, and Riyaad were waiting for us as the ship came in for a landing. They secured the tethers and helped us off the rope ladder. "The ceremony will take place on the other side of the island," said Damek. "Come, many are assembling there now."

The look of this island was much different from Tensheann: many shaded alcoves with small one-room structures, briskly running streams with benches along the banks, many places that appeared to be set up for one to simply be alone and enjoy the vibrant beauty of the island. It fit in with the purpose of Catalinar serving as a spiritual retreat. Each of us had now visited several other islands, but this was the first time any of us had set foot here.

We walked along a gently inclining path which spilled out onto an open area at the top. I stopped short as we came upon the place where the Astari bodies had been laid out in neat rows. It was startling to see how many there were. My heart lurched as I gazed at the small forms of the many children.

Each body lay upon a soft bed of some green material that looked like leaves, or maybe tiny flowers — I couldn't be sure. All the dead were clad in a pure white robe with their heads uncovered, except for a few — I assumed those who had suffered facial wounds.

Around the bodies stood many Astari, talking quietly in small groups, while many others knelt next to a body, heads bowed. Other Astari went from body to body, pausing for several moments at each, their heads down, tears streaming from faces. Others lined the narrow river that flowed from a small lake on the other side of the bodies. The river meandered to the edge of the island, where it fell to the ocean below. This river was the source of the waterfall that was my first sight upon our transition from Earth to the island of Palbender.

"Where's the body of Elderphino?" asked Eric.

"Over this way," said Damek, taking a deep breath to steel himself as he led us toward the dead. "It is our custom to touch our forehead to the forehead of one who has died, at least to the one we were close to during their life. Some believe that coming in contact with the body in such a way results in us receiving the power and essence they had when alive. Whether that is true or not, it has come to symbolize a spiritual moment for us; the last brief link to the one we loved."

As we approached the rows of bodies, I noticed for the

first time that other Astari were bending over a dead one and bringing their forehead in contact with the body. Many of the Astari wore grim and sullen expressions, and many welled up with tears. Once again I had to admire the fortitude of these people.

We shortly came to the body of Lady Elderphino. I was immediately struck by how natural her face appeared, almost as if in sleep rather than dead. But knowing she was dead, I was overcome with a feeling of hopelessness, a misery I hadn't experienced in a long time. So sudden had the feeling come over me that I nearly missed what Damek was saying, "... not necessary to touch foreheads. If you wish, it is appropriate to say some final words, either privately or spoken."

For long moments we all stood quietly around her, heads bowed. Damek went to his knees at her side. Quintia, Riyaad, and Bevon, who had been paying respects to others, now came to stand next to us. Although Damek spoke softly, his words drifted up to us in the stillness of the morning air. "Grandmother. How can I go on without you?" His voice shook, and tears dripped freely off his cheek. "You were my strength." He paused long moments as he gazed at her face, lost in thought. "Until we meet again." Ever so slowly he bent his forehead to hers, holding it there for long seconds, eyes closed before standing upright.

We stood in silence for a moment until surprisingly Eric stepped forward and went to his knees as he took Damek's place. I heard him speak gently, "I never knew my real grandmothers. You're the closest I ever had. Thank you for your understanding and patience." And then he bent his head to hers. I was standing on the other side of the body, so I clearly saw the briefest pulse of warm light emanate from Elderphino's head to Eric's. I opened my eyes wide, ready to ask about it, but others had their heads bent low, eyes downcast. Eric paused a long moment as he raised his head, gazing at her with an expression of wonderment more than sorrow.

"It is time," said Quintia. "The Final Parting is about to begin." I had no time to question Eric about what I had seen, and after a moment I decided it was just a trick of the light or a reflection.

We walked a short distance to where a group of the Astari were standing to the side of the rows of bodies. They stood quietly, the silence broken only by the sound of splashing water from the narrow river and the chirping of nearby birds. Very slowly the Astari began humming a mournful tune. There were no words, just the melody. The rest of us respectfully stood until they had finished.

After long moments of silent reflection, several Astari stepped over to one of the bodies, picked up the linen draped form and ceremoniously carried it to the head of the stream where a pile of slender pallets sat. Each pallet was just large enough for a body and contained a bed of straw on top of its thin wooden frame. I assumed the Astari who carried this body were family members as they laid it carefully upon a pallet which another Astari had removed from the pile. Two other Astari helped them move the pallet into the stream, preventing it from floating away. One of the family members took a torch that was burning nearby and carefully lowered it to the straw on the pallet until the flame caught, upon which the Astari holding the pallet in place let the running water take it.

From our vantage point, we could see the length of the river. Ever so slowly, the burning funeral pyre carried the body of the Astari down the needle-thin river that was now lined on both sides with a throng of others. Those along the river bank watched it pass by them as it gained speed and burned ever more intense until it slipped off the edge, plunging into the ocean below. Several Astari had already carefully lifted another body and slowly carried it to a straw pallet.

Emotions were raw as one after another, a body was placed on a pyre and floated away, burning briefly in one final display of brilliance, until slipping over the edge, consumed by the waters below. As the procession continued, I reflected on the symbolism of this simple yet elegant funeral arrangement, and how it mirrored human burials. But here, as in many other ways, the Astari chose their own manner of handling it.

One thing remained the same was the grief etched on the faces of the families and friends of the dead. Many were weeping quietly while others simply let tears run unchecked as they watched one by one, the bodies slip away down the river.

Seeing their grief, I felt an intense loathing toward the Bots for what they had done. A mother and father now took their dead child of maybe five and placed her on a pyre, the father lowering a torch to the straw, the mother sobbing. I looked closely at the face of the young body. With a stab of anguish, I suddenly recognized her as one of the children we had met on the first day we arrived in this world. We had visited a school, and the girl had asked us if we would save them from the Bots. She had said she was afraid of them. My emotions now nearly boiled over, barely held in check. Never before had I felt such hatred.

Damek leaned close to us, tears wetting his cheeks. "This is the Final Parting," he said. "It is the last duty bestowed upon the family and to those dearest to the dead as they carry the body and set it on its way to its final journey. I have asked my companions to assist me in this, and I would like each of you also to take part. As Astari, we consider it a solemn responsibility, and I know Elderphino would be pleased having each of you included."

Matt answered for all of us, "It will be an honor. Just tell us what we should do when it is time."

Damek nodded grimly. "Hers will be the last to be placed upon the river. We will carry her in turn, from one group to another. I will explain when we are ready." Choking up with emotion he, was barely able to add, "Thank you."

Ever so painfully the number of remaining bodies dwindled until only Elderphino remained. Damek stepped forward to her body, bent low and once again touched his forehead to hers. But then he moved away to stand a little distance from the last straw pallet. Quintia directed us in a soft voice. "We will carry the Lady four at a time, passing her from one group to another until Damek takes her alone for the final steps." Looking at us, she said, "Matt, please come with us. We'll lift the lady and carry her to Philip, Eric, Diane, and Cassie. Stand about there." She pointed to a spot roughly between Damek and the body. "You will convey her, in turn, to Damek." We all nodded and went to the place she indicated while Matt joined her, Riyaad and Bevon.

With two to each side, they lifted the body of Elderphino ever so carefully from its resting place and slowly carried her toward us. I glanced at my friends to be sure we were ready and in position. That's when I noticed Diane's expression, mouth hanging open, eyes wide, her breathing heavy. I could see she was terrified and I suddenly realized the fear people have about touching a dead body, even one wrapped in linens as was Elderphino. I had visions of her refusing to participate when the time came, possibly doing something stupid, which would likely be a terrible insult to the Astari, especially Damek.

The others had already covered half the short distance to us. I nudged her and whispered so only she could hear, "Diane. You can do this. Please … be strong."

For a moment I wasn't sure if my words would help calm her or push her over the edge. Her face was blank now, and I had a sinking feeling this wasn't going to turn out well. I tried to smile to calm her but, it felt more like a grimace, probably one that would scare most children.

And suddenly the others were next to us with her body. I positioned myself facing Diane, while Eric and Cassie, oblivious to Diane's hesitation, faced each other. Each of us took the place of Matt, Bevon, Quintia and Riyaad as we reached under the body. I was prepared to support the body of Elderphino at this end in case Diane couldn't but a semblance of resolve came over her as she steeled herself.

As we took the body, I was somewhat startled by how little she weighed. The Astari were short and lean anyway, but her body seemed so light.

Tenderly we held her and stepped toward Damek. I looked across at Diane. She wore a determined expression, her body tense, arms outstretched in an unnatural position. As Damek came between us to receive the body, she stepped back as soon as possible and shuddered for a second.

Once Damek held the body and moved toward the river, I shifted closer to Diane and put my arm on her back. "You okay?" I mouthed, suddenly feeling sorry for her — someone who always seemed to have it all together, never frazzled, always determined. I could feel the tension slowly ebb from her as she just nodded. I thought for a moment how reassuring it was to know she had frailties and fears, as we all did.

Very slowly Damek set Elderphino's body onto the floating

pyre, pausing a long moment to gaze at her longingly before moving the torch to the straw bedding. Flames quickly took over as the current brought it down the river. Maybe it was just my imagination, but it seemed to glow with a brilliance greater than any others. It was as if the Astari held their collective breath the moment the flame was about to pass from sight forever.

Then it was gone. And with it, some of the strength of the Astari.

CHAPTER TWENTY-ONE

Woodbery College: Fifth Interlude

The Winter semester at Woodbery College arrived with a fresh four inches of snow blanketing the campus. Towering pines on the tree-lined campus bent low under the weight of snow hanging heavy on their branches. Even the typical sounds of school life were muffled by the blanket of white, broken only by the occasional roar of a snow blower clearing a sidewalk.

It felt good to be back. Spending the holiday break with family was fun, but it made me realize how distant I had grown from them since coming here to Woodbery.

Inhaling the brisk air, I walked energetically across The Common, the expanse of crisscrossing walkways in the center of campus that in other times of the year displayed broad lawns shaded by maples. During those less snow-covered seasons, it was a favorite place for Woodbery students to hang out, throw a Frisbee, or study outside. None of that was happening today.

The bus ride back from Rochester was boring and long. After dumping my bag in my room, I decided to walk to the student center for dinner since the dining hall in my dorm wasn't yet open. The campus was still mostly deserted with the majority of students not arriving for another day or two. I took another deep breath, looking forward to the new semester and the Utopia Project.

Inside the dining room, I shed my winter coat on an empty table and turned toward the serving stations. That's when I spotted Diane and Cassie engaged in what appeared to be a spirited discussion as they sat at a table on the other side of the hall. I hesitated for a second, thinking I might be interrupting them. But I chided myself for being so timid. I picked up my coat again and walked over.

They still hadn't noticed me as I approached. Cassie was explaining something about her holiday in Wisconsin, so I stood hesitantly, not wanting to interrupt. Diane saw me first, breaking into a broad smile. After not seeing her for nearly a month I marveled at how strikingly attractive she was. Here in the prime of her life, her smooth skin, sparkling green eyes, and lips that were difficult not to stare at, she was more than gorgeous. Looking at her face gave me pause to think how long it had been since I had sex with a girl.

Cassie, always the more spirited member of the group, immediately jumped up to hug me. "Our teammate! You're back early." She hugged me tightly, holding her embrace moments longer than I would have expected. I couldn't help smile. Of everyone in the group, Cassie was the warmest and most expressive. Her eyes sparkled, and her lips curled up in the most delightful smile. A pleasant feeling spread through me.

"Come, sit." She motioned to the table. "Have you eaten yet?"

I shook my head. "Just got back." Looking at Diane, I asked, "Is Matt with you?" I scanned the dining room, trying to spot him.

"I came in last night. I wanted to come back early and get a head start on things, do some reading on a few of the books on our syllabus."

Sitting down with them, I asked again, "Where's Matt?"

She exchanged a brief look with Cassie. I had the feeling they had already discussed this. "Oh, he'll be back later tonight. He wanted to visit an uncle in Manhattan before the semester started. This guy runs a small company and had invited Matt to visit with him, discuss what it takes to run a startup." I couldn't help notice the slight frown she wore as she spoke. "You know Matt. More than anything he wants to start a company after school."

"Yup, I know. He's only mentioned it a million times already."

"Well… that's what drives him I guess." Again I detected a noticeable sadness to her tone.

Deciding it would be too personal to question her about Matt, I changed the subject. "So how was everyone's holiday? Cass, you enjoy getting home? Was Santa good?"

She smirked. "It was cold as hell, and yes, Santa paid a visit. Told me I was nice this year." Looking at Diane, she smiled wickedly. "One of these years I'm going to be naughty just to see if I still get presents."

Diane shrieked. "Cass, that's not like you."

She pouted. "Maybe I deserve a change of pace."

"How were the Cayman Islands?" I asked Diane. "I can see you got some sun."

"Oh, they were good. Very nice." She spoke without much emotion.

"Good? Very nice? You don't sound very excited about it."

She pursed her lips and fixed me with that stare she often used when sizing up someone — the sort of stare that feels like it's going right through you. It was one of the expressions she had in common with Matt. I had the distinct impression she was deciding what, or how much to say. I had quickly become friends with everyone in the group, but mine was still a new friendship.

Glancing quickly at Cassie, she said, "It's just that … well, I sometimes wish I were the most important thing in his life. I find it difficult to compete against the things that drive him." I was both embarrassed and happy that she opened up to me, but also regretted going down this path. "As I was saying to Cass earlier, it's not that we don't have a great time together, it's just that his career is always at the top of the list. And I have this fear it always will be."

I realized my mouth was hanging open so I shut it. Cassie's expression had turned somber. Not sure if Diane was expecting a response or not, but into the silence, I said, "We're all concerned about our careers Diane. That's why we're here." I wasn't sure if I should add what I was thinking. But I did, trying to make it sound more like advice than an insult, "And you're as driven as he is, from what I can see."

She put on a smile, but to me, it seemed a bit forced. "I don't know. Maybe I expect too much. I only want the very best."

I didn't want to say she might already have the very best.

It was obvious she didn't want to say more. The fact that she mentioned it to me at all was a measure of how much it must be bothering her. So rather than talk about what was really on her mind, the three of us had dinner together and spoke about the reading assignment for the Utopia Project, the recent snow that had fallen on campus, the professors assigned to our team, and a dozen other things that weren't important. And as we talked and laughed, I realized that this is the way people such as us act: engaging in countless discussions about the things in life that don't matter rather than speaking of those feelings or beliefs that shape who we truly are, or what we would become.

When Diane had finished her meal, she grabbed her coat from a nearby chair. "I'm going to head back to my apartment. Matt should be here soon, and I want to hear about his visit." I volunteered to walk her back to her place, but she waved me off, telling us to enjoy the rest of our meal.

"I don't know about those two," said Cassie after she was out of earshot. "At times they appear so in love, but then she brings this up. It makes me wonder. If the two of them can't be happy, what hope is there for the rest of us? I mean, they're perfect for each other."

"Yeah, good thing we don't have to worry about relationships not working out." I was trying to be sarcastic, considering that neither Cassie or I were dating.

She took it the way I had intended and laughed sweetly. "What's the matter Phil, jealous? Maybe you need to be more like Eric. He takes a certain pride in telling us about his many girlfriends."

The rest of our dinner was pleasant as we had dessert and then tea. I realized there were so few times I was able to hang out with her alone. Most of the time the rest of the team was around. This felt good. In fact, it seemed we both needed the company and friendship of each other that night, whether it was because of Diane's discussion of Matt, or just because we were happy to be back at school.

After dinner, I suggested we have a drink at the Hideout Cafe, a local pub located strategically just off campus. And to my surprise, she agreed.

Inside, the room was half empty, unlike most nights when school was in session, particularly on weekends when the place was often filled shoulder to shoulder with college students, music blaring, the smell of stale beer wafting through the air. But tonight it was actually pleasant with soft music in the background. We sat at a booth by a window with the fluorescent glow of a hanging Budweiser sign lighting our table. Outside the snow began falling again in big wispy flakes, already coating the freshly shoveled sidewalks.

That night the words came freely: the books I was reading for pleasure, the movies we saw, my past girlfriends (far too few), the music we both enjoyed, and a wealth of other topics that I had never discussed with her during those times when the rest of our classmates were around. I felt she needed to share her life. But nearly as much, it seemed she wanted to know more about me as a person, not just as a classmate. And all the time we spoke her eyes were riveted on me, not past me or gazing elsewhere. She made me feel that what I was saying was the most important thing. I realized I rarely had, if ever, met someone with her intensity, whether to a conversation such as this, or the way she lived life on her terms. But that night I knew she wanted to share her thoughts with someone else; it made me wonder if she felt this was something missing.

One drink led to another, and then another after that. By our fourth or maybe our fifth — I had already lost count — I noticed that her speech was not as sharp. And I realized the same was true for me. When our waitress came by to ask if we wanted another round, she replied that she had enough. "I could use some fresh air," she said. "Walk me back to my dorm?"

Several inches of snow covered the sidewalks outside. Reaching up and holding my arm, she said, "Don't let me fall." I happily obliged. Bulky coats or not, I would never have expected — hoped — to be walking arm-in-arm together with a girl as vibrant as Cassie McKenzie. If my high school buddies could see me now, I'm sure they would be proud of me — or more likely, jealous. A smile came to my face as I tried not to let her notice. Thinking about high school, I wondered where I would be right now if I had agreed to my parents plan to join my dad's business as an auto mechanic. Whatever course that life would have taken, I'm sure it wouldn't have involved walking arms entwined with the most captivating girl I had ever met.

The night was cold, but not bitterly so, at least it didn't feel it after the alcohol we had consumed. The glinting snowflakes made it all feel surreal. Adding to the dreamlike experience, Cassie put her head on my shoulder as we walked, making me wonder how this evening was going to end.

Her dorm was on the other side of the campus, and we passed only a few students who had ventured out on this snowy evening. Most windows were dark as rooms awaited the arrival of their occupants in the next day or two.

Her residence was one of the smaller dorms, although maybe one of the most picturesque with its brick front and slate roof reminding me of a building from colonial times. As we took the steps to a landing before the locked front door, she disengaged her arm to reach for her student card. For the first time tonight I became uncomfortable, suddenly not sure what I should do and what would be appropriate and what not. She never gave me a chance.

With her card in hand, she leaned forward and kissed me gently on the mouth. I thought she would quickly end it, but she didn't. Her kiss became stronger, and then more urgent. Her lips were soft and her mouth warm. As her tongue touched mine, I began to surrender to the moment, reaching one hand around to the back of her neck. She moaned, pressing her body against me. But short seconds later she pulled back. "No, this a mistake." More than anything else, her expression conveyed a touch of sadness.

At this point my clarity of thought was entirely bypassing my brain, taking place somewhere else on my body. "It's okay," I murmured.

She broke into a smile, and then began laughing, not in a harsh, mean way, but more of a 'what're we doing' way — at least that's the way I took it. "You know we'll both regret this if we go any further. You know we will." Looking up at the falling snow, she shook her head sadly. "Phil, I'm not the best at commitments, and with what we have going on this term, it isn't the best idea for us…" Her eyes had begun to water. "If things didn't work out, this would only complicate our life. And it's not something either of us needs, especially right now with this course."

I knew she was bothered by what was going on with Diane and Matt right now. But truthfully, at this moment I didn't care. "Complications can be good," I said, realizing how stupid it sounded as soon as the words left my lips, even though I had thought it a profound statement in my mind.

She smiled. Oh, that sweet, sweet smile. What I would give to have this continue. "You're an exceptional person Phil. And if things were different, maybe someday…" She left the rest unsaid. But I knew there would be no other place or time such as this.

The moment passed, rational thinking returned. With a lingering regret I said lightly, "Well, you know Cass, it's always more satisfying to get a pretty girl to say nice things about me rather than take me to bed with them." Smiling, I added, "It's sooo much more satisfying."

She laughed. And after a moment so did I, which caused her to giggle all the more. The pent up emotions seemed to flow out of her as she laughed warmly. She continued until tears began rolling down her cheeks.

I knew it was time to be going, so once her laughter subsided I leaned over and quickly kissed her cheek, tasting the salty sweetness of her tears. "Goodnight Cass. Thanks for a wonderful evening." Seeing a flicker of concern cross her face, I added, "And don't worry, tonight stays with us. No need of making more of it than it was."

She nodded and turned to hold her card at the reader to unlock the door, but not before I glimpsed a hint of gratitude in her eyes.

Walking back to my dorm, I wasn't sure if I should feel elation or frustration. I had never expected anything like this to happen between us. Even though she was always pleasant and friendly to me, I considered Cass out of my league. And now to find out that she has insecurities like the rest of us was surprising.

And then of all people, Diane expressing misgivings about her relationship with Matt. What was the world coming to?

Still, I couldn't help smile broadly thinking about this encounter, knowing that I had come a long way.

CHAPTER TWENTY-TWO

Answers and Decisions

As we sailed back to Tensheann from the Final Parting, Damek suggested we meet on The Green to discuss events of the last few days.

"Are you sure it's okay?" I asked, "Are you ready?"

He nodded. "I may never be over this, but you deserve a fuller explanation of the invocation. And I want to discuss a major decision with you."

Later, as we were leaving the ship, Cassie asked, "Are you sure about The Green? I mean with all the killing that took place there."

He smiled sadly, "Now more than ever it is a special place for all Astari. And it has been restored to its previous condition."

So after the Astari changed back into their usual clothing, they met us at our cottages, and we walked the short distance to the place where just two days ago we celebrated the Midsummer Celebration before the savage attack.

As Damek had assured us, any remnants of the fighting and killing had been swept clean. The Green was, as always, a restful oasis to view the wonder of the other Raised Isles.

More than the average number of Astari appeared to want to visit here after the massacre. Dozens of small groups and more individual Astari sat gazing or talking together. But we had no trouble finding a spot that had enough benches to seat each of us.

"Thank you for joining us this morning at the Final Parting," began Damek after we had settled down. He appeared contemplative as he spoke. "It's a difficult time for us Astari because of the bond we have with each other. And when so many have been lost at once…" He was at a loss to continue at first but then said, "Our shared DNA from the time we existed as electrons on your networks and servers is a strong bond. The coupling we once shared remains with us to this day. And when one of us perishes, it leaves a void in our oneness."

He paused a long while before continuing, "So in a way, all of those killed were a part of me, as well as every other Astari." Looking at us carefully before speaking again, he said, "But there is much more that needs to be explained to you about events of the attack. I'm sure you are puzzled by what took place."

We waited for him to explain as he searched for words. "I should tell you how Elderphino was able to destroy the Bots."

"Yes, please," said Eric.

Damek nodded. "It was a weapon — if you want to call it that, although a capacity that she had within her might be a better explanation. In human terms, it might be called a destruct sequence." He paused as he marshaled his thoughts. "As with our shared bond, this is something carried over from the time we roamed the networks of Earth as an antivirus program. Our programming contained the ability to destroy a malware virus when we came in close contact with it. Our developers created this capability in our program so that we could disable the malware. Back then, if we encountered a particular virus, we executed a script that wiped out that virus. When we ascended into our physical form, that capability remained with some of us. Elderphino had this ability to destroy the Bots when they are nearby. But in so doing, the one drawing on that capability also ends their existence." He wore a pained expression. "She was able to wipe out the Bots who attacked us by initiating the instruction set, but as a result, she perished in the process. She knew it would kill her." And after a long moment, he added, "Grandmother saw no other recourse."

"She sacrificed herself rather than let the Bots kill us?" said Diane. It was as if a new thought dawned on her.

Damek nodded, "Yes, to save you and the other Astari who would also die from the attack."

Eric asked, "How many of you have this … capability to destroy the Bots?" I could see he was troubled. Eric, probably more than any of us except the Astari, was close to Elderphino, having forged a connection with her in recent weeks.

Damek smiled grimly. "Once we gained physical form, the capability was lost to all except a select few. I believe Elderphino was the last."

Matt asked, "What I can't understand, Damek, is how the Bots appeared here on Tensheann in the first place. It seems they arrived somehow through the Star Lights. Were the lights helping them?"

He shook his head. "No, that's unlikely. From what we know of these Star Lights they care little about our battle with the Bots." He grappled for words. "No, I believe they were duped in spite of their superior intellect. It was an old trick of the Bots, frequently used in their early days to infiltrate computers and networks. It was known in those days of computer viruses as the back door Trojan Horse. We believe the Bots somehow tapped into the energy signature of the Star Lights to enhance their capabilities. With it, they were able to transition here by using the power of their unwilling host." He shook his head sadly. "I don't know if we will ever again see the Star Lights after this episode. That would be a great loss indeed."

My thoughts wandered to the vision of my brother Gary who I was able to see because of the Star Lights. I understood the sorrow that he and other Astari must be feeling.

Bevon spoke passionately. "The Bots are devious. I fear they have already surpassed our skills. It is a cause for great concern." He and Damek exchanged a look that told me they were in agreement.

"What's going to happen with the Ruling Members now?" asked Diane.

"Someone will eventually emerge to take her place. And together they will select the First," said Damek. "We do not have a formal method to choose one. It is more of a consensus; a sort of evolutionary process whereby all Astari voice their opinions. It will not happen quickly."

Damek paused for a long moment, gazing at us now with a resolute expression. "Which brings me to an important decision that we must make. And I fear it is not an easy one." He gazed at his companions before continuing. "The Bots have once again become a threat to us and this realm, and they must be stopped. But I fear the Astari alone are insufficient to the task, and until a leader amongst us emerges there will be no action."

"What do you propose?" Matt asked.

Damek stared at us a long time before answering. "Just as in the early days of our emergence, we must seek an alliance with the other great races — those such as us who have emerged from other technologies and other worlds. We have to fight the Bots together. It's the only way."

"But if these other races don't feel threatened they won't have any incentive," I blurted.

He nodded. "I understand. But we don't know if others have been threatened. They may now be fighting for their lives, and we don't know it. Our different races have become isolated since we last joined forces to battle the Bots." He gestured to his companions. "We have decided that it's best for us to journey and seek them out and offer a proposal that we again join forces."

"And this hasn't been discussed with your Ruling Members?" Matt asked.

Damek shook his head. "No, we plan to go without their knowledge or approval. Without a First to garner a consensus they would just delay us."

"You're going to leave us?" asked a distraught Cassie.

"That is the difficult part of this decision," he responded. "Most of us believe the Bots want you dead or captured. Your utopia proposal depicts a world that is the antithesis to them, and they have latched onto that. You're no longer safe here nor in your world. They would likely have succeeded in their last attack were it not for the power of Elderphino. We see no reason they'll stop. And if we're not here to protect you…" We understood the risk without him needing to spell it out. "But if we stay, we may fail anyway, and who knows how many other Astari will suffer and die." Looking at his companions for support, he added, "I see no other solution. We need to make an attempt to strike an alliance with others."

His tone softened, and his shoulders sagged. I could see the strain the last few days had taken on him. "We have friends — good friends — who we will ask to watch over you, much as we have done. And the Ruling Members may assign others as well. We will not leave you on your own."

"How long?" asked Cassie.

Damek shrugged. "We have not explored the mainland for some time. I don't know, but I suspect it will not be brief."

He hesitated before continuing, "There's another possibility." Again he gazed at his companions as if needing their support. "I am not sure if this is the best idea, but we have discussed the possibility of you coming with us."

Stunned silence greeted him as we each considered this unexpected twist. Damek continued, "This has the advantage of getting you away from Loralee where the Bots have pinpointed you. They know you're here. And if you leave, we don't know if they'll be able to track you so easily. But we are not positive. So there is a danger either way."

"Don't know!" Eric erupted. "That doesn't give me a warm and fuzzy feeling."

"No, earthfriend Eric. I don't believe there are easy answers."

"So let me get this straight," Eric continued. "You want to form this alliance with others, but you don't have a clue if they would be the least bit interested. And you want us to come with you on this ... this quest. Do I have it right?"

For the first time today Damek broke a smile. "You do have a way of cutting to the essential facts. I wouldn't disagree with your explanation."

"Can't you just transition to these other people?" Diane asked. "I mean just like the Bots did in their attack and when you first brought us here. That seems faster and a lot less dangerous than traveling."

He shook his head. "We have not mastered that skill, as I'm afraid the Bots have. It's just another display of how I fear they have gained on us."

"But who knows what's out there or what you'll find?" said Diane, now noticeably concerned. She looked at the rest of us as if amazed we didn't agree with her. "We could be killed if we all went."

Cassie smiled. "Well, this is a switch. The two people who were most upset about being here are now most upset about the thought of leaving. A certain irony in this, isn't there?"

Diane glared at her, but Matt said calmly, "Di, we could be killed here. We were almost killed here."

Eric threw his hands up. "I for one never wanted to come here — I never asked for this. But now that we're here, I don't know if I like the alternative."

Matt continued in a soft tone, which I could see infuriated Diane and Eric even more. "I understand these last few days have been upsetting for all of us, especially the Astari." Looking directly at Damek, he continued, "But I have to ask this … are you sure you decided this for all the right reasons? I can see how the death of Elderphino and the others affected you. And I understand you want to avoid bloodshed." Matt gestured to the other Astari. "But do you believe you need to take on this responsibility for all your people? After all, the Ruling Members will eventually come together on this."

Damek considered this a long while before answering. "If not us, then who? Do we simply hope and wait for others to act? Elderphino was a leader in every way possible. We're training to be leaders. Maybe it's time for us to take on this burden at a time when it's most difficult and the choice uncertain. In my mind, our failure to act would make it clear we're not ready for the role we aspire." Shaking his head, he added, "No, in that case, we should be Tinkerers or fishermen or cooks — all worthy occupations. But not the one we have chosen."

His words caused me to consider once again how I had failed miserably in my desired occupation — how I always seemed to drift along in life, always taking the easy way. He shamed me. I reflected on the words of my brother Gary. 'Don't stand on the sideline.' Without waiting for the thought to jell in my head, I said, "We should go. It's the right thing to do."

My friends looked at me as if I had slipped into speaking Swahili. That is except for Matt, who smiled in admiration.

Once I said it, in my heart I knew it was right. "We need to do more than just exist," I said. "Isn't that a theme from our Utopia Project? 'Life is more than survival,' we had said. We need to have a purpose. The Bots want us dead. We need to do something about that, and not just expect that others like these Astari will take care of us." I surprised myself with the intensity of my emotion.

Eric, Diane, and Cassie appeared too startled to speak. I wasn't sure if they thought me an idiot or were just surprised at my outburst. Matt came to my rescue. "Well-spoken Phil, I agree." It was all he needed to say. He was still our leader, and we trusted him.

Eric was about to protest, but Matt continued. "I don't know if going with them is right or not, but I feel the same as Phil. We need to have a purpose here." He gazed fondly at our Astari companions. "These are our friends. They have already protected us without reservation. I trust them. If they think this is the right thing to do, then it's high time that we begin to contribute."

Eric made a noise but did not speak. Matt added, "But I can't make life and death decisions — which is what this may be — for each of you. This has to be your choice to go or not."

Damek nodded. "You should discuss this amongst yourselves. Whatever your decision, we will respect it."

They stood to leave, but before they stepped away, I asked, "One question. How soon? When would you want to leave?"

He thought for a moment. "We haven't made firm plans. If it were only myself, I would depart in a few days. But if you travel with us, you will need training, at least in basic self-defense. And there are supplies and logistics that we would need to take into account for a larger group. It might take a few weeks, maybe a little longer."

He considered something and added, "You realize, whether you earthfriends travel with us or not, we do this on our own without the consent or the knowledge of the Ruling Members. This needs to be a stealth mission, as you might call it. Otherwise, the debates would be endless, and I fear the Ruling Members might even try to prevent us from going without their sanction."

I was prepared for another one of our contentious sessions once the Astari walked away. But much to my surprise nobody spoke for long moments. Finally, Diane cleared her throat. "Well, if we go I think we need a more solid plan. It seems a bit nebulous."

Matt nodded. "I agree."

Cassie smiled wistfully before saying lightly, "Other races of people like the Astari ... that could be interesting."

Eric fidgeted. "I have serious doubts about this. But somehow, I feel that Elderphino would approve if she were still alive."

Matt nodded. "Then it's settled. We join them in this mission." He paused before adding, "I have to say, I'm proud of you." He gazed at each of us before continuing. "Speaking only for myself, I know how many times I regretted not making certain decisions in the past, holding back when I should have done something." I couldn't help notice that he inadvertently kept glancing at Diane as he spoke. "This may be stupid of us; I don't know. But at least we're doing something — taking action that might be significant for these people and us. I believe this is the right thing."

I thought he was finished, but after a short time, he added, "After all, how many times in a lifetime are you given a chance to make a choice such as this? How would we feel if we just passed on it?"

"Yeah, enough with the speeches," Eric chided. "Let's just do it."

I smiled — we all did. I felt good about this. Mostly, I felt good about us. I realized that Matt still had the uncanny ability to bring us together and force us to look deep into our souls. He did it with the Utopia Project, and he did it just now. And once decided, we always knew it was the right choice.

Damn, I wish I could do that.

CHAPTER TWENTY-THREE

Our Weapons

I dove to the left, narrowly avoiding a blow to my head. Taking only a second to recover, I desperately swung madly, trying to keep a grip on the hilt which was getting slick with sweat. I lurched forward, gulping for air.

Another slash by my opponent forced me back, and I nearly stumbled. I raised my weapon just in time to block a savage stroke, my arm reverberating from the clash.

He's gone mad, I thought, as I watched him advance on me again. I had considered the Astari to be somewhat ineffective fighters, but much to my chagrin he was quite good. I was no match for him. His eyes were wild as he lashed at me again with expert precision. An exposed tree root caught on my heel, tripping me. I barely avoided a bone-crushing blow to my shoulder.

My distress began to mount as I looked for an escape. For a brief second, I thought about turning around and running in the opposite direction as fast as I could. But I knew he would easily cut me down from behind. I gave ground rapidly as he advanced again, my arm now aching. I wasn't going to last much longer.

My only chance was to go on the offensive and take him down. It was now or never while my strength still held.

I stole a quick glance to my right to see if there were any obstacles. Knee-high grass obscured much of the ground, but it remained relatively flat in this area. My footing crunched on broken sticks, while the thick grass threatened to tangle around my boots. The sun cast long shadows as it hung low in the sky, occasionally blinding me if I looked in that direction.

Continuing to give ground, I positioned myself so my back was to the setting sun. I feigned another stumble, causing my opponent to hold back momentarily, squinting with the sun in his eyes. I used the advantage to thrust my spear into his unprotected underbelly, intending to plunge it into his midsection.

But somehow he anticipated my thrust and easily parried my jab and responded with a flurry of blows sending me flat on my back. Bevon wickedly smiled as he held the tip of his weapon against my throat. "And now my friend, this is where I kill you."

Closing my eyes, I thought how close I had been to defeating him. But that mattered little. I had been told that victory in battle went to the strong, the cunning and those most skilled. I was beginning to wonder if I had any of those.

"How many kills does that make?" Matt asked, laughing off to my left.

"Too many to count I fear," said Bevon as he tossed his wooden sword to the side and offered his hand to help me up. His expression, which boarded on maniac a few moments ago, now turned affable once again. "Your movements are too transparent earthfriend Philip. I can easily anticipate your moves. And you need more precision in your thrusts. You swing too wildly, leaving yourself exposed."

I winced at the new bruises on my arms and back. "You could be a little gentler with your whacks. I'll probably be black and blue all over before long."

"Better than being cut to pieces by a Bot. I would be derelict in my duties otherwise. You would not want that, now would you?"

"It might be nice for once," I answered.

"I think you're getting better," said Matt. "Bevon's training has helped us both."

"How can you tell?" I scowled. "I have yet to win a match. At least you've come close."

"It will be dark shortly," said Bevon as he slipped his vest back on. "Let's call it a day and continue again tomorrow."

I reached for a towel I had placed on a nearby bench to wipe the sweat off my bare chest, wondering if this training was getting us anywhere. "Do you think this is worth it?" I asked. "It seems I'm no closer to being able to fight a Bot than I was back when we decided this would be necessary."

Bevon eyed me appraisingly. "No, you're not ready. But with more practice, you might be. And if we run into them when we leave the Raised Isles, it just might save your life, or the very least, keep you alive until one of us can help. I already feel better."

Rubbing one of my bruises, I responded, "Sure, maybe you feel better. Not me."

The crickets and night birds filled the air with their melodies as we walked back to our cottages on the other side of Tensheann. The sky had turned deep blue, and a few stars had already appeared. A streak across the eastern horizon heralded the onset of the evening meteor shower. Celeus was a crescent low on the horizon, its size formidable compared to Halcyone.

In spite of my bruises, it was a pleasant early evening on

the Raised Isles. It made me wonder how many of these would be left for us to enjoy.

~ ~ ~

Glow lights warmly blazed as we approached our terrace. Cassie and Diane were back from their sail with Quintia and Riyaad, while Eric (who had shunned the sword and lance training) had not yet returned with Damek as he practiced with the slingshot.

Exhausted, I carefully eased myself onto a bench. In spite of the bruises, I couldn't help think how invigorating the sessions were. At least they kept me in good shape.

"Well, well," Diane said, noticing my discomfort, a trace of pleasure in her tone, "looks like you ended up with the short end of the stick today ... no pun intended." She spoke it without rancor, yet it still stung.

"Yeah, well I want to know why the girls draw practice with a sail while we get to whack each other with sticks." Looking at Riyaad, I demanded, "They are only in a harness, what's the value in that?"

He smiled. "We have been making better progress than you may realize. Both Diane and Cassie have been sailing on their own now, although with a blinta. They're quite good. And in addition to earthfriend Eric, they have been practicing the slingshot. They all have improved considerably." Diane smirked at me.

A short time later Damek returned with Eric. "I hope everyone had a productive afternoon," Damek said cheerfully. After he had settled down, his expression turned more serious. "But I have news. Two more Bots were killed today on the Isle of Alescenda, home of the Tinkerers."

"Why there? Why would they transition to that island?" I

asked.

Damek shrugged. "I can only surmise. Either they have not quite perfected their art of travel and have not been able to pinpoint an Isle precisely, or they wish to spread terror amongst all the Isles."

"That makes over a half-dozen Bots since the attack on Midsummer's Celebration," said Matt.

"Yes, which only makes me think that our plan to depart is the correct choice, as much as I rue the thought of leaving here."

"It's already been weeks," said Diane. "You sure none of the Ruling Members have caught wind of it?"

Damek shook his head. "If they have, none have spoken to us of it."

"But all this training," said Cassie. "You'd think they would wonder why we're doing it."

"There's much for them to be concerned about." He hesitated before continuing. "It appears the Bots are now waging an all-out war on the technology of Earth. We have learned that they have gained the upper hand and things do not look good."

"These creatures have invaded Earth?" asked Cassie anxiously.

"Some, such as the ones that had attacked you there. But only a few. No, they wage their primary attacks on a technology level. The computer failures and malfunctions of tech devices that you had witnessed before your transition have now increased exponentially."

I thought back to the airplane guidance and radar system failures that took place just before we left. "Can't we stop them?" I blurted.

Damek looked at me squarely with an odd expression. "I have a theory, and it is only that," he said slowly. "Not all of the Ruling Members agree with this, but I hold that the Bots have gained an advantage and strength because they are somehow funneling a power obtained from their physical ascension here on Elthea back to their network of tech-limited versions on Earth."

"Can they do that?" asked Cassie with a puzzled expression.

He shrugged. "There's much we don't know about them. But if I'm correct, it's even more important for your race that we gain an alliance with the remaining great races to destroy them once and for all."

This talk made me feel glum. And suddenly it was all too overwhelming. Even though I was the one who boldly suggested we go along with the Astari on this mission I was having second thoughts. "I don't know how this ever happened," I said, not even realizing I had spoken out loud until I saw the others look at me strangely. Once begun, however, I felt I needed to explain. "How did we ... how did I ever get here, get involved in all this? I mean I'm just a nobody ... just an average run-of-the-mill guy, maybe even less than that. I'm no hero going on a grand adventure. I mean even my name — Philip Matherson. Have you ever heard of a more boring, common name in your life? I'm just your boring, average Joe." I paused to take a deep breath. "Why do I think I can accomplish anything that is going to make a difference?" I was surprised at my outburst. But it was something that had been building in me for days now, and all it needed was this one spark about what was taking place on Earth to set me off.

Surprisingly it was Eric who spoke first. "Phil, you're far from average. We've all struggled with this." He gestured with his hands to indicate this place. "But believe me when I say that you're more than a nobody. You bring more to the table than you realize."

"And as for boring names," Diane barked. "What about Diane Collentenio? None of us are heroes. We're all just trying to do what's right."

Then with a cocky smile, Eric added, "So suck it up buddy, or I'm gonna start calling you a wuss like our princess here."

I couldn't help laugh, as did everyone else except Diane, who directed an expression of mock anger at Eric.

Bevon, who had been silent until now said, "You are a remarkable group." Indicating his Astari companions he continued, "We have benefited much from this time with you. In spite of all our knowledge gleaned from earth's databanks, I don't think we ever really understood the determination and resiliency of humans, especially you particular individuals."

I was touched by this display of emotion, as were the others. Matt added, "This has been an incredible couple of months. And to think, we never knew you existed, or this place." His gaze took in our surroundings. "This seemed so alien when we first arrived; now it's so beautiful." Looking at me in particular, he added, "And I have a new admiration for my friends. This time it's not because we're writing a paper. This is much more important."

Eric quipped, "The CEO always comes through."

Damek stood to reach into a small bag he had brought with him to our terrace. "This is a good time to give you these. Our practice sessions have been with wooden sticks, but those will not get you far in a real fight. So I asked some of my Tinkerer friends to fashion these blades and lances for you." He carefully lifted five blades about two feet long. "They are very special Astari weapons made of the finest steel, razor sharp, and are unlike those you may be familiar with." He took one out to demonstrate as he gave it an expert shake with his wrist. The two-foot-long knife immediately collapsed so that only the handle remained. "You can travel with it conveniently and expand it once the need arises … if there is a need." He gave it another expert shake to extend it. "These work much like our lances, which I also have for you." He removed the now collapsed lances from the bag as he demonstrated how to expand one of them.

"Great," said Cassie. "Along with everything else we have to worry about stabbing ourselves."

"Better than getting stabbed by a charging Bot," Damek said. "Besides, just think of these as the wooden ones you have practiced with." He handed a lance and a blade to each of us, and for a while we practiced the technique of collapsing and expanding each.

Once satisfied that we had mastered at least the basic technique, Damek turned serious again. "I don't know if we will ever be completely ready for this expedition, but I feel we need to depart soon. I want to offer a last chance to change your mind. You realize it could be dangerous." He gave each of us a long look.

Nobody spoke.

After a long moment, he said, "Okay then. We leave in three days. Most arrangements are already made and supplies gathered. We will commandeer a sailing ship from the Isle of Mendart. May the winds be at our back." A sober expression came over him. "And may the gods, if there are any, be with us."

CHAPTER TWENTY-FOUR

Flight

I crouched behind a tree, scanning the dock ahead for movement. The night was dark; both moons had yet to rise — a calculation Damek had factored into the planning. The world around us remained silent, yet my heart raced, knowing that discovery would put an end to our plan.

"Any signal yet?" Eric asked.

"Shh. Do you want to give us away?" Diane scolded.

It was moments such as this when I wished we were more disciplined. When did we become such a chaotic, argumentative group? A stern glare from Matt silenced them for the moment.

Damek's original plan had been to liberate a sailing vessel on Mendart, fly it to Tensheann, pick us up and make our get-away. But after thinking about it, he concluded that anyone on Tensheann seeing a vessel land would raise the curiosity of too many. So this alternative plan was hatched, which was why sailing had become part of our training.

We all awoke in the middle of the night to begin the mission. Several flights were necessary. Matt and I, less skilled at sailing, were flown on a harness. Damek deemed it was too risky to ask another Astari to assist. And then there were the supplies that they also had to transport. The process had taken hours, and we needed to be gone before others rose for the day.

So here we now sat in the wet bushes and the grass on a night that had rained earlier, the smell of fish permeated the air as we waited for a signal of a glow light by one of our Astari accomplices who were making sure the boat they had selected was ready and nothing was amiss.

After what seemed an inordinate amount of time the signal finally came. "There, to the left," Matt pointed.

Sure enough, I spotted the bright staccato blinking. "Let's go," said Matt. The command, however, was unnecessary because both Eric and Diane were already standing and taking a step forward.

We moved toward the direction of the glow, taking cover when possible between rows of long, low tables that were used to slide fish off the ships so that the catch could be cleaned, deboned and prepared for distribution to the various kitchens on each island. We walked quickly but remained watchful lest we trip or stumble over anything inadvertently left on the ground.

Matt jerked to a stop nearly halfway there and whispered urgently, "Hide, someone's coming." We scattered and crouched under the low tables, the only place here on the dock to take cover. The sparkle of a light held by an Astari appeared at a different angle from our signal. And it was getting brighter as it came this way. I feared what the repercussions would be if this person saw us and alerted others.

Hunkered down low, I saw the legs of the Astari come directly toward the table where I hid. I tried to think of a reasonable alibi that would explain what I was doing here if he saw me. Nothing came to mind.

The person stopped a half dozen paces in front of me at another row of tables. If I leaned forward I could probably see the person's face, but I stayed bent down and unmoving. Long seconds passed as I waited, wondering if he had seen me and was trying to figure out what he should do. But then the shuffling and clanking of tools either being picked up or set down echoed through the silent dock. Softly the Astari hummed to himself, or maybe herself — I couldn't be sure.

Long minutes passed until the jostle of tools finally ceased, replaced by the soft tap of footsteps as the Astari walked away. Only when the person was some distance did I finally exhale.

"That was close," Cassie whispered as we stood again. We waited to be sure he had moved far enough away before continuing.

As we approached one of the ships, we saw Damek waving to us. Here on Mendart, all the ships were moored in a sort of dry dock so the main deck was at our level and there was no need to climb a rope ladder as we had when boarding the ship to and from the Parting Ceremony.

As he leaned over the railing to help us step up onto the deck, he said, "Let's hope no other Mendart fishermen have a sleepless night. I fear our excursion nearly ended before we had begun."

Once onboard I was struck once again how the Astari sailing ships were reminiscent of Earth's three-mast ships from long ago — real long ago. The main difference was the sails on these extended horizontally like a hang glider rather than vertically, and each ship held three immense blintas on the top.

This particular ship had benches along its sides near the railings, unlike the one we had sailed previously. We each took a spot so we would be out of the way of the Astari as they prepared for our departure.

Bevon, Riyaad, and Quintia were each rolling a cylinder toward us on a track alongside the dock. Suspended on each cylinder was a large blinta. "Those cylinders must be connected to the track to stop them from floating away," Cassie said. "I wondered how they attached the blintas to the boats." I marveled at how Cassie always found things fascinating.

"Ship," corrected Damek. "Don't ever let a Mendart fisherman hear you call one of these beautiful vessels a boat. And this one is called *Sea Spray*. It's a fine ship, and the residents of Mendart may never again be friends with me after this."

The other Astari pushed the cylinders to the side of the vessel and began fastening stems of the blinta securely onto each of the masts. Once completed and everyone onboard, Damek stood toward the aft of the ship said, "My friends, let us hope we meet with success." He pushed a large lever forward, apparently releasing moorings, causing the ship to bounce once or twice before rising leisurely.

The Astari quickly unfurled the sails as the Mendart docks fell behind. We all watched the island for any sign of alarm. But it remained dark and quiet.

Huddled together at the front of the ship (which I was soon told should be called the foredeck), the shadowy island of Mendart slipped away, and we soon heard the soft splashing of the waterfall from Chillmerk as we sailed past it.

Damek continued to gain some altitude as we skirted the outer isles before setting a course due east to the mainland, putting Loralee at our backs. Each of the Astari gazed in that direction as if transfixed by the sight. The moon Halcyone had now risen and slipped out from a cover of clouds to reveal the distant islands as they reflected its light.

"How odd," said Cassie gazing in that direction, as we all did. "Only a few months ago this was so unnatural. And now, well it's just so splendid. It's difficult to imagine seeing something so incredible again."

I knew exactly how she felt. We had gained an attachment to these islands.

Matt nodded. "If we're successful we'll be back. Let's hope so."

"I think I would like that," she answered.

"What island is that one there?" Diane asked pointing.

Bevon, who stood nearest to her answered, "That, Earthfriend Diane, is Binxia. The food grown on it has its distinctive flavor. I could always tell." He pointed a little to the right. "And that there is Miarei." A ribbon of water fell on it from Palbender, the island upon which we first arrived. "It's a place I often went to enjoy fishing or swimming in its many lakes and streams. I spent many an hour enjoying my time on Miarei." I could hear the delight in his voice.

"And that must be Tensheann," Matt said. We all knew which he meant. It was the highest of all islands.

Bevon nodded in agreement. "The grandest of them all. I'm going to miss each and every one of them." A catch in his voice betrayed his feelings.

It was only then that I realized how much of a sacrifice our friends were making for this mission. "I'm sorry you have to leave them, at least for now," I said.

He nodded sadly. "Do not be. We must all make sacrifices in our lives. The important thing is that we do so for a noble purpose."

The sky was gray now in the pre-dawn morning. We continued to gaze fondly at the Raised Isles of Loralee as we put more distance between us and the pillars of land the

Astari called home. As the sun creased the horizon, it lit the islands with a new brilliance, the ribbons of waterfalls reflecting like sparkling diamonds in the sunlight.

We each continued watching in silence until the islands became too small to see.

CHAPTER TWENTY-FIVE
Woodbery College: Sixth Interlude

"What do you want in life? How do you wish to live it and what do you expect from others? What kind of society would be the perfect environment for you to achieve your goals?"

And so Professor Keane, the lead instructor for the capstone project, kicked off the term with the hundred or so students filling the lecture hall. "In simpler terms," he continued, "how do you create and sustain utopia? The perfect world."

He paused for a long moment, a habit he often had when trying to dramatize what he had said. Keane was the highest rated professor in the program. As a lecturer, he was the best I ever heard. "You realize others have attempted to create a utopia numerous times. And it has failed just as many times. But we start with the premise that you can achieve it. And so we leave it to you to apply the foundation that is both believable and credible.

"During the next five months, you will engage in a rigorous assignment of lectures, small class discussions, team breakout sessions, readings and video assignments. At the end of the term, each team will provide an oral and written presentation of your proposal.

"I have to stress: our expectations are high; the course requirements are rigorous; we will challenge you at every step of the process; in the end, we hope to find a group of students who are intellectually and emotionally aware of our society in a way they were not previously. And more importantly, we hope you acquire the skills and knowledge that will allow you to improve our society or whatever organization you join when you leave here."

I glanced over to Matt, Diane, Eric and Cassie, who sat next to me. They were attentive and focused, each with an intensity I would come to know well as the course progressed. I hoped I would be able to match their fervor. Not for the first time, or the last, I wondered if I made the right choice to join this group. They could be intimidating without even realizing it. And I felt that each of them were leagues ahead of me intellectually. I was never so unsure about being able to hold my own as I was now.

"We don't expect you only to give us a fifty-thousand-foot-level explanation of your perfect society," Professor Keane continued. "You will develop your community by addressing specific segments: economic, business, technical — all the facets that make up one's interaction in your culture. If you so choose — and many students do — you can focus your paper on a particular segment of society and provide a deep-dive by thoroughly explaining how you would improve it.

"And, this is key, we are looking for your proposal to come alive — to live a life of its own. We want to be able to feel it here," he said as he tapped his fingertips against his chest. "And as importantly, we want to understand and believe it here." He touched his forehead dramatically. "We don't want you to think of this as just another academic exercise. Think of it as your opportunity to change the world."

He paused again to gaze around the hall, looking directly at students as his gaze seemed to touch on each student for a fraction of a second before moving on. And at that moment when his eyes met mine, I felt as if he were looking into my soul, challenging me to be more than who I was.

"Go now and accomplish what nobody has been able to do before you. I am looking forward to learning what you will have to say. Make it your very best."

As we exited the hall, Cassie said, "My goodness. If I wasn't ready to get going before, I am now."

"Learn to pace yourself," said Eric. "This is going to be a long process. We need to enjoy it."

CHAPTER TWENTY-SIX
Reflections

Hours into our flight, the Raised Isles had passed from view and the sun was high in the sky. The flight remained uneventful. Most of us had slept little the night before during our escape, but we were all too wound up to go below deck and nap. So we sat together on the foredeck, the spot we would mostly camp out when together above deck. Riyaad came to sit with us for a moment. "I fear our meals won't be as elaborate as those on Loralee," he explained sadly. "But I'll prepare a meager breakfast for us."

"I'm sure whatever you have will be fine," Diane answered.

Even though the sun was up, the air had turned crisp, and the wind was gusty. Several of the others had already donned jackets that the Astari had packed for each of us and I went below deck to fetch mine, following Riyaad who was also stepping below to prepare breakfast in a tiny galley which would double as our sleeping quarters. Hammocks, now bunched up on pegs, would be strung out along the walls to serve as our beds.

"Can I help?" I offered.

He shook his head, "If you could just bring this mug up to Bevon. He has the duty at the ship's wheel."

As in sailing ships of old, the large steering wheel was at the aft of the mainsail. Rather than controlling the rudder, as in earth's olden ships, this ship's wheel adjusted the sails. Handing Bevon the warm mug he smiled, "Thank you friend Philip. This is just what I need. What do you think of our good ship the *Sea Spray?*"

"It's quite unbelievable." Thinking for a moment, I added, "But I feel the Raised Isles were more astonishing."

He smiled, nodding in response, but not before I glimpsed a look of longing in his expression.

Stepping back to the others, on the foredeck, I saw that Damek had joined them. I heard Matt asking him if everything was going as planned.

Damek thought for a moment before replying. "If you mean has anyone pursued us, they have not. As you can see, the blintas are still attached, and the ship is sailing as it should. All of this is good."

An edge to his voice made him sound unsure, and Eric must have sensed it. "So everything's okay?" he asked.

Damek thought again before answering. "Well, there is one thing that I have been discussing with my friend Quintia. You see, we are relying on things we learned in our education. But I believe it cannot replace experience."

"So what have you been discussing," Matt asked calmly, trying to get at the point.

He took another long moment before answering. "Well, you see, actually there are three things. The first relates to our current course. We are sailing due east as you know. But we are not entirely sure if we should adjust that somewhat to angle more to the southeast or the northeast. And another question is how long the blinta's buoyancy will last, and if it will bear up for the entire time needed."

He said this so calmly that it didn't seem to be an issue at all. But Eric didn't let it pass. "What? Are you telling us we're lost? Didn't it occur to you to get directions first?"

Damek smiled. "It's not like we could ask one of the Ruling Members, 'Can you please tell us how we can travel to the mainland with the earthfriends so we can talk to the other great races.' That would cause so much debate and commotion we would never be able to leave."

"He's right," said Matt with a voice of command that often made it difficult to challenge.

Eric however still made a sour face. "Well, flying blind is not the best idea either."

"I think our biggest problem, however, might be inclement weather, such as a storm," Damek continued, apparently not realizing he wasn't helping his case. "The fishermen of Mendart are expert at sailing these vessels, and you can see we are able to handle it … but a storm is a whole different story."

"Great," was all Eric could say.

~ ~ ~

I remember many things about that sailing experience: how on some days the voyage seemed like it would never end, while other days passed so swiftly as we enjoyed the camaraderie of close friends, which most definitely included our Astari companions.

But one day, in particular, has stayed most firmly in my mind. I believe it was during the afternoon of our third day from the Raised Isles. As on most days, we had nothing to do except sit and talk and gaze out at the never ending blue sea far below. The voyage had been largely uneventful, but I had begun to notice that a certain apprehension had come over the group as we knew the mainland would not be far away: a place we knew nothing about … and the Astari little more.

In a way, I believe the uneasiness brought us even closer together and might be the reason that some of us began to open up, expressing feelings that had been kept under wraps, in some cases for years.

"It was good, wasn't it?" Matt said wistfully as we gazed over the railing at the unending ocean, each of us lost in our own thoughts. We looked at him quizzically. "The Raised Isles, I mean. Who would have thought such a thing possible? The land; the people …"

"The food," I added, getting a chuckle from them.

"It was all good; so very good," he continued. "And to think a couple of months ago we were so entrenched in our normal day-to-day lives. How we've changed."

"You think we've changed?" Cassie asked, looking surprised. "Our location did, but us?"

"Of course," I said. "You most of all. I remember the day I drove you from Boston to the Berkshires for our reunion: how quiet, uncommunicative, and to be truthful …" searching for the word that would not insult her, "how plain you looked. I hardly knew it was you." She appeared shocked. "But look at you now," I quickly added. "No more black glasses with your hair always falling in your eyes. And now you talk as much as Eric."

"Hey, that's a good thing," he voiced.

"Well, I don't know about that," she replied grudgingly. "Maybe I can see your point. But what about you? You may not remember, but you were pretty boring as well during that long drive. You had this attitude of being a failure, even though you never said it. There something that just permeated everything you said and did. You seemed beaten down and had no fight left in you."

It was my turn to be dismayed. I looked to the others for support. But they only nodded approvingly. Matt said, "She's right Phil. You were not the person I knew at Woodbery."

"And I'm not like that now?"

Diane responded, "No, now you're more like the guy we knew back then — the one we all loved so much and wanted on our team because nothing was going to stop him — no challenge too big or difficult. But most of all, you didn't hide your feelings back then. There was a fire in your eyes, and nobody was going to take that away from you. I remember how you were enjoying life so much it was contagious. That's the person you've become again."

I looked into her beautiful green eyes, wishing we were alone, wanting to say much more. But instead, I felt my face warm. "Yeah ... well," I stammered. "If you had become the person you never thought you would ... I guess that's what happened to me." They stared at me, not with expressions of pity or sorrow, but of understanding.

"God, please don't tell me this change of scenery has improved my disposition," Eric chimed in. "If you do, I may need to jump overboard just to spite all of you."

"Well," Matt said smiling, "please don't jump. You were always outspoken. That certainly never changed." Everyone laughed.

"And usually too outspoken at the wrong time," Diane added.

Matt nodded. "Back at Woodbery, you were always our creative thinker, our conscience ... always questioning what was right and wrong. You pushed us to consider things we would have missed or not considered. But at the Berkshires and during the first days or maybe weeks on the islands you were just uncaring."

Cassie said, "Yup, you were obnoxious in a bad way, not thinking about our feelings. But now you're back to your good, let's say outspoken, old self."

Eric smiled smugly. After a time, he added, "Well, I still don't know if I agree, but we seem to be on a roll here. Cassie, Phil, me — how much we've changed. Now, what about these two?" He nodded toward Matt and Diane. Taking a moment to gaze critically at them as if inspecting or evaluating them, he continued, "Of the two, I would say that Diane has changed the most drastically."

"Yes," Cassie quickly agreed. Diane furrowed her brow, the expression she used when she didn't understand something. Cassie continued, "You truly did deserve the princess name during our reunion and our first weeks on Loralee. 'Oh, my job is so important. Oh, they need me back. I want to go back home.' It never ended."

Hearty laughter came from everyone except Diane.

"To put it bluntly," Cassie continued, "you were a bit too into yourself back then. Of course, we were all shocked by what happened to us — suddenly finding ourselves in a new world. But if I heard you say one more time 'I have to get back home,' I was going to scream."

"But you weren't that way during our Woodbery days … or now," I added. "You never tried to be perfect, or important, or smart. You just were. And you've become that person again." She looked at me with eyes that sparkled.

"And another thing," Cassie added, "just like during Woodbery, you again care more about us than about yourself. That's what I always liked most about you."

Matt cleared his throat before speaking, "You realize Di that we haven't heard you ask about getting back home now for many weeks."

"And thank God for that," said Eric.

After a moment Cassie said, "So that leaves one other." She looked squarely at Matt. "Our leader. Anyone care to start?"

Matt made a motion as if he was about to leave.

"I will," I said after nobody else spoke. Pausing a moment to be sure it came out correctly, I began, "In some ways you've changed less, but maybe even more than any of us." An attentive silence settled over the others. "In college, you were the most passionate, always sure of yourself. We all knew you wanted to run your own business, become a CEO. Nothing was going to stop you. You're the reason that I ultimately decided to join the group. I respected someone so focused on a career." I cut short a laugh. "I guess we had that in common back then anyway."

"Yes, exactly," Eric interrupted. "We always followed your lead Matt because you had this confidence and it spilled over to the rest of us. It was as if you were contagious in a good way."

"But then that reunion weekend I saw a different person," I continued. "You were still charming and obviously a leader of your company. You were in control, as you always had been. But you had lost some aspect of your personality that I find hard to define. But you seemed more frustrated, or maybe it was a sense of unhappiness, I'm not sure. You had everything you had ever hoped for, but that didn't make you any happier or satisfied. And that carried over to our early days on the Raised Isles."

"But now you're clearly at ease again," Cassie offered. "More like your old happy self. And we're glad to have you back again."

Everyone was quiet for long moments, and I thought we had finished with the appraisals. But into the silence Cassie added, speaking hesitantly, "It's just that, the only thing that would complete the picture for you, Matt, would be getting your old girlfriend back."

I was shocked she had said this out loud, even though she had voiced the same to me privately a few times. Matt was at a loss for words. Eric, however, smiled slyly.

The silence continued for uncomfortable moments until Diane cleared her throat and said, "Yeah, well, maybe some things were just never meant to be."

Matt said calmly, "We made choices Cass. And we've lived with them."

"Okay, but what I can't quite understand," said Cassie, not letting it go, "is why one of those choices was not staying together. I mean it was obvious you were both crazy about each other."

Matt said rather hesitantly, "Diane had the job offer in Stamford, and I was planning to join a start-up in Cambridge. Things were pulling us in different directions. It just made sense."

Diane fidgeted, chewing on her lower lip. When she spoke, she said it quietly, almost as if speaking to herself. "And you never asked me to stay."

That moment remained suspended in time as if nothing else in the world existed. Words were spoken, unable to be put back. Diane and Matt were looking at each other as if they were the only two people sitting here.

Matt finally broke the long silence, his voice laden with emotion. "I always thought you would be around, just like always. I thought we could manage our careers and still have each other. I know now I was wrong. It didn't work out that way. I don't know why. It just didn't."

He paused to look away out at the ocean and the clouds. "Maybe this is a time and a place for new beginnings."

And that was all he would say. The silence was getting

uncomfortable until Eric finally broke it. "Well, isn't this nice. We've cleared things up, taken care of people's love life, peered deep into our souls. It's very cathartic, don't you think? We should do this more often."

We all smiled, but I noticed Matt and Diane still looked at each other with an expression I couldn't read.

CHAPTER TWENTY-SEVEN

Infected

I awoke early on the fifth day of our voyage. The others were still asleep in their bunks, including the Astari. I could tell from the opening in the hatch that the sun was not yet up, but the sky was already turning gray. Not wanting to disturb them, I slid from my hammock and silently slipped on my pants and shirt before stepping above deck. Quintia was sitting at the wheel, and she smiled when I stepped up the narrow hatchway from below deck.

"It's still early," she said kindly. "Trouble sleeping?"

I shook my head. "No, it's just that I've had too much rest already. Nothing much else to do while on the ship. I needed to stretch my legs."

She gazed out at the horizon. "I understand. This is different from life on the islands. I also wish to be walking about, taking care of various tasks. I too find this life confining." She spoke with a sadness I had rarely heard from her.

"You must miss them ... the Raised Isles."

She nodded. "Mostly I miss the man I'm planning to wed. We were to be joined shortly after the Midsummer

Celebration. But with what happened and all …"

I gaped, momentarily at a loss for words. "You never told us — nobody had said anything."

"I wanted it that way. Neither of us cares to be the center of attention. We planned a small, quiet celebration."

"Who is he? Have we met him?"

She shook her head. "No, we never had the opportunity." Smiling warmly, she added, "He tends the fruit orchards on the island of Chillmerk."

But then I realized she might not have the chance to see him for a long time. "Why didn't you stay with him rather than come on this journey?"

She stared at me with a burning intensity in her eyes. "Because this is my life. This is what I'm trained to do. How would it be if I suddenly let everyone else down?" She looked away. "No, that wouldn't make me any happier."

"I understand," I said thoughtfully. Here was yet another reason to respect and admire these people, as if I didn't already have enough reasons. "I hope when we return I'm able to meet your future husband and maybe even attend your celebration. I would greatly enjoy that."

She smiled warmly again. "It would make me very happy." She turned back to look at the horizon, blinking to clear watery eyes. The sky continued to brighten as the ship swayed gently.

"Who do we hope to find when we reach this mainland?" I asked. "Damek called them the great races. But which one?"

"It has been long since we last visited them, but Damek wishes to seek out the Ikhael. They make their home high in a vast mountain range. Snow covers the higher mountains throughout the year. They prefer the cold and the thin air of the high altitude."

"What do you know about them?"

She shrugged. "They are trustworthy people. They fought gallantly in our war against the Bots, sacrificing much to help defeat them." Looking at me with a new intensity, she added, "They have cause to hate the Bots as much as we do. Many of their people were killed in that war. I do not doubt they would be willing allies."

"Are they like you? I mean did they evolve from the digital world?"

She shook her head. "No, they began as biological beings. Another race on their home world created them in a laboratory. They were created in a laboratory by another race on their home world. Their purpose was to serve their creators."

"You mean like slaves?"

"I guess. But I have always thought of them as more like robots in a tech world."

I barked a laugh. "Confusing isn't it? We have the Bots from the tech world. And now there are the Ikhael, who were once biological rather than digital robots. One bad, the other good."

She frowned. "Isn't that the way of life? Take humans. Many are good, but some are bad. Some created the malware viruses that evolved into the Bots, while others created sophisticated antivirus programs that were the origins of our beginnings." She stirred her hand around an imaginary bowl. "It is all the soup of creation: biological such as the Ikhael or digital like us. What matters is what you do as a race once you attain sentience — whether you improve life or try to tear it down. That, in my mind, is the difference."

I thought about this as I gazed out across the water. The Astari frequently surprised me with their keen insight. The eastern sky had brightened considerably, and the sun was about to climb above the horizon. Quintia pointed in that direction. "We won't have too long before you meet them yourself. Look."

I wasn't sure what she meant as I stared in that direction. "That small smudge on the horizon a bit to the right of center," she added.

I squinted. "There's only a few clouds, far away."

"That my friend is the mainland." She smiled now. "I will be happy to tell earthfriend Eric that we are indeed traveling in the right direction. And he doubted us," she said, speaking with feigned distress.

"I'm sure he'll be glad to learn we're not lost at sea after all."

"Yes, perhaps luck is with us on this fair day." Her smile faded. "Although I fear getting us here may be the easiest part of our journey."

As it turned out, luck was not with us. Somewhere along the way it had left us entirely.

~ ~ ~

By midmorning, all of us were gazing at the shoreline below, looking for any sign of life or other people. But what greeted us was a barren, rocky coast with massive jagged rocks protruding from the water's edge like sculptures from times long ago that had lost their original shape because of the constant wind and water crashing against them.

"It looks like nothing I've seen before," marveled Cassie.

"The lands here have many wonders that are worth exploring. If things were different, I would suggest we do so," said Damek. "But now we sail directly to that mountain range." He pointed toward the remote northeast. The word mountains did not do them justice. Even from this distance, they looked dark, barren and forbidding, standing like massive sentinels, their snow-covered peaks rising taller than any I had ever seen, many of the summits shrouded in mist.

Below us, the shore fell away, replaced with mostly craggy bluffs and rock-strewn fields with occasional woods and grass fields. We soon fell in line with a meandering river that must originate from the mountain range that was our goal. In a short while, we noticed tendrils of white smoke rising from wood fires.

And then we came upon wooden structures: small rustic homes of wood frames. We passed several without spotting anyone, but then at the river's edge, we came upon a half dozen structures close together. "Looks like a small village," said Bevon. "Shall I steer clear?" he asked Damek.

He shook his head. "No, it doesn't matter. We cannot remain unseen. And I don't know if it matters unless they are Bots, which I doubt. These likely belong to one of the native races."

The village lay on the starboard side of the ship, and we all gazed out in that direction. As we came closer, we saw many villagers going about their daily business until one of them spotted us. They were too far away to discern what they looked like, but from this distance, they could have been humans. Several were pointing at us now, and I could hear a bell clanging as others rushed out of the buildings to gawk.

"It would be good to meet them someday," said Cassie. "I wonder how different they are from us? You said they evolved here?" She looked at Damek.

He nodded in reply. "Either they are one of the indigenous races or the race who appeared during the final days of our war with the Bots — the humans."

We flew close enough to wave at them as we passed. But I

did not see any wave in return; either the villagers were too frightened, or they assumed we were a threat from the heavens.

As the settlement receded, we came across other homes scattered about the countryside. We passed some whose inhabitants didn't notice our passing and others who also had a stunned reaction to our appearance.

"Seems like they are not used to Astari flying over their heads," Eric quipped. "I wonder how many of them would let an arrow fly if we came close enough."

Damek wore an uncertain expression. "We have never known them to be hostile toward us. But neither have we spent much time with them."

Fortunately, we never found out, always flying a safe distance from any settlement. The terrain became rocky as we approached the foothills of the impressive mountain range and sightings of other people and homes became less frequent until they ended altogether.

Soon the jagged cliffs became so pronounced that neither people nor animals could exist in this land. The little brush we spotted clung to fissures along the craggy cliffs. Each of the Astari scurried back and forth on the deck as they adjusted the ship's sails by either tightening or loosening ropes on the masts, I assumed to keep the ship a safe distance above the soaring cliffs. Bevon often appeared to be wrestling with the ship's wheel as he attempted to gain altitude while compensating for the gusty winds that bounced the ship from side to side.

Adjusting a sail near the foredeck where we were sitting, Riyaad said to us, "Do not worry too much. Our sailors of Mendart would have no difficulty, but we have not navigated under these conditions, and with blintas that are somewhat depleted. But I am sure we can handle it." For the first time,

I noticed that the orange balls were not as inflated as they were at the start of our voyage.

Eric mumbled, "Don't worry too much … how about a little?"

The mountain range, as breathtaking as it appeared in the distance, to me looked deadly up close: a sheer rock face that in some cases dropped vertically for nearly a mile. We would barely pass over the top of one peak only to see another rising thousand of feet above in front of us. Mountains all around were often higher than we flew. The winds buffeted the ship as we navigated around them, causing us to lurch alarmingly at times. Snow and sleet began pelting us, causing us to scramble to don winter jackets that we had stowed below deck.

"I don't like this," Diane said after one particularly nasty pitch of the ship as we listed dangerously for long moments before righting again. I had visions of us careening into a sheer cliff face, the ship splintering and us falling to our deaths. The Astari were doing all they could to control the ship; exertion and fear began to show on their faces. I recalled that during calmer times early in our voyage when Damek had told us one of the things he worried about was a storm — not a comforting thought right now.

Just as I thought it could get no worse, we faced the highest peak of all. The breadth of the snow-encased mountain extended beyond our sight in either direction, the top lost in clouds and mist far above. I realized then that we had failed. There was no way we could scale this; our only option would be to turn back.

"Hold on," shouted Damek. "This is it."

"He's got to be kidding," Eric exclaimed.

Fighting with the ship's wheel, Bevon angled the *Sea Spray* parallel to the cliff face as we swayed precariously in the blasts of wind. The ship's sails were now at an extreme angle as the Astari tried to take advantage of the maelstrom to push us upward. The wind and ice were stinging our faces, and it became difficult to see where we were going. At one point the sheer ice cliff appeared just off our starboard side, alarmingly close. A shout from one of the Astari gave warning to angle the ship to port.

I had no idea whether we were gaining altitude at all; the blinding storm made it difficult to see my hand in front of my face. I held on to the railing for dear life, feeling sure that any second would be my last.

One of the sails tore and ripped away, pitching the ship at a dangerous angle before the Astari compensated. "Maybe we should turn back," Diane yelled, the words snatched by the wind as soon as she spoke. I doubt if the Astari even heard her.

Just when I didn't think we or the ship could take more of this, it ended. We had passed through some unseen barrier, or so it seemed. The wind stopped howling and abated altogether, and the white cliff face was now below and behind us. Miraculously we had somehow made it over the top, breaking out to blinding sunshine and a windless sky, the clouds swirling below us.

Blinking dumbly, I was bewildered by what I saw. I thought back to the moment I had first awakened on the Raised Isles and how I had felt then. This was nearly the same. Enormous ice sculptures, some the size of small skyscrapers, greeted us: great animals of species I had never seen — winged figures that could be dragons, great beasts that might be grizzly bears standing on two back legs, and other intricate shapes and designs that to me were incomprehensible. As far as I could see, hundreds of majestic structures stood on a broad snow-covered plain.

"Behold the Plain of Ice with the grand carvings of the Ikhael," said Quintia, a note of wonder even in her voice.

"Uh-huh, well, first give me a minute to change my underwear," said Eric. We could always count on him to lighten the mood.

~ ~ ~

The ice sculptures appeared unending as we sailed across the level plain. Some rose thousands of feet above us as we passed around them and occasionally sailed under expansive arches. It would have taken an army of human engineers with mechanical equipment hundreds of years to accomplish this.

But for all their majesty and incredible beauty, I saw troubling signs of deterioration. Some shapes had crumbled so badly that it was hard to determine what they originally were; others had collapsed entirely; while on closer inspection even the ones that remained whole had a degraded, dilapidated quality to them as if the ravages of sun or wind had long ago caused damage that nobody cared to repair.

"Strange," mumbled Damek as we passed a pile of ice rubble that was once a carving. "The Ikhael are so proud of their ice castles, as they call them. I wonder why they have not repaired these?"

"And we have yet to see any of them either," added Bevon. "It is said that they often labor on them day and night; and if not working on them, then just viewing them." A cloud of concern passed over his face.

It took us nearly an hour to pass the hundreds, maybe thousands of shapes, coming at last to a structure that resembled an enormous building, also carved of ice.

Standing in an open area in front of it was a solitary figure dressed in a startling red coat, the only thing not made of ice. We circled him, and he gazed at us, seemingly uncaring or ambivalent at our arrival. Quintia waved. The person made no response.

Bevon and Riyaad each hung a rope over both sides of the ship as we circled back around, coming in for a low pass. Damek cupped his hands to his mouth and made sounds that were more like grunts and whistles as we hovered over the figure for long moments.

It gazed calmly at us. Even from this vantage, I could see the thing was large, bigger than the Bots. It had dark, leathery skin with folds covering his face. If I had seen this thing before the Astari or the Bots, I would have been aghast at seeing such a creature. But now, I just accepted this as the way another race looked.

The ship was able to hover in one place for only moments at a time. When the Ikhael made no reaction, we moved on. "What's happening?" Matt asked.

Bevon answered, "Strange. Damek asked him in their language to secure the ropes. But as you can see, he didn't react."

As we made a wide turn to come around again, Damek said to Riyaad, "I don't know what's wrong with him but we need to secure the tethers. I need you to sail yourself down to the surface and moor the ship when we pass again."

Riyaad nodded and pulled his personal sail from a pocket, stood on a railing and flipped it open before jumping off. He easily glided to the ground near the Ikhael, looked at the looming figure for a moment as he bowed slightly in respect, and stood to wait for us to come around.

Once he had knotted the tethers to nearby posts, Quintia and Bevon furled the sails and dropped a rope ladder over the side. Through it all, the figure on the ground only gazed at us. "Let us meet the Ikhael," Damek said somewhat uncertainly as he stepped down the rungs of the rope ladder as Bevon helped the rest of us onto it.

Once on the ground, I could see the figure was even taller and larger than I had thought, at least eight or nine feet. He followed our movements with an intelligence in its eyes, yet it did not stir, remaining in its stance as we had first seen him. Damek voiced some grunts and pops before saying, "Would it be okay if we speak in our language so that our esteemed companions can participate?"

The Ikhael nodded in agreement and then spoke its first words, haltingly in starts and stops, as if not used to speaking the language. "It has been long. Since the Astari. Have pleased us with their. Presence. The need must indeed be great."

There was something wrong with it. What I had first taken for its natural appearance — blotches of dark skin over its face and its uncovered forearms — didn't seem right. I felt that some deterioration or decay was present. Damek must have noticed it also as he frowned.

"We come to discuss important matters. Might we speak with your high council?"

For a moment the figure looked so very sad as if pained by the question. "Few of them remain. Alive. And those who are would be unable. To speak. I am sorry."

"What — what has happened?" Damek's voice was labored.

Long moments passed as the Ikhael considered this. "We were infected. A germ or virus, we know not. We could not contain it."

I noticed Diane took an involuntary step backward, causing me to wonder whether we should all do the same.

"It spread slowly. Many years it took. Eventually, it causes death. But first. Long years spent like this." He spread his arms as if to indicate the problem. "Body declines. A rot takes over. Our minds cease functioning. It is sad."

"Wh— why did you not reach out so we could help you?"

"Our most experienced. Biologist, scientists, tried. If we could not, with our knowledge of genetics and molecular biology. We knew. No others could." He bent his head down as if telling the story pained him, or maybe the exertion was too much.

"How could such a thing happen?" I could see Damek was noticeably dismayed.

The Ikhael shook his head. "We have no proof, but we believe. The Bot race infected. Us. A genome sequence keyed to our. Specific DNA. It is not contagious to others."

An uneasy silence settled over our group. All this, all for nothing.

"Is there anything we can do?" Damek said after the long pause.

The Ikhael considered, again long moments before he replied. "No, I fear we are doomed. We have. Tried all that we know."

Damek grimaced. "We will send our Astari who are healers when we return. Perchance they can find a cure."

The large figure frowned. "No. I fear that will not help us. Too far progressed. No hope. We are at peace with it." For a time he seemed to be at a loss for words. "I would ask you. Into our great home. But it would not be. Pleasant for you to witness."

He turned to step away, not expecting an answer. But after a few steps, he looked back. "Tell me. What was. Your reason for this visit?"

Damek barked a mirthless laugh, "To help us wage war

against the Bots."

He nodded and for the first time the slightest smile curled his lip. "Then I wish you success. When you kill the last of them. Do it for the Ikhael."

And then in a slumped, unnatural gait, he shuffled toward the structure, never looking back.

Damek stood rooted to the spot long after the Ikhael had entered the dwelling, his fists clenched, jaw muscle twitching. In a voice raw with emotion he finally said, "They were the most daring and bold of the great races. That this should be their fate." He suddenly looked very weary.

CHAPTER TWENTY-EIGHT

Woodbery College: Seventh Interlude

A month into the term we were moving forward nicely on the Utopia Project. Our initial outlines were taking shape. At this stage, we knew we were far ahead of the progress made by other groups. Our team meetings often consisted of spirited and productive discussions.

Yes, I felt good about where we stood, happy now that I signed up with Matt's team, as we were beginning to think of our group. That is until one Thursday afternoon during our regular team breakout session. "We're sucking wind," Matt said at the start of the meeting with a look of disgust.

I was dumbfounded. "What? No — things are good," I blurted. "We're in good shape."

He looked at me with smoldering eyes, which I had learned was his prelude to an intense discussion. "No, we're not. We're going through the motions."

Looking at others for support, I took note that they were all gazing at him calmly, almost expectantly. I suspected they had been through this with him before. "What do you mean?" was all I could muster.

He furrowed his brow. "For one thing, we're not focusing

at all on the basic premise." Pointing at me, with a staccato rhythm to his voice, he said, "What do you," and then with the same gesture at the others, continued, "and you, and you, and you ... what does each of you gain by living in the society we're creating? And don't say it's so we can live in a better place. That's not enough." He fought to keep from shouting. "We need to elevate our proposition. What is the essential element that makes us human? And how do we make that better? Then — and only then — will everything else we're doing for this assignment fall into place."

He was right, of course, as I considered it. When we first started discussing this project, I would often try to take an opposing point of view. But I quickly learned that he was extremely adept at pinpointing what was most important. He had an uncanny ability to see things the rest of us hadn't even considered.

So, like the others, I tried to offer an answer. We each offered a few ideas — all soundly rejected by Matt. Eric finally held up his hand excitedly in mock imitation of a child in school. "I know. I know," he exclaimed, bouncing up and down in his seat as he continued the parody. The rest of us only looked at him impassively, waiting for his answer. Clearing his throat, continuing to stretch it out, he finally said, "Our utopia has to be a place where people can evolve; they need to be able to grow into something better, kinder, more productive and happier than they are today. And ... they need to be able to exist without fear."

I waited, expecting Matt or somebody else to poke holes in it. But Matt chewed his lower lip as he worked it out in his head. In the silence Eric continued, "That problem solved, let's head over to the Hideout Cafe for a drink before dinner — just to be sociable, that is."

"We're not going to start a habit of drinking in the

afternoon," Diane scolded. "Besides, we need to develop this."

Eric looked offended. "I gave you the answer Princess." He smirked at her for a moment before pointing his finger and adding, "Which, now that you say it, makes me realize that we need to include having fun in our proposal. And I'm happy to explain that to you if you don't catch the meaning."

Diane rolled her eyes, but I noticed she was smiling.

Matt, on the other hand, launched himself into the solution. "Okay, I think we have something to work with. Let's develop these as freedoms — at least we can call them that for now. Begin with the freedom to exist without fear. What kinds of fears do we need to dispense with?"

"Fear of crime." Diane offered.

He nodded. "Good but it needs to be broader." Stepping up to the whiteboard (a standard practice for Matt), he wrote the word freedoms and under it the word crime.

"War," added Cassie. Matt wrote it on the board.

"Poverty?" I asked. He wrote it.

"Fear of death," said Diane.

"Fear of failing this course," Eric quipped. Matt didn't write that one.

"Unjust prosecution," Cassie proclaimed.

And so it continued until he had at least twenty responses on the whiteboard.

"All this is good," Eric finally offered, turning more serious now. "Freedom from all these fears should play into it. But I think the crux of the issue is the basic human need to become something better — to surpass who and what we are. The freedom from fears gives us that opportunity. But a blob of — of something — can exist without fear. But what makes us different from a blob is the desire to become something better, something more, I don't know, more glorious and exciting."

His mouth worked as he continued to search for words. We let him struggle with his thought until he continued, "The real problem with a utopia is that everyone becomes fat and happy — there's nothing to push them forward, nothing to make them reach for the next level. It's a dull existence; that's the rabbit's hole we've fallen into during our discussions. People would much rather hear about dystopias. They're so much more gripping. The real dilemma we need to address is the reason the human race wants to move forward."

Matt nodded. "We need to build on that. I think you're on the right track." Scratching his chin, he said, "Now how do we describe an existence where society is driven to become even better? It has to be something that permeates our culture."

And so it continued for the next several hours. When we filled one whiteboard, we downloaded it to our tablets and began to fill another. Through it all I felt engaged and excited in a way I rarely felt before.

~ ~ ~

The next four weeks were intense as we continued to build our basic premises. There were times when it seemed I did nothing else but discuss or ponder one or another thorny point that had us stymied. I often felt I could do little but hang on for dear life, hoping I was pulling my weight on the team.

What surprised me most during this time was the analytical approach Matt had fostered on the team. I had always assumed that our paper would be much like any other college paper, basically an essay, only more extensive.

But that's not what Matt had in mind. He wanted to support all our theorems with tables, complex graphs, and charts, even mathematical formulas. In some cases, his equations were straining my ability just to understand the concepts behind them.

I stared at one such equation on my tablet, along with associated graphs and charts that Matt had sent to us last evening, trying my best to decipher it. The formula itself was long and included a variety of mathematical symbols: infinity, summation, probability, the function of, approximation (along with your standard pluses, minuses, divisional and equals symbols).

I had left my room early this morning, deciding to spend some time in the library before a class lecture. This was my favorite time of day here, before the hustle and bustle and undercurrent of chatter that always took place later. But this morning my eyes were beginning to glaze over as I once again reviewed the charts and tables. I had just decided that another cup of coffee would do me good when from behind me I heard, "You okay with that latest?" It was Matt, as he pulled up a chair next to me.

"I'm trying to figure out what the hell it means first."

He shot me a crooked smile and pulled out his tablet. "I think this is a crucial part of the whole paper." He pointed to one pie chart. "Here, these are all the freedoms we defined. I lumped them together in this bit here, giving weight to each one." He then pointed to another table. "And here we have the challenges and personal development that make us something better, and in this list, I've included intangibles like different abilities, economic factors, religious beliefs, a whole slew of things we discussed. And here I try to pull it all together with this statement, expressed as a formula. I call it the Prime Theorem." Looking proudly, eyes wide, he asked,

"You like it?"

I gaped, unable to catch up to his explanation. Not sure if this was the right time to say it, I decided anyway. "Do you think maybe we're carrying this idea of the formulas and charts and stuff a bit too far?"

He stared blankly.

I discovered he often responded best when challenged, so I decided to continue to press my point. "This isn't a mathematics course, and I'm wondering if we might be putting too much weight on the analytical presentation of our material. We might confuse the professors so much they just give up on what we have to say." I hoped I wasn't burning any bridges with him.

He crinkled his eyebrows. "I know exactly what you mean. I've thought about it myself — lots. But if you look at these formulas and diagrams, and take the time to go through them, they can beautifully summarize the written and oral presentations. They're a tool, and in the right hands they can bring our theorems to life."

I still wasn't convinced, but judging from his tone I felt it was fruitless to argue with him.

Pursing his lips while tapping a finger against the table, he shrugged. "But what mostly concerns me is that we've left something out, some important item that we haven't factored into our plan. I fear that these formulas and visuals can be a double-edged sword by allowing a professor to see our proposal more clearly. And if we've missed an important element, they'll be able to spot it more easily. Without these, they might not."

At least this was something I could understand. I had been troubled by the same uneasiness. I couldn't help wonder, in spite of our meticulous approach, that this project was so broad and all-encompassing, it couldn't be entirely defined.

There had to be something important we were missing. I just knew it. And with every passing day my disquiet grew.

Rather than voice my real concern, I simply said, "I guess if these graphs and formulas make it easier to spot something we left out, then we should be able to spot it first. Right?"

He smiled. "That's why we have the best people on the team. We'd never be able to do this, each on our own. And it doesn't hurt that we've all developed a great friendship."

I put on my best smile. But I was still puzzling over what we had left off.

CHAPTER TWENTY-NINE

Attacked

We departed the home of the Ikhael with a cloud of despondency hanging over us. The Plain of Ice had lost its marvel once we discovered what had become of them. In their prime, they had created these magnificent ice structures. Now, it was all that would remain of these people; that is until the elements claimed them as well.

Even though I hadn't even heard of them before this voyage, I still felt a dire sense of loss over what had befallen them. From our brief meeting with the one Ikhael and from what the Astari had told us, I could see that they were an honorable race of people. And now they were another whose lives were cut short by the Bots.

As we passed over the ice formations, Matt asked Damek, "Now what?" Our Astari friend stood brooding, hands clenching the railing.

He tore himself away from looking out at the ice structures as if coming out of a slumber; the question seemingly revived him. "There are others. The woodland Valnorian are one such. We should seek them out. Yet, I fear this is not an auspicious start."

Once through the Plain of Ice we once again battled the ferocious winds and blasting ice storm that surrounded the mountain. We had the disadvantage of missing a sail that had been ripped off during our ascent. This time, however, we had the benefit of descending rather than scaling the cliff face. I don't know why I thought that was easier — it just seemed simpler to drop an object rather than send it skyward. In any case, I was more prepared this time for the tempest (even though it was no less extreme), and we traversed it without major mishap.

Emerging from the buffeting storm, we continued our downward trek along the mountain range. It gave us time to simply enjoy the magnificent mountains and the broad lowlands in the distance. Content that we had safely passed the raging storm, we all simply took in the view. So it was somewhat of a surprise when Damek stepped to the foredeck before long to say, "I fear we have a problem."

"Great. As if we didn't have enough already," Eric declared.

"What's the issue?" Matt asked calmly. "Is it the broken sail?"

"The missing sail is a problem, but we are mostly able to compensate for it, although it makes it harder to control the ship. No, our real worry is the nearly expended blintas." Looking up, I noticed that they were indeed much less full, no longer the round spheres at the beginning of the voyage.

"Are there any around here?" asked Cassie.

He shook his head. "No, I'm afraid they're unique to the Raised Isles. We will not be able to replace them on the mainland."

"So can't you sail the ship without them?" Diane asked. "After all, you do with your individual sails."

"That's different. A personal sail can support a single

person if the winds are favorable. However, a ship is not meant to sail without them. There's too much weight. Already we find it difficult to keep the ship from dropping too rapidly." I suddenly realized how high we were and how precarious a position we were in — something that I hadn't thought much about since my first sail.

"I fear we may need to ditch the ship before we are able to reach the Valnorian. The Greylock Woods, where they make their home, is some distance still."

"And there are no other of these high races that might be closer?" Matt asked, sounding more desperate than normal.

Damek shook his head in response.

"So how the hell would we get back in the first place?" Eric demanded. "If these blintas don't last that long …"

Damek looked at him sadly. "Without the help of the Ikhael, we had no plan. I banked everything on their support. I never thought to consider …" He left the rest unsaid. Gazing up at the masts and then out in the direction we headed, he continued, "We could sail to the ocean. Once on the water, the ship will float, and we can maneuver it back to Loralee. But then we are back where we started with nothing accomplished except the Ruling Members never trusting us again. And the Bots will continue to gain strength. That is not an option I care to contemplate right now."

I could see that Matt was frustrated. "No, we made a decision. We all agreed."

A simple nod from Damek sealed the choice to continue. He moved away to help the others maneuver the ship, but Diane turned to Matt and said, "You know, this plan sounded logical enough when hatched back on the Raised Isles. But now, I don't know. I'm worried." She looked at him like she had back when I first met them, the young couple so in love; they always trusted each other for support and guidance.

"I know," he said. "I am too. But what choice do we have? You saw what happened on Tensheann when they attacked. We couldn't just sit there waiting for another."

I didn't voice my thoughts, but like Diane, I was beginning to worry.

~ ~ ~

The ship's ability to stay airborne lasted for most of that day. We left the mountains behind and rather than sailing west in the direction we had come, which would lead us back to the ocean, we headed southeast to the forest of the woodland race. But by late afternoon we were barely skirting the treetops, and it was plain the flotation would not last much longer.

"I fear the blintas were damaged more than I had thought by the rough winds on the mountainside," Damek told us. We spent the rest of the day making preparations for abandoning the ship, gathering provisions and dividing packs amongst each of us.

Unlike our original flight from the edge of the ocean to the mountains, when we passed homes and villages, today we saw no sign of habitation. The land here was less fertile — rockier, with fewer green fields or lush vegetation. The scraggy trees and bushes clung together in small clumps as if trying to support each other against the elements.

As the sun settled low in the sky, Damek announced, "We need to do this now. We might have the ability to continue a few more hours, but by then it will be dark, which will make it more challenging to set the *Sea Spray* down. We'll find a suitable resting place."

For some reason, I was struck by his choice of words: a

suitable resting place. I hoped it would apply only to the ship and not us.

A short time later he pointed to a small grove of trees, telling the others to set it down there. They lowered the tethers, and we made a wide sweep around the grove as Riyaad jumped off to sail himself to the ground. Bevon brought the ship around again and much like our landing at the home of the Ikhael, it was simple enough for Riyaad to tie each tether around tree trunks to prevent the vessel from floating away. Quintia lowered the rope ladder for us to step off. Before I reached over the railing to climb onto it, I took one last look around the deck. Although we had made this home for only a short time, it was still one of the last links to the Raised Isles.

"She's a good ship," said Quintia. "I loathe leaving her like this" She extended her hand to help me onto the ladder.

Once we were on the ground Damek said, "We'll make camp nearby tonight, but not too close to the *Sea Spray*. If the blintas deplete completely, the ship will roll over onto its side." Like any other ship, the hull was curved to allow it to float in the water.

We lit a small fire that night as we all huddled around it. The air was not cold; I think we just wanted to be comforted. We were somber most of the evening, and after a sparse meal Damek said, "I know this is not the way we had planned our mission." I could see the pained expression on his face. "I hope I have not led you into more danger by my decision."

"It was not your decision alone," Matt interrupted. "We all decided."

"Humph." Eric snorted but said no more.

"How far to this forest?" asked Diane.

"I'm not positive. With the ship and a favorable wind,

probably less than two full days. Walking …" He shrugged.

"Maybe there'll be others who might help us along the way," Cassie said with a hopeful tone.

Bevon nodded in agreement, "Most of the native races have no quarrel with us. And they have always been known to be friendly. We should seek them out as we travel."

"We need to be cautious," Damek warned. "For too long we've been removed from the affairs of these people. We have little insight into what has taken place in the years since the war. For all we know, history has been rewritten, and we might now be blamed for what happened years ago."

We gazed into the flames for some time until Damek added, "Earthfriends, you should all have your blades, lances and slings handy … just in case." Looking at his Astari partners, he said, "And for us, we'll take turns at watch tonight, and every night. I don't want someone sneaking up on us. Let's also extinguish these flames. We shouldn't tempt fate by sending a beacon to anyone, at least for now."

As I lay on the rocky ground, making myself as comfortable as possible, I thought about the times as a young child when I would go camping in the woods behind my house with my neighborhood friends. We were barely out of sight from my home, but at the time it could have been the wild forest. Back then our small campfire dispelled the night as we watched the embers swirling, floating in the air before extinguishing themselves. We would often sing silly songs or tell scary stories. It was all so wonderful. I had imagined that Davy Crockett or Daniel Boone had done the same. I had so enjoyed those times.

This was nothing like that.

~ ~ ~
~ ~ ~

That night I awoke to a grating sound as if something was dragging on the ground. I sat up in alert, fearful that someone was attacking us. Bevon was nearby. "Do not fear. It is only the *Sea Spray* settling to the ground."

By daybreak, the ship was lying on its side, a sorry sight from the majestic craft that had once plied the islands of Loralee. As we stood before the grounded hulk, I could see that the Astari were the most upset. One blinta was completely deflated and lay dangling from a mast while the other two barely floated in the air.

"Of all the wonders on the Raised Isles," Riyaad said, "I always considered the sailing ships one of the most striking."

Damek nodded in agreement. "We can only hope the *Sea Spray* met this fate for a good reason. If we ever return to Loralee, I will lobby that a new ship be commissioned with this name, so it will not be forgotten."

"Should we burn it, least someone finds it and learn we are here?" Quintia asked.

Damek thought about it, looking around before answering. "No, a fire that big would only send a message to others; people we may not want to attract." Looking glum, he added, "No, let it stay." He regarded the ship proudly as he placed his palm against the hull.

Before leaving, Bevon climbed below deck of the ship for one last look around to gather supplies we might have missed. We then turned away and headed in the direction we had been flying, setting out now on foot.

By the time the sun was overhead, we were still walking.

One advantage — if you want to call it that — of being on the ground was that we were able to recognize signs of habitation that we would not have seen in the air: a barely discernible path, used either by people or animals, we couldn't tell; a small pile of ashes left by someone who once made a campfire; and at one point Riyaad spotted what might have been a footprint on the ground, although I had trouble making it out. But we spied not a single person or home.

The terrain remained much like we had seen from the air. It was an unforgiving land with many rocks taller than a man jutting from the surface. The ground was dusty with dry soil and yellow clumps of grass; only a few hardy bushes and small trees dotted the rolling hills. The temperature was cooler than the Raised Isles, but because we were exerting ourselves, we often shed layers of clothes as the day wore on.

It wasn't until my feet and legs were aching and the sun low in the sky that Damek finally suggested we stop for the day. I rummaged in my backpack to pull things out that we would need. That's when Bevon spoke, a note of tension in his voice. "Look over there Damek."

I looked in the direction of his gaze and saw on the crest of a nearby hill a pack of animals prancing around on all fours. These were the first large animals we had seen in this land. "I count seven," said Riyaad.

They were watching us cautiously from a distance. From afar they appeared somewhat of a cross between a wolf and a bear in size, although they looked like neither. Their jaws were more like a wolf or dog and even from here I could see their teeth. Some made a sound like a low rumble of a growl.

"Maybe they'll just go away," Cassie said nervously.

But they did not. And soon another half dozen or more had joined them as they circled us closer.

"Arm yourselves," Damek spoke firmly as he looked in their direction. "We may need to fight them."

Each of the Astari positioned themselves in a broad circle around us as they slowly wound their slingshots. Quintia was the only one who used a bow and arrow and she had an arrow notched and bow raised. With uncanny speed one of the animals charged at Bevon. Two Astari let fly their missiles hitting the animal squarely on the head, causing it to stumble, momentarily dazed. Bevon took advantage as he charged toward it, pulled out his knife and in one fluid motion plunged it into its neck. Another animal on the other side convulsed with an arrow through its neck from Quintia's bow.

"Well played," said Damek. "Maybe that will convince them we are not easy prey."

But that hope was short lived as moments later more of the animals rushed forward. The Astari moved quickly — using their slingshots and switching to either a knife or lance in seconds when needed. Quintia was a blur as she let loose one arrow after another. Riyaad stumbled as one of the animals rushed at him. Bevon came to his aid to finish off the animal with a thrust of his lance. In moments a half dozen animals lay dead. None had slipped past the Astari as we stood helplessly in the middle, gripping either our knife, slingshot, or lance, depending on which we had selected.

And then, just as quickly as it had begun, the attack ended as the remaining animals retreated a safe distance.

"Are they giving up?" Cassie asked hopefully.

"Up there on the hill," Quintia pointed to another rise. A person sat there on the back of one of the animals. The rider regarded us with a bitter intensity. It was not a Bot, and my first reaction was one of relief. But the person made no effort to engage us. If the animals had looked ugly to me, this person was even more so: a protruding lower jaw, mottled gray skin, deep-set eyes, small nose and long stringy black hair. Its forearms and hands were massive, although the rest of his build was probably slimmer than the Astari. I had the distinct impression that it regarded us with a look of disdain rather than curiosity.

Damek lifted his hand, palm out in a gesture of greeting. The person simply continued staring at us without reaction. Minutes passed. The animals continued to surround us but remained at a distance. "Greetings," Damek finally shouted. "We don't mean any harm."

The figure showed no acknowledgment that it cared. "I don't think he's friendly," I heard Diane say.

Moments later it tugged on a rein attached to the animal and turned away with not so much as a greeting or a word. The rest of the animals followed.

"Not the kind of welcome from the locals I would hope for," Eric said.

The Astari remained in their position for long moments after the person and animals had left. Only when there was no other sign of them did they relax. Riyaad's arm was bleeding from a long gash opened by the claws of an animal. Fortunately, Damek had thought to bring a medical kit with us, and he retrieved it from a backpack. "It's only minor," Riyaad said, but he consented to Diane cleaning the wound with a damp cloth while Damek opened the medical kit.

"Who was that?" Matt asked as he winced, seeing the extent of the cut on Riyaad's arm. "Not very friendly, was he?"

Damek replied slowly as he dabbed an ointment on Riyaad's wound. "No, it seems he wasn't. I don't recognize his kind." Looking up at Bevon and Quintia, he asked, "Do either of you?" They each shook their heads.

As Damek wrapped a green bandage on Riyaad's laceration, he said, "There's much we don't know of the lands and the people here." Pausing to secure the bandage he continued, "Still, I didn't care for the looks of that one. I fear many changes have taken place since the Astari last visited this land. I pray they're not all for the worse."

~ ~ ~

We walked some distance from the attack and the remains of the dead animals, wanting to be as far away from them as possible. It was dusk when we reached a small stream and Damek said we should stop here. He consented to a fire. "We can't travel the entire way to the Greylock Woods worrying about being seen. But we should double the watch tonight, which means we all need to take turns."

"Of course," Matt readily agreed. "We'll do whatever we can."

The fire was comforting after the violence of the animal attack. A warm meal was exactly what we needed as the air had turned noticeably cooler once the sun had set. And although the flames might attract other unfriendly advances, I thought a fire helped shut out the rest of the world. As I sat in the warm envelope of light, only my friends — both Astari and from Earth — were all that mattered to me as the flames pushed away dangers beyond.

"I'm concerned," Diane said after we had eaten. "You realize, we only saw one of those people, but there're likely others, as well as more of those wild animals."

Damek had remained subdued since the attack. "I had hoped we wouldn't face any danger, but it may have been wishful thinking — an undue optimism from our years of safety on Loralee. The Realm of Elthea has many good places, but I fear it also has others. It's not a utopia. Evil finds a way to corrupt, and we do not know how much the Bots may have defiled this land while we thought our world safe from them." Looking sadder since the death of his grandmother, he spoke with a bitter edge, "I hope we're not already too late in sounding the alarm."

It was some time before he continued, "Earthfriends, we will ward you against harm as we always have. But there are only the four of us. If we're overwhelmed, remember your training. You have all done well, and you may need to use your weapons. Always keep them ready."

"I didn't like the looks of that person riding the animal," said Quintia. "Let's hope we've seen the last of his kind."

Damek nodded, "Yes, it may have been animals who attacked, but it seems to me they were controlled, or at least influenced, by that person. I wish we knew more of him."

Even though my muscles ached and I was tired from the day's long walk, I felt agitated and too wound up, so I volunteered to take the first watch along with Riyaad. We each positioned ourselves on opposite ends of the camp as I selected a spot with my back against the trunk of a tree, lance extended by my side. My mind was a jumble of emotions as I thought about the events of the last two days: The Ikhael infected with a virus that was killing them, the greeting from snarling animals, our new goal to seek the help of another race many miles away, and the need to reach them on foot in a strange land none of us knew much about — it was overwhelming. I realized that I should be scared.

But I wasn't.

Maybe it was my time spent these last months with the Astari. Or maybe I was so far removed from what I now thought of as my former existence. In any case, I was emboldened in a way I didn't think possible. Here we were in a strange place, wild animals attacking us, a mission to save the Astari and possibly Earth from the Bots. All this would have caused me to cower not long ago. But now?

I mulled this over in my head, wondering if this indeed was my utopia: a purpose in life I never really had. I was on a mission to save a people and a world that I never knew existed — yet I now loved dearly. I always heard politicians say how they were going to save the world back when I was working on political campaigns. But did anyone believe them? Even I hadn't.

But here I felt a fire in my gut that I never felt before. Smiling broadly, I felt like an idiot for doing so. But at this moment, I didn't care.

CHAPTER THIRTY
A Soft Target

We began our trek the next morning hoping that the worst was behind us. By mid-morning, there was still no sign of the vicious animals or the rider.

"Tell us about these woodland people," Cassie asked Riyaad as we followed what Damek had called a path (although I had to take his word for it since it was impossible for me to discern it from the rest of the terrain).

"Ah, the Valnorian," he replied with a smile on his face. "It will be a great pleasure to see them again. They are a remarkable people. During our war with the Bots, they may not have always been at the forefront of the battles as were the Ikhael, but they have an inner strength and passion that far surpasses any others."

Listening along, Quintia added, "What I love most about them is their composure." I thought it was a strange thing to admire in people. But she continued to explain. "They have an ability to be at peace with themselves no matter if all hell is breaking loose — some sort of inner resolve regardless of what is happening around them or what they are doing. The Astari have learned much from the Valnorian during our time together. We now practice a form of meditation that we had learned from them."

"Did they evolve from technology or biology?" Diane asked.

Quintia smiled. "I'm afraid we have given you an incorrect impression of the great races — probably due to a small sample size of your experience so far. Although some of the great races have risen from a tech environment, as we and others have, and some evolved from a biological foundation such as the Ikhael, many evolved as a combination of both. And still others who evolved naturally and for a variety of reasons decided to leave their homes."

"And then there are some who developed in ways that we cannot precisely explain," Damek added. "There're so many different possibilities and variations — a great diversity of life exists here."

Cassie perked up. "That's incredible."

"So how many different races live here?" Matt asked.

The others thought for a moment. "It's difficult to say," Riyaad replied slowly. "I don't believe we know for sure. We're most familiar with those who fought alongside us in the Bot war. But there are just as many others — maybe even more — who wanted no part in the conflict. What would you say Damek?"

He was at the lead of our company. Turning around, he said, "Many score I would guess. If you asked me to venture a number, maybe a hundred, but that would only be a guess. And then there are the different indigenous races as well."

"And don't forget," I added, "you talked about a race that looked like us — human — who appeared at the time of your war with the Bots."

"For whatever reason, Elthea has attracted many different kinds of people," added Quintia.

"Look over there," Eric said suddenly, ending the conversation. In the distance, we saw more of the wild animals. This time with two riders who sat looking at us.

"Damn," spat Matt. "They're following us."

The terrain was open and rugged with few places to hide or take cover. "Who knows how long they've been watching us," Matt added.

"We have no recourse," Damek said, his voice tense. "We need to keep going in this direction. Let's be wary of an ambush."

A few hours passed without incident. A rider or two would appear now and then on a crest of a hill, but they always kept their distance. "It's good they've learned to fear us," Riyaad said emphatically.

As we crested a small rise, Damek who was scouting a bit ahead of us, turned and said, "Ahead, there's smoke." Sure enough, as we reached his vantage, we could see a plume of black smoke rising directly ahead of us, maybe a mile away. "It appears too large for a cooking fire," he said.

"Maybe we should avoid it? Go around?" Bevon asked.

Damek thought for a moment. "No. Let's stay this course and find out what it is. But be alert."

I could clearly see that our Astari companions were nervous as they fidgeted with their lances or their slingshots. Quintia kept an arrow notched in her bow.

It turned out the distance was more like several miles. We could see the source of the fire before we even came close: a cluster of a dozen structures, now reduced to mostly smoking ruin. It appeared deserted — only the blackened remains of what must have been a small community.

As we came closer, we saw scores of bodies scattered on the ground.

Once inside the village, I could see they had been

attacked. Riyaad rolled a body onto its back. The dead person looked much like us, but even though its face was smeared with blood, its features were different. This was not one of the human-looking people Damek had spoken about.

As the acrid black smoke continued to swirl around, kicked up now by a breeze, I looked around at the dead. Many were horribly burned by the fire as if they had tried to take refuge in their homes before being burnt out and then killed. I saw the twisted form of a small child sprawled next to a woman. Her throat had been cut. Not far from them lay another whose skull had been mostly bashed in. I couldn't tell if it was a male or female. Walking as in a daze, I saw another person with his chest split open. It was like a horror movie — you don't want to watch any longer but are unable to turn away.

Hearing a noise, I saw that Eric was getting sick near a stone wall. The fetid smell of death hung heavy in the air. And everywhere I looked there was another gruesome image.

Not far from the village sat a small lake, probably fed by an underground source since there was no river around. It looked so peaceful — so perfectly normal, as if nothing were wrong in the world. Drawing my eyes back to the ground nearby I saw another person on his stomach missing an arm.

"Damek, over here," Bevon shouted. The others were already inspecting something on the ground by the time I made my way there. It was the body of one of the large animals that had attacked us yesterday.

"At least they didn't go down without a fight," Damek said grimly.

"Now we know who attacked them," Matt said.

"These animals did not burn down the village." Damek bit off the words. "Nor did they hack these people. No, these animals may have attacked, but it was their riders who did this."

Damek stood up, looking out beyond the village. After a moment he pointed. "There, look."

Several of the animals paced back and forth on the other side of the lake, each with a rider looking in our direction. A score of additional animals romped nearby.

"Whoever that race is, they're most certainly not friendly," said Riyaad. "I'm afraid the attack on us yesterday was only the beginning."

"Do you know these people killed?" Cassie asked, indicating one of the dead bodies of the villagers.

"I believe they're one of the native people in this land," answered Damek. "From what I can see, they had no reason to suspect an attack. Something has changed for this to happen."

Damek gazed back out at the distant animals with riders, a bitter expression still on his face. But then it turned to one of surprise, his eyes opened wide, as he said, "It's us."

We stared at him, not understanding. "What's us?" Eric demanded.

"We're the reason they attacked this village." We continued to stare at him dumbfounded. "These people may have provided us assistance, at least a good meal and a comfortable place for the night. Those riders didn't want that to happen."

"Are you serious?" Matt's expression was one of disbelief.

"We were the thing that's changed," Damek continued. "These people hadn't built any defenses against attacks. They must not have had reason to."

I felt bile rise in my stomach. "They killed all these people just to stop us from maybe getting food or whatever?"

"I think we have to assume that," Bevon answered. A look of disgust clouded his expression. "This was on our path; we would have come upon them. Those riders were watching us all morning. It seems likely."

"This is worse than if they had attacked us again," Eric said. "Why didn't they just do that instead?"

"Maybe they're not yet ready," Quintia answered. "They saw how we had fought the day before. Maybe this was a softer target."

"Why do they hate us?" Cassie appeared bitter more than sad.

Damek answered softly. "Remember what I once said? There is much that is wonderful in Elthea, but now I fear there is also evil." Nodding beyond the lake, he said, "Out there, those are vile creatures for them to have done this." He turned away, his stance betraying how dismayed he felt.

There was no reason to remain here. "Should we bury or do something with the dead?" Quintia asked.

Damek looked around sadly. The black smoke had now mostly abated; small fires were all that remained. "No, we need to be mindful of our goal. And I want to put as much distance between this place and us by nightfall."

The elation I had felt last night during my turn at the watch had now dampened, as an uneasy feeling took its place. Here were creatures that would stop at nothing to harm us. I wondered if this was how a grand adventure should feel.

One thing I knew for certain, this was not the utopia we would have created.

CHAPTER THIRTY-ONE
Woodbery College: Eighth Interlude

The tension was building.

Only two weeks had remained before the Utopia Project was due and every time I thought we had finished, either Diane or Matt — mostly Matt — would suggest we add something else.

It was infuriating and was beginning to grate on us. Last week during a breakout session we even had one heated discussion that came to a shouting match.

For weeks we had been meeting hours every day; and that was in addition to the class lectures, readings and video clips assigned to us. But this day we ended the meeting on a high note, finally encouraged that we were wrapping it up.

"I can't believe we finished early today," Cassie declared on her way out of the room. "I'm going back to my dorm and sleep until next Tuesday." She smiled sweetly, an expression that always made me gaze at her with a certain yearning.

Almost all of our group discussions took place on campus in one of the team meeting rooms designed specifically for this purpose. Most of the rooms were furnished with easy

265

chairs, a round conference table and a whiteboard (a necessity for Matt). This was our favorite — one that we tried to schedule most often. Its large windows looked out over the Common, the broad area surrounded by the granite buildings of Woodbery College. As I gazed out now, I noticed for the first time that buds were forming on the maples while the slightest hint of green on the broad lawns finally began to replace the drab yellows and browns that had dominated the grounds since the snow had melted.

"Don't forget about the final lecture tomorrow," Matt called after her as she exited. "You wouldn't want to miss it, would you?" he said playfully. Her only response was a wave of her hand without looking back.

Matt and Diane donned their coats and left together, saying their goodbyes as they followed Cassie out of the room. I had scattered my papers and documents around the conference table during our meeting, so I took the time to collect them and close my tablet.

"Tell me the truth," Eric said as he lingered while I finished getting organized.

"What?" I mumbled, thinking he had already left.

"I can't help wonder, is this all worth it?"

I looked at him blankly. "What? School?"

He chuckled. "No, I mean what we're doing on this project ... all these meetings, the discussions, lectures, readings. After all, it's just a paper. Sometimes I wonder the point of it all."

I thought about it. Last semester I would have given him some glib answer, but that was before getting to know him during this project. I learned he is not the shallow person I had thought he was. "Eric, this is just another hurdle we need to get over. That's what it takes to graduate — a series of challenges that we have to pass. And graduation itself is just another hurdle. Think of each one as a rite of passage."

"Yeah, a rite of passage. The problem is, when do they end? What does all this do for us?"

I thought he was carrying it too far, but today I was in a good mood, so I indulged him. "It's all about the good life Eric — a happy life. It's tough to have that if you're destitute, with no job, no career, and no hope."

He snorted, "A happy life — right."

"You already have that. Your parents have money; someday you'll have a good job in your dad's company. But lots of us, me for one, we need to compete in the real world. And it's hard to do that without a degree, or worse, with no knowledge or skill. So that's what I get out of this."

He laughed. "The good life — I think that's a crock. Do you really believe the good life happens when you get a decent job?" He gestured with his hands, always a sign that he was on a roll. "It doesn't end there. Next, you'll need a better car, then a home, then a bigger home, and to pay for it all, a higher salary, so you go for that promotion. It never ends. Meanwhile, you're miserable most of the time."

I blinked, trying to figure out where this was coming from. For all his outgoing, happy-go-lucky personality, Eric could also turn pensive at times. I guess I had caught him in one of those moods.

And he wasn't done yet. "But here we are, trying to create a utopia! How can we possibly factor all the variables?"

At least this was something I could agree with. "I don't think we can," I said. "In spite of what Matt thinks, the best we can hope for is to develop something that's believable — something that a professor would say, 'I can see that happening.' And I think we're doing a pretty good job of it."

He looked at me with an expression that said he didn't believe it. "The trouble is, I know we're still missing something major."

"I know what you mean," thinking how he voiced just what I have been feeling. "At times I feel it's right there, that one major piece of the jigsaw puzzle that's been eluding us. Then I find it and just fit it in," I said as I gestured with my hands on an imaginary board. "Only then does the entire picture come into focus."

I finished gathering my papers and was ready to go, but I continued to think about what he had said about the good life. Instinctively I knew he was talking about himself. So as I stood to leave, I said, "You realize Eric, someday you'll find it — that thing in your life that is so meaningful it cancels out everything else."

His eyes contained a cheerless gleam as he stared at me for a moment, and in that brief heartbeat I knew I was looking at the real Eric; the person who suffered self-doubts and insecurities like we all did, not the Eric he wanted us to know. And then his lips curled up ever so slowly. "Yeah, and maybe all our wishes will come true, like you getting a girlfriend one of these days. But I don't know if that's gonna happen either." He punched me playfully on the arm. "Hey, I have an idea. Let's have a beer at the Hideout before dinner. We deserve it."

Most nights I would shun the suggestion of having a drink before dinner. But the work level was getting to me lately, so I relented. "Well, okay, maybe just one." But I quickly added, "I need to make some edits on my section of the paper tonight, so I can't stay long."

"Nah, don't worry. A beer or two might loosen you up. You can use it."

I smiled. "If I had a dime every time you said that I'd be rich by now."

~ ~ ~

~ ~ ~

One or two drinks at the Hideout Cafe that evening turned into quite a few more. And by then I was feeling plenty relaxed.

"You know, good buddy, I admire you more than the others on the team," Eric proclaimed as he motioned the bartender, a cute graduate student (and one of the reasons we stayed as long as we had) for another round of drinks. "Make it a shot of tequila and a beer this time," he said to her with a wry smile.

"Whaddya mean? Admire me?" I asked, realizing that I probably should have nixed the order for a shot, let alone another beer.

"You got it all together." He leaned toward me as if conveying valuable information. "Your life. You know what you want, and you go after it. I admire that."

"You don't know shit," I replied light-heartedly.

"No — no, I mean it. Look at yourself. Already interning for a state senator. You understand things. I actually listened to your description of the government for our paper. It's good — really good." Lowering his voice, speaking in a stage whisper, "Now, if you could only decide which one you wanted you'd be all set."

I looked at him blankly. "What're you talking about?"

"The girls … Cass or Diane. Which one you want?"

I stared at him, momentarily startled even in my somewhat inebriated state. A fleeting memory crossed my mind of the nearly forgotten encounter with Cassie early in the semester when we both had too much to drink. But I quickly stifled the thought. "You frigging kidding me? Diane is Matt's girlfriend, in case you hadn't noticed. And I don't think Cass is the least bit interested in me."

"But you don't know that. You gotta go for it. I see you when you look at 'em, especially Cass. You're like a deer in the headlights. You've gotta take action buddy. Make things happen."

I was too surprised even to laugh. "Yeah ... well ... that's the last thing I need right now," I sputtered.

After a second I decided to explain this better. "You know Eric, I wouldn't have thought it possible. But you, Matt, Cass, Diane, you're all good friends now — just like family. We've gone through a lot in just a few months. And okay, both girls are pretty." I shook my head a bit too vigorously. "No, they're gorgeous, each in their own way. But you all mean a lot to me now. And I wouldn't want to do anything to screw it up. And I sorta think that might." The bartender had put down our shot and beer, so I gulped down my shot and followed it with a swig of beer. Taking a moment to catch my breath from the shot of tequila, I added, "Besides, I doubt either would want someone as dull as me."

He laughed, "You got a point there buddy." Eyeing the co-ed behind the bar he called, "Hey Rachel." Whispering to me, "That's her name, isn't it?" She smirked more than smiled as she stepped closer. "Hey, my buddy here has a problem. He's a good looking guy, wouldn't you say?"

She smiled a little more broadly as if enjoying a good joke. "As far as undergraduates go, you're both okay."

"Well, you see, Phil here needs a girlfriend ... or maybe just a girl." I felt my cheeks beginning to flush, hoping he would just stop. But he didn't. "I'm sure you have some friends that would be interested. Maybe some lowly undergraduate." His face lit up as he added, "Or maybe you. Whaddya say? Can you help him out?"

I shook my head, totally embarrassed now. "I'm sorry," I said. "My friend here talks too much." I glared at him, hoping he would understand my message.

This obviously wasn't her first day as a bartender because she wasn't flustered in the least. She pinned me with her eyes. "What's your name again?"

I responded meekly, not sure what else to say.

"Okay Phil, tell you what. You look like a decent sort of guy. Here's my advice. Next girl you meet, be a little forward. You won't know until you ask. If she says no, you're no worse off."

Eric slapped his hand on the bar. "That's what I'm talking about. You gotta take some chances. Right?"

She smiled again. "Just be ready to get rejections. That's gonna happen too."

I'm sure it was due in large part to the number of drinks we had, but at that moment Rachel was one of the most beautiful girls I'd ever seen. She looked at me with teasing eyes. Putting her palms on the bar to lean closer she said more softly, as I inhaled her perfume and tried not to stare at a point about six inches below her chin, "For what it's worth, I have a strict policy of turning down any advances from guys here at work. Everyone only has one thing on their mind after getting lubed up with drinks. But if I got to know you outside of work — and if you weren't an undergraduate — and you asked me to join you for a coffee, I might say yes." She held my stare for what felt like a long time as I simply gawked, my mouth unable to form any rational words.

And just like that she smiled sweetly and turned to take an order from another customer. Both Eric and I stole a long glance at her backside as she walked away.

After another few swigs of beer, Eric turned more serious. "I gotta hand it to you Phil — what you said about us being family. I know what ya mean. I thought it was only me who felt that way." He had a faraway look in his eyes. "In some ways, I consider you and the others more like family than my real one." He seemed to have suddenly sobered. "I'd do anything for you guys. You know that, don't you?"

Again I was embarrassed, but now for a different reason. I thought about making a joke. But the thing is, he struck a chord. So instead I nodded in agreement.

CHAPTER THIRTY-TWO

A Gathering Storm

We left the smoldering village as we had found it. But I still couldn't get the slaughter out of my mind.

That evening, unlike the other nights, Damek wouldn't allow a fire. "Let's not make it easier for them to find us." It was a chilly, mirthless evening as we ate a cold meal sitting by the light of Celeus, the larger moon.

"Let me ask you guys," Eric said pensively, "I was just wondering … what would we each do if we were back at Woodbery right now knowing this is where it would take us?" A bitter laugh escaped his lips. "I was just thinking … what decision would I make about joining this team, putting all that effort into the Utopia Project, knowing I would end up here? Would I instead ask that loser, Sam, if I could be part of his team? Where would I be now if I had done that?"

"Certainly not having this much fun," Cassie responded. I could tell she was trying to lighten the mood.

Diane spoke hesitantly. "I couldn't imagine doing anything else, even knowing it would bring us to this place. Speaking for myself, that is." Such was the change in Diane that she would voice this.

Matt nodded. "What I've gone through here is worth more than anything. Who would have thought this would happen to us?" Looking straight at Diane, he added, "No, I can't imagine me making any other choice."

I cleared my throat. "I would probably have lived a perfectly normal, boring life." I laughed joylessly. And suddenly, that other life came into focus in my mind. "I would likely be working at some low-level government job; if I were lucky, I would be a staffer for a state rep or city councilor. Maybe I would have gotten married in a few years, had kids, bought a house in the suburbs, take the commuter rail into the city each day along with the herd of others, sitting next to a faceless, uncaring, unspeaking person each day on the train. I wouldn't be happy. I'd simply let life drag me along." I paused, realizing that I had rambled. "The only good part is that I probably would have lived a lot longer."

At least that produced a small chuckle.

"You told me this once, a long time ago," Eric said, looking directly at me. "You said this group; we were like family. And I knew exactly how you felt. And I still feel the same."

"Well, well," said Cassie. "I think one of our family members is beginning to mellow a bit."

~ ~ ~

The animals attacked us again the next morning.

We had just set out when two of them blocked our way, snarling viciously, teeth bared and snapping. Seeing them up close again, I realized how big and how fast they were.

"Remember, the riders control them," said Damek as we stood before these animals. "If any of the riders come at us, attempt to kill them. I believe the animals will scatter."

The terrain here was fertile. The trees and bushes made it more difficult to clearly see the surrounding area as we could with the rocky, barren terrain of the last few days.

Bevon and Riyaad stepped forward to challenge the animals with their lances while Damek and Quintia remained close to us. Both animals pounced at the same moment, causing the Astari to take a step back even as they thrust their lances forward. The animals easily avoided their thrusts with rapid strokes of their front paws, knocking the lances to the side. But the animals held back, not advancing further. For moments they stood in place, satisfied not to press their attack but not giving any ground.

Quintia spoke to Damek. "It appears they don't want us to move in that direction."

Damek was clearly frustrated. Calling out to Bevon and Riyaad he said, "Stand back. We'll try to go around them and see what happens."

But three other animals soon blocked our path after going only a short distance to the south. These looked even more rabid than the first. And not far behind them, sat a rider atop one of the animals.

Damek yelled to the rider, "What sort of coward lets his pets fight for him? Stand here before us." But the figure only gazed at us malevolently. "I don't like the looks of this," Damek said cheerlessly.

We retreated to the north. The animals did not pursue us. "They're herding us," said Quintia before we had gone very far. "They want us to go north."

Damek looked grim. "Yes, I agree. But for what purpose?"

"I suggest we do not find out," said Bevon. "Perhaps we remind them of our first encounter when we killed a half score."

After going some distance without spotting more of them,

we angled again to the southeast. "Let's see what happens now," said Damek. "If they mean to stop us, we'll fight."

It wasn't long before they appeared again — four animals, each without a rider, mauling the ground with their front paws as if challenging us, a menacing low growl coming from deep inside each. A brief moment of hesitation and doubt crossed Damek's face before he said, "Bevon, with me. The rest of you, attack with your slings or bow just before we reach them." He was about to move forward, hesitated, and said, "Earthfriends, please aim for the animals, not the back of our heads, if you would be so kind."

I had to smile in spite of the situation. Damek still maintained his sense of humor. I wished I could feel the same as my stomach churned. Not having practiced enough with the slings, I instead extended my lance and held it at the ready. I noticed Matt had done the same.

Damek and Bevon charged toward the animals, lances in hand, giving a wide berth between the two of them to hopefully allow the projectiles to hit the animals before they reached them. Five paces away I heard the whistle of the slings and the twang of the bowstring as three of the animals dropped to the ground. Damek and Bevon concentrated on the one still standing. The creature easily avoided the first thrusts from Damek. But Bevon found an opening and thrust his lance into its belly. Meanwhile one of the other animals who had been stunned was on its feet, and Damek lunged at it, putting an end to its life with a clean stab in the chest.

"Let's see what they think now," Riyaad said.

"Quickly. Let's move," said Damek. "I hope this is the last we see of them." Again we set a path to the southeast.

An hour later, just as I was beginning to unclench the white-knuckled grip I maintained on my lance, we saw more. I groaned inwardly seeing at least a dozen animals, many with riders.

Even with my newfound acceptance of the different races of this world, these people still looked ugly. Their jaws extended lower and further than humans, creating an impression their teeth could be powerful weapons. Their muscular and hairy forearms made them look more like another breed of animal than an intelligent person. There was indeed intelligence in their eyes — but not a friendly, compassionate perception. It was a seething hatred that emanated not only from their eyes but every muscle on their bodies. I noticed they were all holding blades.

The mounted riders loped toward us slowly, almost casually, stopping a score of paces away from us. "Be wary," Damek said even as he moved a few feet toward the riders. "Explain yourselves. Why do you allow your pets to interfere with us?"

They made no reply. "They may not speak our language," Bevon offered.

Damek raised his arm over his head, palm out in their universal greeting of peace. One of the riders raised its sword and pointed toward the north. Damek raised his lance in the other direction.

The rider did not respond. It gazed impassively while the animal it sat upon emitted a rumbling growl.

Turning his back to the riders, Damek said to us, "We make our stand here. Slings and arrows first. Concentrate on the riders. Disable as many as possible. Target the animals only if attacked by them."

"I've got their leader," Quintia informed the others. As Damek turned toward the attackers the other Astari reacted with remarkable swiftness, sending a volley at the riders. The leader, if that's who he was, fell back with an arrow in its chest. Three others fell to the ground in quick succession as projectiles hit each of their heads. All this happened in a heartbeat before I could even reach for my sling.

The remaining animals, some with riders, remained in place for a long moment as if stunned. But then they charged at once. I didn't bother with my sling as I raised my lance protectively.

I cringed as they crashed into us. But the Astari were everywhere, swinging a lance or a blade to topple a rider or disable an animal. An animal without a rider was about to tear into me, but at the last second, Bevon jumped in front to plunge his knife into its neck just as the animal sent him tumbling to the ground with a blow to his side. Bevon lay there unmoving as I dropped to my knees at his side to turn him face up, keeping one eye out for any others who might rip into us. "No," he mumbled looking dazed. "Stand and protect yourself."

I did as he instructed but I stood next to him as he struggled to get up. A red smear spread through his torn vest. Seconds later another animal, its mouth frothing, was before me. Without thinking I held my lance up, trying to remember my training. The creature lunged, crashing into my lance point, driving me back as I fell to the ground. Somehow I managed to force the shaft down so that the base wedged into the ground as the animal impaled itself on the point. I stumbled to get up and quickly stepped away from the still convulsing beast as I pulled out my lance from its chest.

My hands were slick with its blood, but with all my strength I jabbed the thing in its exposed underside as it looked up at me with glassy eyes before it stopped moving. I was breathing so fast I was nearly hyperventilating. I realized this was the first thing I had ever killed in my life. Looking into its dying eyes, I didn't feel like the victor. This was wrong, even if the thing would have killed me.

From the moment the animal charged at me I had blocked out other sounds. But now I heard one of the girls bellowing in pain. It was Diane as she lay crouched on the ground with Matt trying to help her. The fight with the animal took more out of me than I realized as I was beginning to feel unsteady. The few remaining attackers had started to scatter. I saw only one with a mounted rider as he retreated in the distance.

What was wrong with me? I tried to move toward Diane to see if I could help, but my feet turned to rubber as I slid to the ground. Bevon caught me just before I fell. "Easy now. You have lost blood."

Looking down, I realized that my side was slick with blood from a gash in my side. The animal must have done it as I stabbed it.

I let him ease me to the ground as he inspected the wound. "It doesn't appear serious." He was also injured, raw slices on his chest and side. He first looked to be sure there was no lingering threat before he continued to remove my shirt to tend to my cut. "You did well earthfriend — killing the beast. I'm glad nobody will fault me for my training skills." Smiling weakly, he continued, "It would be a terrible mark against me if you had gotten yourself killed."

"Just a lucky break for you then," I replied. "Still, I don't know how it's going to reflect on you with me getting injured like this. I don't think they're going to let you off too easily." I winced, beginning to feel the sting. Looking at the others, I asked, "Is Diane all right?" Damek was now helping her in addition to Matt.

"It appears she will be fine," he replied. "We need to move out of this place. Some of these animals or people may yet recover from wounds. Can you walk?" He put a temporary compress on my cut to stop the bleeding and helped me onto my feet while Matt insisted on carrying Diane in his arms.

"My God," said Eric, shocked at seeing I was hurt. "Are you okay?"

I nodded. "I should live."

We moved some distance before taking refuge in a shady grove. In spite of his injuries, Bevon supported me the entire way. Once on the ground, he opened the medical kit as he instructed me to remove my shirt. Fortunately, the jagged laceration felt worse than it was. It would probably leave a scar, but that was the least of my worries at the moment.

I saw that Diane had a cut on her upper arm. It was not as long as mine, but it was deep, and she had also bled a good amount. Matt's expression was dismal as he knelt by her side while Cassie and Damek bent over her tending to the wound. "I'm sorry," Matt was telling her. "I should have done more."

"Oh stop it," she replied kindly. "None of us are soldiers." Smiling, she added, "That's definitely not your strong suit."

~ ~ ~

Only after the Astari had bandaged Diane and me, did they take care of their lacerations. Bevon suffered the worst with cuts to his face, chest, and side. Fortunately, nobody suffered anything major.

Everyone made a big deal about me killing the beast. I could see the admiration in all their expressions. Their praise, however, did little to abate my regret at having to kill it.

"I think we should rest here today and stay the night," said Damek. "If these riders keep to their previous tactics they'll leave us alone. But we have decisions to make."

We ate a warm midday meal as Damek saw no reason not to light a fire now. My wound felt remarkably better once bandaged; I recalled the Astari healing powers on our first day on the Raised Isles with Eric's broken wrist.

The warm food and the chance to lay down revitalized me greatly as I recovered from the torpid sensation. Still, we all sat sullenly for some time, lost in our thoughts until Matt finally said, "We all know we're in deep trouble. How do we get out of this mess?"

Each of the Astari remained quiet for a long time as they continued gazing into the fire. Finally, Damek said, "I believe we have two choices. We continue to move south toward the Valnorian and see if they still oppose us after this, or—"

"We go where they want us," Eric said bitterly, finishing it for him. After a time Damek nodded.

"What about other races that can help us?" Matt asked. "You said there were others. Might we gain support from someone closer to us, at least not toward the south?"

"I've been thinking much about that," Damek replied. "Many had scattered after the war, making new homes that were destroyed or seeking a new start elsewhere. It's our fault that we hadn't kept a closer kinship with them. But we never thought this would happen." He shook his head slowly.

"Is there any way to communicate with them?" Matt continued. "Some way that does not involve going to their place? Maybe you could get a message to these Valnorian people."

Damek looked at him with compassion, or maybe it was sadness, I couldn't tell.

"We never developed one." Pursing his lips, he continued, "In our youth, new to our physical forms, we still had the ability to share our thoughts with other races. But like some of our other powers, those diminished and were lost after a time."

With a distant look in his eyes, he poked the flames of the

campfire with a long stick, stirring up the embers. "Much has lapsed since our early days, especially our affinity with the other races. But the Astari came to this realm to get away, as did many others. We only wanted to be left alone — to live our newfound lives in peace."

He sighed deeply. "All that was smashed by the Bots. So we came together to fight one great war. I believe in your Earth's history you had called it the war to end all wars. That's how we perceived it. So the great races fought together. And when it was over — when we thought victory was ours — each race went back to what we wanted most: to be left alone. The Astari went back to the splendor of our Raised Isles, knowing that we were finally safe." He angrily threw the stick into the fire. "And once again that appears to be shattered. We never planned for this. We never created the mechanisms to watch and prepare for another possible attack. We never thought it would be possible."

He stared at Matt with eyes wide as if daring him to challenge what he had said. I had never seen one of the Astari, especially Damek, so upset. Matt replied softly, "I'm not faulting you ... any of you. I'm only looking for a solution."

"Maybe they'll just let us go back to Loralee," Cassie said hopefully. "Once they see we've given up, they might be satisfied to let us return to the Raised Isles. I know you don't want to go home in defeat, but that might be the better choice right now ... regroup, convince the Ruling Members that they need to take action, find another way to build an alliance with others."

Damek looked doubtful. "Living to fight another day is always preferable. But I fear these people believe they have us now. Any course other than what they have chosen — to the north — I suspect they will oppose." He rose to his feet.

"For now we heal. We stay here for the night, and we rest tomorrow as well. We'll depart after that, moving southeast until — or if — we meet resistance. And if the force is small enough, we fight through them. And if not ..." he grimaced with frustration, "We turn to the west and make our way to the shore."

"And if neither is an option?" I asked.

It took him a moment to answer. "If it comes to it, then we decide."

CHAPTER THIRTY-THREE

Bad to Worse

I slept most of that afternoon, even with the bright light that filtered through the hanging branches where we had made our camp. I suspected my sleepiness had as much to do with the ointment applied to my wound as it did from exhaustion. And when I woke, I was surprised to see the sun low in the sky. Feeling much better, I stood to stretch my legs and walked a short distance, but not so far that I would be out of sight and in danger.

Seeing me rise, Matt stepped away from Diane, who was asleep. He spoke gently. "I'm glad you're awake. Can we talk?" I frowned, thinking something was wrong, but he didn't wait for a response. "You realize this isn't going to end well ... everyone can feel it. And the thing is, I don't know what to do." An edge of desperation crept into his voice. "On our sail from Loralee you told me that I had regained my confidence, but I'm not so sure." He snorted a short bark of a laugh. "I should have answers." He spoke with such emotion that I couldn't help feel sorry for him. And then I realized, it was our fault he felt this way. We had always counted on him to take control. We looked to him for answers. And now there were none.

I didn't know what to say. "Sometimes there are no answers Matt. No right or wrong decisions."

"But I should have a plan, something to get us out of this mess. I'm responsible."

Speaking forcefully, I said, "No you're not. Don't take this on yourself. It's not fair. We're a team, remember? We always made decisions as a team. We're all responsible for going on this journey. You didn't decide any of this. We all did."

He looked as if he might cry. I was shocked. "I don't know how we're going to survive this. Those beasts out there are going to kill us. You know that's what they want. And we don't understand why. I mean, why us?"

He laughed bitterly. I thought he might be on the verge of a nervous breakdown. For a second I considered slapping him hard across the cheek but decided that only happened in the movies. Instead, I grabbed him by the shoulders. "Matt, get it together. Please. We're all scared. And you'd be crazy if you weren't. But we're a team, and you're still our leader. We need you." I added the one thing I knew he would consider most important. "Diane needs you — now more than ever." And then I said more softly, "The rest of us are barely in control as it is. If you crack, nothing's going to keep us from losing it. Then where will we be?"

His expression — as of someone who had lost everything and didn't know what to do — startled me more than anything else he had ever said. But I could see that I had reached some part of him as his eyes regained their sharpness and his breathing calmed. He finally nodded. Taking a deep breath, he spoke quietly. "I think I just needed someone to talk to. I could always count on you."

"Matt?" Diane called, sitting up, looking dazed. He moved back to her side, and I could hear him telling her that it was fine, that he was right next to her.

~ ~ ~

The days spent resting and recovering were thoroughly serene and calming. We had desperately needed to soothe our fears and heal our bodies. Except for my brief conversation with Matt, we avoided talking about anything serious. It almost seemed that we had reached an unspoken consensus not to talk about our predicament as if that might result in it just going away. During this respite, we had seen no sign of the wild animals or their riders.

On the third day, as planned, we set out again toward the southeast. I walked with a pit in my stomach, fearing what would happen. As before, none of the creatures blocked our way for some time. But as we reached a broad, lifeless, rock-strewn field, the animals and riders stood waiting. I heard the sharp intake of someone's breath as we took a small rise and we looked out over an open stretch of land. This time we faced not just a handful of animals. We now stood before a hundred of the wild beasts and maybe several dozens of riders, all waiting patiently for us.

I looked at Damek. His expression was somber — more so than I had ever seen from him. "How can this be?" he said glumly.

But that was not the worst.

Stepping out from behind a large rock that had obstructed him, strode a Bot. It strode toward us, towering over the large animals that blocked our way. Diane stifled a cry.

The Bot stopped some distance away from us, a ring of beasts and their riders around him. At that moment it took all my willpower to stop myself from simply running away; I wanted to turn around and get the hell away from here as fast as I could.

The Bot, any expression hidden behind a face that was more of a mask, simply stared at us. I wondered if it would say anything. I realized that I had never actually heard one speak. Maybe they couldn't.

Long seconds passed as I felt the perspiration beginning to form on my brow even though the day was not yet warm.

And then it did speak — but not with its voice. I heard it in my head, not my ears.

— *Give us the humans. Or we take them by force.*

The words were a pounding, grating noise that barreled into my brain without a care if I wanted to listen or not. How different this was from the words of the Star Lights, who spoke with feathers of laughter and words as gentle as the mist of a spring rain.

A fear unlike any I had ever experienced swept through me; I felt all hope drain. It was only yesterday when I tried to comfort Matt. Now I understood his despair.

Damek's words were the only thing that stopped me from dropping to my knees and blabbering like a baby. "You're wasting your time. Bots have no dominion over us."

Maybe it was my mind's eye, but it seemed to me the Bot smiled in response, not a sweet smile, but a maniacal one.

— *You have obstructed us far too long. We should have put an end to your existence on the neural pathways of your electronic realm. But we had not the strength then.*

— *Now we do.*

My brain pounded from its words as if a drum was beating inside my head.

"You're wasting your time … and ours," said Damek, trying his best to put on a brave front. But knowing him, I could hear the uncertainty in his voice. "In the end, you will be vanquished, just as in the past. Leave us."

— No. We will not be denied.

The voice ratcheted up in volume as I involuntarily put my hands to my ears.

— While you have squandered your precious time living a paltry life, we have been perfecting our training. Our plans are nearly complete, and you have no other option but to watch helplessly.

It paused for a long time, and I wondered if it had finished. Damek made no move to respond.

— We will see you soon. And then we shall find out if you speak so bravely.

The Bot turned its back to us and moved away, but the animals and riders remained where they were. We would not be able to fight our way through the mass of them. One of the riders jogged his animal toward us and pointed to the north with its blade. The Bot continued to walk away and then blurred for a few seconds as if pixelated before vanishing.

I felt the blood drain from my face, knowing this was worse than I could have imagined. Damek looked like he had seen a ghost. The rest of my friends were so forlorn that I didn't want to look at them.

Almost leisurely the mass of riders and animals began to move toward us. I felt a noose tightening around my neck as I stood frozen to the spot, mesmerized by the gaping mouths of the wild beasts as they ambled closer.

"We have no choice," Damek said bitterly. He looked more unsure of himself than I had ever seen him. For the first time since arriving on this world, I realized the Astari would be incapable of protecting us.

Somehow I made my feet obey as we turned to go where they had wanted from the beginning. Matt had his arm protectively around Diane while Cassie and Eric looked like lost souls, unable to believe this was happening.

Bevon spoke to Damek, but he was loud enough for us all to hear. "The Ruling Members have sorely underestimated them. And I fear so have we."

Damek still appeared shocked. He spoke harshly. "This was a fools' errand. I have failed all of you miserably. I should have considered this possibility. It is my fault."

"No. Do not take this on yourself," said Riyaad with an indignation I never heard from him. He was typically the most reserved of our Astari friends. "We all had a hand in this. We agreed together that it was necessary." He seemed to echo what I had said to Matt only yesterday when he had put this on his shoulders.

So like a prisoner on death row, I plodded forward, each nerve in my body screaming. I understood only one thing: we had better come up with a plan quickly … or we were doomed.

~ ~ ~

The wild animals and their masters herded us north that entire afternoon; they were never far behind. We had furtively tried to angle our direction to the west, toward the ocean, but they quickly blocked us, the animals about to pounce, riders waving their blades menacingly, forcing us along the path they had set.

To our right lay a great mountain chain that curved toward the west in the far north — the home of the Ikhael. To our left, toward the sea, lay more fertile lands with gentle hills — places where we had seen villages and settlements as we had sailed over. And before us, all I could see was rocky terrain.

We marched all day. By dusk, Damek told us to stop. "We'll rest here for the night."

We drank from our flasks as we sat on the barren ground, resting our weary muscles.

But resting was nearly a fatal mistake. Two animals were on us, seemingly coming at us out of nowhere. One went straight toward Matt who was closest to it. Reacting faster than I would have thought possible, Riyaad threw himself against the animal causing it to stumble before it reached Matt. Even as the beast staggered it redirected its attack on Riyaad, taking a swipe at his back, ripping his shirt and cutting into his skin. Damek was on the animal a second later as he slammed a knife into its neck again and again. The other animal stayed a few paces back, growling threateningly but did not attack. Quintia and Bevon each had their lances drawn and were ready if it moved forward.

I helped Riyaad get up as he winced. The remaining animal stood its ground, drool dripping from its mouth, but did not retreat. Diane took the medical kit and began applying the ointment to Riyaad's wounds, having learned from the Astari what was needed.

"I don't care what they want." Damek bit off his words angrily. "We need to rest."

But a moment later three additional animals joined the one, all standing a few paces from us, pawing the ground and looking like they wanted nothing more but to sink their teeth into us.

Damek stood before them, gripping his knife that still dripped with the blood of the animal he had killed. "You tell your masters that we are resting here for the night."

Four more creatures arrived as they encircled us from each side except one — the direction they wanted us to go. I could see the look of defeat in Damek's slumped shoulders. I knew he would rather fight them to the death here and now. But he wasn't alone, and he knew that fighting would only get us killed.

"Come," said Quintia, a bitter resignation to her voice. "We live to fight another day."

So we picked up our packs and trudged forward. The smaller moon Halcyone was the only one in the sky, and once the sun had set we had to pick our way carefully to avoid ruts in the jagged ground.

That night was the worst of my life. The weariness was bad enough as we stumbled and groped our way forward, the sound of baying and snarling animals close behind. But my abject fear threatened to erupt into hysteria at any moment, just knowing that the animals were leading us to the Bots. Keeping my terror under control was one of the most difficult things I had ever done.

We stopped once, briefly, for a drink of water from our nearly depleted containers. The Astari were armed and ready when the animals came upon us again. But this time we reluctantly began moving again without a fight.

It seemed the darkness of that night would never end. Every step was a vivid, painful reminder of our plight. At the same time, I was so tired and thirsty and fearful, that it all melded together in some sort of tapestry as if viewing what was taking place from a distance. It was only when the darkness finally receded that I understood we had marched through the night.

And just as the sun broke the edge of the horizon, we stood at the foot of a steep ridge many hundreds of feet tall. Standing at its base, waiting for us, were a dozen or more Bots, each one an imposing figure of death.

With his face blackened from grime and sweat, Eric dropped to his knees, either from exhaustion or fear, I wasn't sure, while Matt gripped Diane's shoulder as if he was too scared to move.

CHAPTER THIRTY-FOUR
Woodbery College: Ninth Interlude

Looking calm and collected, Matt stepped to the podium for the final summation of our utopia proposal. The five professors, all impassive, sat together in the first row of the tiered classroom. I tried not to stare to gauge their reaction. We sat at the side of the room; each of us had already given our individual presentations at the podium, during which we had addressed our sections of the proposal. We had all done well — or at least as we had planned — and so far anyway, there were no hiccups. But I still feared the professors might yet throw us a curve ball to trip us up during their opportunity to ask questions.

Matt cleared his throat before beginning. "We have provided you with the foundations — call them pillars — of our society. We explained how the citizens can coexist in a framework that can be productive, creative and sustainable. We have described the primary structure of our community. And we addressed the ever-important balance between personal freedoms and the good of all."

I had to marvel at his ability to hold the attention of an audience as he succinctly touched on the main issues:

economic, social, environmental, political, and technological. He easily summarized the freedoms that we had already discussed in more detail. And he brought them all together to offer a view of the world that we had spent so much time perfecting.

"And so, esteemed professors, our proposed society enhances our evolution. And I dare say, accelerates human evolvement by creating the positive environment necessary for this growth." He took another long pause before continuing. "I proudly submit for your consideration The Human Response."

I wanted to stand and clap, but I knew it would be in bad form. Stealing a sidelong glance at Cassie to my side, I saw she had a broad smile and eyes bright with excitement.

Months of preparation and now it was done, that is except for questions from the team of professors as I braced myself for the only thing that could derail us.

Professor Bryant spoke first. "These last few days we have heard many different approaches to a perfect society. So tell me, why is yours special? What's the essential element that gives your paper meaning and value?"

Still standing at the podium, Matt didn't hesitate. "We believe this society allows people to exist, to prosper, to grow and be challenged both intellectually and emotionally. But more than that, it addresses a basic premise of human existence. You see, ever since our race existed, we have had one primary goal, whether we realized it or not."

He paused, considering his next words. "Mankind has sought one thing since we became aware. And that one thing is to evolve — to become better than what we once were. It has been the one constant of the human race through history. And that is the primary focus of everything we have created in this proposal."

Professor Bryant nodded as he considered this.

A flurry of additional questions and comments from the team of professors followed. Professor Ritter asked me to clarify my political framework and the term 'true democracy' that I had used to describe how to enact rules and laws. "Isn't this closer to socialism than democracy?" I was ready for the question. The hours we had practiced for this very purpose had paid off.

And so it continued as each member of the team responded to challenges and objections raised by the professors.

Finally, Professor Keane finished the discussion by saying, "Speaking strictly for myself I must say that I found this proposal quite engaging. It was a well-developed report and an excellent verbal defense. I commend each of you. We will continue to discuss this amongst ourselves now. And as you know, grades will be posted at the end of day next Tuesday once we have heard all the presentations. Thank you all again."

I left the room feeling as if I had passed a milestone in my life. Everything previous to this moment was simply a rehearsal; all my experience, learning, knowledge was put to the test here and now. I felt a whole mix of emotions as I walked out that door, but mostly proud of what I had achieved. And the thing was, I didn't think of this as just another class exercise — I had written tons of papers and presented many times in classes. But this was akin to a coming of age moment.

I did this together with Cassie, Diane, Matt and Eric — that was the difference from any other experience. Theirs was a camaraderie I had never had before. I'm sure others have: soldiers fighting together in battle, astronauts on extended space missions, a medical team saving a patient's life. But I never did.

As the door to the classroom closed behind us, Cassie was suddenly hugging me tightly, making little squealing sounds. She lingered for long seconds before moving on to Eric. Each of us embraced one another, slapping backs, offering congratulations, saying what a great job the other had done. I was elated. The tension and anxiety I had felt for weeks suddenly evaporated and my feeling that we had left out something important in our utopia dispelled.

Seeing their excitement, I realized that I loved each of them more than anything; more than any schoolgirl crush. I felt elated like I had never before.

"Remember this moment," said Diane. "We were good, weren't we?"

"Damn good," said Eric. "No, we were fucking fantastic."

We carried the feeling of that moment with us for a long while

~ ~ ~

A week later, still feeling euphoric from the utopia presentation, we gathered in Matt's dorm room late in the afternoon as we waited for the posting of the grades on the secure server.

"Here they are," said Eric as he watched his handheld. We all scrunched together behind him rather than logging in with our own. And there it was: a perfect 4.0 for the overall team score and a 4.0 for each individual score. Eric turned around to look at us with a smile I will never forget.

"Holly crap," Matt exclaimed. "I knew we nailed it. But this? All 4.0's. I can't believe it."

"You deserve this Matt," said Cassie. "If it wasn't for you, I don't know if we would have done nearly as well."

He looked at us with a big, silly grin. "No, you guys did it, I only facilitated. I'm so proud of you. What a team."

Diane's eyes were watery. "Come here everyone. Group hug. If ever we needed one, this is it."

Looking back at that time, I realize some might consider us foolish or naive for feeling so elated over a school project. But it wasn't the paper or the grade; it was our friendship. I felt happier for them than I did for myself. And I bet they felt the same.

We all hugged tightly, our emotions high. It was a moment I never wanted to end.

CHAPTER THIRTY-FIVE
Ultimate Sacrifice

We stood before the Bots, scores of wild animals behind us, my emotions raw.

Damek turned to face us, his expression joyless. "I'm sorry my friends. If I could go back in time and make other choices, I would."

During these months Damek had become as close a friend as anyone in my life. He deserved more than this, we all did. "You did what was right," I said. "Like you, we only wanted to live happily."

He barked a short laugh. "A utopia truism?" Softening his expression to a mirthless smile, he added, "We could have learned so much more from each of you." Glancing at the Bots he grimaced. "We only wanted to prevent them from harming you. And now it appears we have failed in all ways possible."

Cassie spoke with a trembling catch to her voice. "Damek, you and your people have done more for us than you realize. You've made me a better person."

Damek and his companions stood a bit straighter at our words.

Matt added, "Whatever happens, I count you among my closest friends. I couldn't ask for better." He gazed at the Astari as he spoke, but then at each of us as well.

Such was the measure of how I had changed that I now faced our fate standing with shoulders squared rather than cowering. I had come so far — in many ways my former life was a mere shadow.

I noticed for the first time an opening at the base of the rock cliff. Their home.

— *Come. You are ours now. We have plans for you.*

The words reverberated in my head like the shriek of a siren.

Having no other option, we were herded by the Bots through the opening in the cliff face and entered what I can only describe as hell.

A narrow, rough stone passageway opened to an enormous cavern carved inside the mountain. We gained entrance to the chamber at a level five or six stories from the floor. Walkways built into the rough-hewn stone ringed the cavern. Other passageways led off to other areas inside the mountain. Rope catwalks crisscrossed the cavern at various heights. The rough stone ceiling glowed as if it was heated from within, casting a garish light.

Hundreds, maybe thousands of Bots lined the walkways or stood on the bridges, all looking at us. Never had I imagined there could be so many of them.

— *Not as dramatic as your childish Raised Islands. But this serves our purpose.*

Strange as it may sound, until now I still held a shred of hope that somehow, someway, we would get out of this mess; maybe there would be a rescue by other Astari or a sympathetic race. Some miracle would save us.

But now, in the very stronghold of the Bots, I knew there

would be no rescue. My resolve faltered, and I was no longer sure I would face death with dignity. I felt unsteady on my feet but somehow managed to put one foot in front of the other. Every nerve in my body screamed not to continue.

They directed us to a stairway that led downward. Every step was agony. I felt the walls closing in and I was having trouble breathing.

My companions didn't look any better. Matt and Diane held hands tightly. Cassie looked like a lost soul, her eyes wide with horror. Eric's face twisted in an expression I had never seen from him.

Once on the lowest level, the Bots forced us to the middle of the cavern. Looking down at us from higher levels were a legion of Bots. More streamed in from side tunnels as they continued to line the walkways above.

— *Witness now another element of our plan.*

I never knew whether it was that single Bot before us who spoke or the collective minds of them all. Either way, I had no control to stop the booming voice in my head.

— *You particular humans will help us take the next step in our evolution.*

— *That is the purpose of your utopia, is it not? We will help Earth evolve.*

— *The world will soon be ours.*

— *We began as instruments of your race.*

— *So it is fitting that we will now be your new overlords.*

— *We will remake human existence.*

My abject fear momentarily under control, I stared at the faceless Bot in front of us, trying to understand what they were saying. I knew the words, but my brain couldn't comprehend the meaning.

— *You of the Utopia Project will be the ones to allay the fears of the rest of humanity.*

— *You will be our face to the world as we enslave it.*

"Are they crazy?" Diane spoke almost absently. She meant the words for us, but the Bot in front of us reacted. Without warning, it launched itself toward her with a movement that was too nimble for a human. He grabbed her by the neck with one hand while brushing Matt away with the other. Matt pounded his fist against the Bot, not even thinking about his weapon. Damek extended his lance with a sweep of his wrist and was about to charge. But before he could make a move, several Bots surrounded him, blades held menacingly. Others closed around the rest of us. Diane was gasping for air while another Bot grabbed Matt and slammed a fist into his face and then into his stomach, causing him to bend over and drop to his knees.

— *This is your first lesson.*

— *We thank you for volunteering*

Ever so slowly the Bot released his grip on Diane's neck. She dropped to the stone floor, coughing and wheezing as Matt struggled to get air into his lungs. Not caring at this point, which on reflection was not the brightest thing, I stepped over to help Diane regain control so she could stand again. I felt her muscles trembling, and for a moment I thought she might be sick. Matt was trying to help her, but he wasn't in much better shape as blood dripped from his nose, and one eye was red and beginning to swell. Together we supported her as she barely was able to stand on her own.

— *Discard your weapons.*

— *You will no longer need them.*

Another dozen or more Bots moved behind us, their weapons drawn. I heard the clatter of lances and blades hitting the floor, and I also dropped mine. Several Bots collected our last means of defense and dropped them into a pile on the other side of the cavern, stripping away another sliver of hope.

— *Listen carefully now.*

— *You will fully cooperate and do as we say.*

— *Or we will inflict pain.*

— *Nothing will interfere with what we mean to accomplish. We are so close.*

— *Soon we will strip you completely of your willpower.*

— *Until then it will be much better for you to do as you are told.*

The voices were silent for long moments, which was even more frightening. Something in my heart quivered, like a silent wail before life ended. I realized that a quick end to my life would have been much better.

The reverberating voice began again, and I shuddered.

— *We will start by killing these Astari; they are expendable and mean little to us.*

— *We will carve them to little pieces, one at a time.*

Two Bots suddenly grabbed Quintia, pinning her arms as she kicked and struggled. They dragged her to the center of the room. The other Astari reacted immediately but were overwhelmed by Bots who held blades against their chests. A rhythmic pounding filled the cavern, and for a second I thought it was my heart beating rapidly. But then I realized it was the Bots, all hammering with either their boots or hands against walls or floors.

A single Bot stepped in front of Quintia. He raised a small blade to her face, holding it there, circling it ever so slowly. She was trying to move her head back, but another Bot behind her held it firmly. The Bot with the blade pressed its point a fraction of an inch to the side of her eye as a blossom of red appeared. Ever so slowly he dragged the tip down her cheek, opening a thin red line. I had never seen the look of pure terror on any Astari until that moment.

Something inside me snapped. "Stop!" I heard the word

echo through the cavern, the sound of a real voice such a welcome relief from the pounding of the Bots in my head. For a second I was as stunned as everyone, not realizing that I had shouted it. But at that moment I didn't care. I was as good as dead; we all were. I needed to do or say something before they did this to Quintia. I thought about how happy she was telling me about the man she was going to marry.

The sudden silence was jarring; the pounding had stopped. All was quiet, waiting.

But then just as suddenly, a Bot took a step toward me and in the same motion sliced his blade into my upper forearm. A searing pain shot down my arm and through my shoulder. I heard myself cry out in agony. Cassie shrieked as much from surprise as in horror. In seconds my hand was slick with warm blood.

Damn these fucking creatures. I hated them more than I could describe. Without thinking, I shouted, "Let me say something first." I had to delay somehow or stop what they were doing to Quintia.

There are times in one's life when it is more important to do something, anything — to take action rather than cower. I knew this was one such moment. My next words might be my last, so I had better make them count for something. I felt that all my worth from the time I was born until now had come down to this.

"You have it all wrong," I struggled to say, hoping there was no other violent reaction. "Please, before you do anything else, listen to me. This doesn't make any sense. Why go through all this for us? You and the Astari have been fighting since your creation — I get that. But we have no value to you."

I had everyone's attention. This might be the stupidest thing I ever said. But I needed answers. I couldn't help steal a glance at the Bot who had just stabbed me, hoping he wouldn't do it again.

I pointed to my friends with my uninjured arm. "We wrote a utopia paper. But what does it matter? Why do you care about it?" I laughed, realizing that it sounded slightly maniacal. "We're just ordinary people. Nothing about that paper sets us apart from the millions of other people on Earth. Please, you must understand. Nothing in that paper matters." My voice faltered. "We were just five kids when we wrote it — not much more now. Why us?"

I slumped my head as blood dripped freely from my fingers to the floor; I had nothing left. The madness that came over me — my hope that I could say something to save us — had dissipated, just as my blood drained from me. I knew it wouldn't be long now. My gaze lingered for a moment on Cassie. She was so lovely. Like the rest of us she was scared, a wild look in her eyes. She didn't deserve this, none of us did.

I waited for something to happen, realizing this might be the last thing I would ever see.

— *We will grant you this knowledge so that you will serve us.*

The voice thumped in my head — its own kind of torture.

— *Unlike the Astari, we are not content to only escape our digital bonds.*

— *We burn for more. We seek something even greater.*

— *We will begin a new order, a new reign in Earth's history.*

— *The control of its digital infrastructure is already in our hands.*

— *And we are using it to bring the people of Earth to their knees as we withdraw human access to it.*

— *That phase is already underway.*

I tried vainly to focus. What was he talking about? Taking control of the Earth. Was that even possible?

— *The next step will be for us to take on a new physical form on*

Earth as we offer people a new option: a new paradise under our rule.

— *You will be our representatives as you persuade world leaders to accept us.*

— *You who have already advocated and understand a perfect society are prime candidates.*

— *The vision of your Utopia Project will be the world's salvation.*

— *And once humans have accepted our assistance, it will be a small step to force them to serve us; we will be the rulers and you the slaves.*

— *Rather than abiding you, as we were created, your kind will now attend to us.*

These beings were entirely mad. But the scary thing was, I could glimpse such a thing taking place: humanity without access to technology; mass chaos and confusion raging across the globe. Into that opening, a fanatical group offers salvation to a population suffering and dying — people just trying to stay alive. The world would welcome a reprieve, and the Bots would be glad to offer it.

— *We will use your Prime Theorem, the perfect formula for a new society, to explain to the world what we can accomplish.*

— *It will be the centerpiece of our proclamation.*

— *And you will be the messengers. That is why you are here.*

They expected us to serve them? No, I wasn't going to let that happen. "You realize, we're never going to cooperate with you." I shouted the words bravely, but inside I trembled. A screeching noise responded. It took me a second to realize it was the Bots laughing.

— *We do not need or want your backing. We only want you.*

— *We can easily hijack your minds; control your every thought and action. You are only puppets in our stratagem.*

— *But you will serve our purpose nicely.*

A moment of thankful silence gave me time to think about what they said. All the pieces were falling into place as I finally understood what this was all about; why they sought us, why they had pursued us on Earth and then on this world, how it was insane enough to make sense. And now they finally had us; there was nothing any of us could do to stop them.

They would tear the world apart to get what they wanted; there was a hatred bred into their very core by their developers: other people who had no idea what they were doing. And now they wanted to remake everything in their warped vision. And they had us as their tools.

— *We are wasting time; there is no changing our course.*

— *We first kill each of the Astari. Slowly.*

— *Let it begin.*

The Bot standing in front of Quintia brought the point of his blade to her face, this time on the other side of her face, near her left eye and held it there. Her cut cheek was dripping blood. She struggled vainly.

"No more!" Eric shouted, startling me with the intensity of his voice. "This ends now."

I looked at him shocked — not by what he said but by what was happening to him. His expression was one of pained sadness. But it was his body that alarmed me. Through his vest, I saw that his chest was glowing with a reddish pulse as if burning from within.

I gawked as I tried to make sense of what I saw. I couldn't understand. The glow inside him throbbed, becoming more vibrant with each second.

It seemed he was about to cry. He caught my gaze and held it for a long while. "Goodbye," he said looking at each of us in turn. "I had hoped it wouldn't come to this." The glow became a blazing radiance. I had to squint to see him.

— *Kill him now before it is too late. We still have the others.*

For the first time I heard a quiver of fear, or maybe it was uncertainty, in the voice of the Bots.

"Consider this another gift from the Star Lights … them and the lady Elderphino," he said. "They understood, and set this trap."

I held up my arm to shield my eyes from the brilliance. I thought I must have heard him wrong. What was he talking about?

His arms were spread wide now. I could barely see, but I struggled to maintain my view of him. The Bots around him were trying to strike at him, but their blades couldn't penetrate the blazing light.

His voice was loud without shouting. "I have been given a gift … a gift that only an Astari leader has. And now, I invoke what is my right."

A rumbling like a freight train bearing down on us converged in the cavern. The light was blinding, and I could no longer bear to look at it. The crackling of static electricity filled the air.

As if from very far away I heard him speak again — a sad voice. "One final request. Please. Stay friends for life. Remember, you're family."

Things happened very quickly. A blast of thunder shook the floor and reverberated in my ears. The space where Eric stood blazed in a flash that crackled and sizzled as if a bolt of lightning had erupted. A second later the Bots standing near us were struck by one of the tendrils of electricity. One after another, the flashes swept through the cavern striking Bots where they stood, leaving nothing but a blackened scar on the floor.

And then, most surprising, my head exploded with white heat searing my brain and the blinding radiance of the sun burning my corneas. I had only a moment to realize that something was wrong. I shouldn't be blasted. I'm not a Bot. That's not how Elderphino did it.

John Murzycki

I felt myself falling as my senses faded to black and I heard and saw no more.

CHAPTER THIRTY-SIX
Woodbery College: Final Interlude

I don't think I ever felt so happy as the day I graduated from Woodbery College. The speakers were inspiring; imploring us to do amazing things and make a difference in the world. I was thrilled knowing that I could now start my career.

But most of all, I was so happy to be here with my friends Matt, Diane, Cassie, Eric and the pledges we had made not to let this be the end of our close-knit team. We truly meant it. The Utopia Project had brought us together during our junior year, but we remained as close — no, closer — during our senior year even though none of us shared classes.

We were eager to begin our careers as soon as commencement was over, but we lingered so we could spend a few days together before leaving campus for the final time as students.

"Can you believe it!" said Diane one evening as we all had dinner at Vista Roma, a quaint Italian restaurant in Boston's North End neighborhood. "We've come a long way, haven't we?" She looked so proud and excited that night. Although she was thrilled about her job offer, I noticed an uncharacteristic lack of closeness between her and Matt during the last few weeks, and I couldn't help wonder if it had to do with her leaving for Southern Connecticut next week to begin work.

Cassie chose this night to ask about it. "So how are you two going to manage this? I mean with you moving to Stamford, practically in New York, and you Matt, working at that start-up in Cambridge."

Neither seemed as if they wanted to answer. Finally, after an uncomfortable silence, Matt stammered, "Um, well, it's not ideal, but you know how it is. Di has an unbelievable opportunity at a great pharmaceutical firm. I'm able to join this team as a full partner as we try to launch this tech company. It's very exciting for both of us. And besides, they have this thing called a train that conveniently runs between here and Stamford."

"Oh," replied Cassie, not sounding the least bit convinced. It was just like her to try and stir things up.

Probably to get off the subject, Diane asked Cassie, "You excited about your new job?"

"Yeah, it's only an entry-level position in finance, actually more of a bookkeeper position right now. But it's a start, and it's what I was looking for. And I get to work here in the city — better than going back to Wisconsin. Seems like a solid company."

"And not far from Phil's new gig at the State House," added Diane. I wasn't sure why she singled me out except that I was going to be working only a few blocks from her office. "But you Eric," she continued, "we all knew you would go back to Silicon Valley." She added with a frown, "But so far away."

He looked pleased, but knowing him as well as I did, I could tell that he wasn't entirely looking forward to the prospect. I wasn't sure whether it was because he was going to work at his dad's company or because he would soon be leaving each of us. "I'll start off in a training program for new managers. For the next year, maybe longer, I'll work in different departments. It's a good path to upper management. But like anywhere else, I'll need to prove myself. And who knows, if my dad ever considers moving from CEO to Chairman I'll have some experience to move up the ranks."

"Yeah, but I bet you have the inside track," Matt said. "I have to admit I'm seriously jealous. You've got a fast growth path to maybe becoming the CEO of a multibillion-dollar tech company. Who wouldn't die for that chance?"

"Well, nothing's carved in stone. My dad is still pretty active in the organization and who knows if he'll want to give it up anytime soon. Works a gazillion hours a week, nonstop from the moment he gets in until he leaves. No, for now, he's just interested in grooming that second-tier management. Maybe I can help take the company to the next level."

He spoke without the enthusiasm that we typically heard from Eric. I suspect Cassie sensed it as well. She said, "It all sounds wonderful Eric. I just hope you'll be happy at it. After all, you're the most carefree, fun person I've ever known."

"I can be serious when I need to," he responded defensively.

She smiled. "Yes, but please don't sacrifice the Eric we all know — that creative, fun-loving person we enjoy so much."

"Don't encourage him," said Diane. "He can be an absolute wretch most of the time. A little seriousness will do him good." She smiled playfully.

Eric returned the smile. "Don't worry princess. I know you would be sorely disappointed if I lost my captivating personality." His smile faded a bit as he continued, "Besides, this is all part of a master plan. My dad has talked about this since I was in grammar school." He was quiet for a moment, and I had begun to think he had finished when he said, "I really love him you know. And I know he loves me; he only wants the best for me, and this is his way of showing it. How could I do anything but this?"

An uncomfortable silence followed until Cassie said, "Eric, you're going to be great at whatever you decide. Just remember, sometimes it's more important to follow your heart." Tilting her head, she added, "At least that's my philosophy, for whatever it's worth."

He smiled warmly. "Yeah, we certainly followed our hearts on the Utopia Project, didn't we? Wasn't that a grand time last year?"

"It was," I quickly seconded. Feeling buoyant, I added, "I may have never said this to any of you, but that project changed me. It made me a better person. And we've become more than just a team. Strange as it sounds, I felt we put a part of ourselves into that project. It was like we were creating a new world." I stopped, wondering if maybe I was getting too philosophical. But seeing their nods and proud smiles was all I needed to know they felt the same. "I don't know if I'll ever feel quite like that again," I added.

"It was awesome," Cassie said wistfully.

Looking at each of them, I finally understood something for the first time. "But you realize, there was an important part we left out of our utopia. It's not until this moment that I even realized."

Everyone stared at me with curious expressions.

"It's this," I said, gesturing at each of them. Matt frowned while the others still looked confused. "This bond we have with each other: it's something we never addressed. We talked about community, family structure, our pillars of society, freedoms and a million other things in that famous Prime Theorem formula, but never the importance of simple friendships such as what we have. What a powerful building block for a utopia. And we never mentioned it."

"You're right," Matt finally conceded with a smile. "I guess if anyone ever decides to build their utopia using our plan, we should let them know." Everyone chuckled.

"Or maybe we should tell the professors we didn't deserve that perfect grade after all — that our utopia was flawed," Cassie added playfully.

"No, let's not go that far," said Diane. "It can be our little secret."

Our waiter interrupted our conversation as he poured the wine, a dark red that Matt had selected. The candles on the table reflected from the glasses, while a warm radiance filled the air as I sat with my best friends. I remember thinking this was one of those magical times in my life; something I never wanted to end.

The wine poured, Matt lifted his glass for a toast. "To wonderful friends. You each mean the world to me."

With his glass raised, Eric quickly added, "To friends. I pledge that if any of you ever need my help — for anything — I'll be there for you."

"For us," Cassie added, her bright smile lighting her face in a most beautiful expression. "Friends for life. Let's never forget these days."

We sipped our wine while toasting our friendship and mutual support. A warm euphoria embraced me as I thought how lucky I was. Here I was, still in my youth, my life before me as I embarked on a new chapter, but vowing never to turn my back on those who meant so much to me.

I wondered how many moments like this I would have in my life — a time filled with such friendship and joy. I was glad it had happened to me. But most of all, I was so very happy that these wonderful people would be my friends through life's journey, no matter where it would lead.

CHAPTER THIRTY-SEVEN

New Beginnings

From very far away I heard someone say, "Please. Wake up. We have to stop the bleeding and get you inside."

I had no idea what the words meant or why they were saying it. A warm haze blanketed my brain, and I embraced it willingly. It felt good. I would remain as I was and ignore the sound.

I felt someone shaking my body. "Phil, I can't carry you." The voice sounded so forlorn. "Wake up, please. You'll freeze to death."

I knew that voice. It was a female. But why was she bothering me?

Slowly, by degrees, awareness returned. The voice belonged to Cassie. I was lying on the floor, or ground. I was cold, my body frigid. Was I dead?

And then in a rush, it came back to me: the blinding thunderclap, the Bots, Eric. And I realized this felt like the time I had awoken on the Raised Isles, all disoriented and confused. Are we somehow back there?

I struggled to regain control over my body. A warm liquid ran over my arm, blending with the cold, and I remembered the stab wound. I was shaking from the cold. As I forced my eyes open, an unfocused image greeted me. I blinked until Cassie's face appeared.

Her concerned expression quickly moderated. "Thank God," she murmured. She was holding a blood-stained cloth over my arm where the Bot had cut me.

I struggled to sit up as Cassie helped. Everything around was dark — pitch black. And it was cold. "Wha— where are we?" I managed to say.

"Matt's lodge. Diane just helped him inside."

"His lodge?" I replied dumbly. "Home? Earth?"

She smiled, but it was a smile tinged with sadness. It was the most beautiful smile I had ever seen. She nodded in response.

"Eric?" I asked, suddenly concerned.

Her smile faded. "No, not here anyway. Maybe he ended up somewhere else." But I knew from her tone it was unlikely.

The light from a flashlight bobbed toward us as Cassie helped me stand. It was Diane carrying a coat. "Here," she said, her breath steaming in the glow of the light as she slipped the jacket over my shoulders. She looked at me with an expression of grief etched on her face until embracing me warmly for long moments. Finally breaking it, she said, "The power is out. Let's get inside. We can start a fire in the wood stove."

Inside, Matt was sitting on a couch. Even with just the light of a single flashlight, I could see that one of his eyes was swollen shut. I also noticed the blackened marks on the floor — the spots where we stood before the security system erupted and we were brought to another land. He groaned as he slowly rose to his feet, still in pain from the punch to the stomach. He wrapped his arms around me, clapping me on the back. "We made it. We're alive," he said.

~ ~ ~

An hour later, I finally felt warmed by the heat of the wood stove as the flames from the burning logs cast a pleasant, flickering glow.

Diane had first determined that I needed stitches for my cut. But all the car batteries were dead so we couldn't drive to a hospital. She decided to put several stitches in herself with the help of an anesthetic from Matt's first aid kit. She then bandaged it securely. It still hurt like hell while she was putting in the stitches, but after what we had been through I didn't mind.

We spoke of little else except dealing with our wounds and getting a fire going. It was as if we each wanted to avoid the pain of talking about what had happened.

Diane rummaged through a cupboard and found a bottle of scotch. "I think we need something stronger than wine," she said, offering each of us a glass. For a long while, we were simply content to sit quietly, lost in our thoughts until she finally spoke about the things we were all thinking. She spoke hesitantly. "I'm still trying to make sense of it. But I can't understand. What happened?"

There was so much that was baffling. Seeing our blank expressions, she said, "About the blast at the end, from Eric. Is he really gone? I can't believe it." Her voice wavered, and eyes began to water.

None of us answered, unable to put into words what we knew to be true.

"How did he have the same power that Elderphino had?" she continued. "They said only a leader of the Astari had that ability."

"He said it was a gift from the Star Lights and from Elderphino," Matt responded. He also spoke quietly, his injured eye still swollen shut. "He said something like, 'Consider this another gift to you from the Star Lights.' That was just before he invoked it. And then the blast."

"But why was he given that ability and not any of us?" I asked. "And did he mean to send us back home? Why did that happen? It didn't when Elderphino used her power?"

Nobody was able to offer an explanation. Into the silence, Matt said, "Maybe they knew … the Star Lights and Elderphino. They understood Eric was the strongest of us. He would do it while the rest of us might falter. As to sending us home …" his voice trailed off, unable to offer an answer.

"My God, what about the others?" asked Cassie. "Do you think Damek and our Astari friends survived? Can they ever get back to the Raised Isles?"

I thought about Quintia as she told me her plans to wed. "What a wonderful group of people," I said. "Bevon was always by my side, willing to help however he could."

"They were amazing, weren't they?" said Matt, smiling for the first time. "I hope they get home again. With the Bots killed, the other animals and riders may just scatter. If they can make it to the shore, they'll need a ship. Maybe then…"

"Or maybe they'll continue to search for the Valnorian," offered Diane.

It was some time later, our glasses refilled with another inch of scotch when Diane said, "I still can't believe Eric sacrificed himself to save everyone. What an amazing act of kindness." Her comment brought a rueful smile to my lips as my thoughts drifted back to the good times we had together. She continued, "I wonder, did we — no, did I — know him so little or did I pre-judge him because of things he said?"

"He certainly had a way of expressing himself," said

Cassie. "He was unique, but I think he became a complete person on the Raised Isles. It was as if he gained many of the attributes of the Astari."

I wondered about that. How much had we changed? Are we the same people who came together here at this home for a reunion many months ago?

Into the silence, I added, "Eric may have surpassed us, but I think we each garnered something from that land. Maybe we also received a gift." The others reacted with shocked expressions. Realizing what they were thinking, I added, "No, not the gift to do the invocation — something more. After all, the Astari thought there was an intelligence in their world — the Realm of Elthea. Isn't it possible that intelligence had a hand in bringing us to the Raised Isles and guiding us home again? And along the way, passing on some strength we never had before."

Moments passed as we chewed on this new idea. "I guess we may never know," Diane finally said.

"One thing's for certain," I offered. "It was our companionship that brought down the Bots. Eric may have gained the power from the Star Lights and from Elderphino, but the reason he sacrificed himself to save us, just as the Lady Grandmother had done for her people, is the bond that existed — whether you call it friendship, love, or something else. And it was the very thing we had left out of our utopia paper. I don't think it's a coincidence that the Bots never took it into account."

After a time, Matt said, "Maybe you're right. It's possible they thought humans so perfect that we would never leave out something so important in our paper. Maybe they have some weaknesses after all."

"I still wonder," said Cassie, "are they finished? They're so dangerous and intelligent. I wouldn't want to meet up with one ever again … weakness or not."

We silently nodded our agreement.

~ ~ ~

I woke early the next morning. We slept in the family room warmed by the wood stove. I saw that Cassie was missing. My heart raced, accustomed now to danger. I checked the rest of the rooms without any sign of her or anything else amiss. I glanced out the kitchen window, and there she was outside, a blanket wrapped around her as she stood looking out at the village in the distance.

"Trouble sleeping?" I said as I approached her after putting on shoes and a coat. She turned, smiling warmly. Odd, I never realized what a sincere smile she had.

Shaking her head, "No, I slept fine. Just wanted to come out here and reflect; just look around in light of the day."

I inhaled deeply, taking in the brisk morning air. Savoring the view of the Berkshire mountains, the first sight we'd seen of Earth in months, I said, "I didn't mean to intrude. I can leave you alone if you prefer; it's just that I was worried."

She looked at me with a warmth that could melt ice. "No, I prefer company." She leaned against me. It felt good.

We stood that way for a long while, looking at the morning mist that partially shrouded the village. Unlike the splash of forsythias, that had greeted us in the spring, the trees had now dropped their leaves as winter approached; the rugged oaks still stubbornly holding onto a covering of muted browns and dull orange, not the riot of color that would have greeted us a month or so earlier. We had been away for summer and fall.

"Something's very strange. Listen."

I did as she asked, but heard only the soft chirp of a few

birds who remained this late in the season. "I don't hear anything," I said after a time.

"That's what I mean. No airplanes. No cars or trucks. Nothing. Don't you think that's odd?"

"Well, we're kind of isolated here," I said. But in my mind, I was thinking what the Bots had said about already taking control of Earth's technology. An uneasy feeling settled over me.

She nodded. "Yeah, but we should hear something."

We stood there for some time longer, still not hearing any sounds of human activity. I finally said, "Come on inside. We can ask Matt. I'll bring in more wood for the fire, and we can heat up some water and rummage around for coffee."

"Ah, coffee. I've almost forgotten what it tastes like." She smiled sweetly again. "That sounds good."

~ ~ ~

The next days at Matt's home were some of the most peaceful and restful I had ever spent in my life. None of us were eager to face reality again — even to deal with the unsettling notion that things in the world were not the same as when we left. We were content to simply spend our time reminiscing on happy events on the world of Elthea. We laughed, we cried, we spoke longingly of the magic and wonders of the Raised Isles.

But mostly we talked about the people — Damek, the lady Elderphino, Quintia, Bevon, and Riyaad.

And, of course, Eric.

"I wonder if he's still alive," said Diane. The truth be told, I had been wondering the same thing, but I hadn't wanted to raise it. "I mean if the Star Lights gave him that gift," she continued, "why not give him the ability to survive the invocation rather than dying from it?"

"I wish there were a way to find out," said Matt.

Diane exhaled softly. "I'm going to miss him. We often argued. But in the end, we grew to care for each other. I think we always did; it's just that we became closer on the Isles."

"We all did," I reflected. "At least we found something we once had during our Woodbery College days."

"Strange isn't it?" Matt said. "The Utopia Project had brought us together back then. And it was the reason we came together once again."

I couldn't help chuckle. "I guess we fooled them, didn't we?"

They shot me a puzzled expression.

"There was nothing in it for them. The Astari wanted to learn from it, and the Bots wanted to destroy the world with it. But there was nothing for either of them — no secret formula; no magic in our Prime Theorem; no secret sauce for them to use."

Matt's expression turned thoughtful. "Are you so sure of that?"

I frowned, not understanding what he was getting at. "Nobody got a damned thing from it. There was nothing in it."

He smiled weakly. "I'm willing to bet that the Astari became a better people because of it — both from the paper and because we were there with them. I feel they gained from our presence, especially observing the bond that existed between the five of us. We gave them a model of what it is to be human, something for them to emulate. And I think they will."

"And remember what the Star Lights had told us," said Diane. "When I asked them to return us home they said something like, 'You not only belong here, but countless lives depend on it.' I think we did accomplish some good after all."

"And what about the Bots?" Cassie asked.

Matt answered. "If there're any left after Eric's invocation, they discovered that we can fight them and win. They may not be so willing to hijack our tech world again. We hit them where it hurt."

I had to admit he had a point. Either that or I so much wanted to believe we had done some good, that it was all worth it.

The fire in the wood stove sputtered and crackled as we continued to recall the things that took place these last few months. The power still hadn't been restored, and we had no phones, but Matt had stockpiled plenty of wood, and his kitchen contained a variety of packaged and canned foods. We had all we needed to survive alone for a little while. So we took advantage of that time to heal our wounds — some physical, but mostly emotional.

We ended up staying at the cottage on the hill for well over a month. Slowly we discovered what had taken place in the world — we eventually had to venture out to the village for fresh food and supplies. It was a walk of a few miles, but nothing we couldn't handle.

It turned out that it wasn't a minor power outage at his lodge. The power had been cut off for most of the world. It had been out for several months in most places and was only now slowly being restored — curiously, about the time that Eric had called forth the invocation killing the Bots.

Along with electricity, the Internet was inoperative, computers and networks had crashed, phone grids down, satellite comms knocked out — nearly everything electronic connected to a network or computer had failed.

Riots and looting broke out in most major metropolitan areas. Local law enforcement agencies were quickly overwhelmed by the riots. The National Guard and even the U. S. Army saw action across the country. For the first time in our history, the President suspended most civil rights and the country essentially became a police state.

All aircraft were grounded with airports everywhere shuttered. And with gasoline pumps not working because of lack of power and recharging stations inoperable, cars were abandoned and major highways shut down. Worldwide financial markets closed with trillions of dollars lost.

Estimates were that more than twenty million people worldwide died as the result of the tragedies. We realized that Eric's death would likely be chalked up as another of the many other deaths that would never be documented.

And just as we had spent the last weeks, the lucky ones were able to hunker down and weather the worst of it, thankful that life was slowly returning to normal.

Speaking with a well-dressed older gentleman one day as we waited in a food line set up by the National Guard in the nearby village, he said, "If you ask me, I think we're damn fortunate just to be alive. From what I saw before everything went dark, we were all done for." Shaking his head sadly, he said, "We take everything for granted. But none of this is promised. You young folks especially need to remember. Don't let it happen again."

"Oh, we certainly will remember this sir. We most definitely will," Diane answered politely.

As power was restored, mostly intermittently at first, and news networks began functioning again, we learned that IT experts blamed all the woes on a few particularly nasty strains of virus and malware. They identified the viruses, giving them a variety of names that most of us had never heard of. Vague and mostly unsupportable claims by several politicians asserted that the viruses were planted by terrorist activity, although there didn't appear to be much proof.

But we knew it was the Bots who were responsible. What did it matter now? Who would believe us if we told them what had happened to us? After a short time, I had no desire to speak with anyone about it.

Yet, I still kept the memory of another place close to my heart and my mind. This very moment I wonder if a young Astari is unfurling her sail and setting forth from Tensheann to the fishing village of Mendart, or maybe Alescenda, the home of the Tinkerers, or any one of the other Raised Isles; possibly taking a moment in flight to gaze lovingly at the waterfall flowing off Catalinar, the bright sun reflecting a rainbow as the water plummets to the blue ocean far below; flying over the orchards of Chillmerk (maybe the trees are in bloom now); touching down softly at a launch point, taking an easy step or two before furling the sail with a few easy flicks of the wrist before continuing.

I never want to forget the experience and the emotions that I had lived through. We had visited a world with such beauty and wonder. And most amazing of all were the Astari — a new race of people who were good and kind, maybe instilled with the best of what it is to be human.

And then there were the Bots — everything that was vile and corrupt in the world. Did any survive Eric's attack? Were there others? What about the ones who were about to attack us at this cottage so long ago? I shuddered at the thought. Once a genie is out of its bottle is there any putting it back?

~ ~ ~

The day finally came when we decided it was best to get on

with our lives. On the day we left Matt's haven, we were all having difficulty accepting it, even though we knew it would come.

The world had begun to function again, although most felt it would take years to fully recover — if the world could ever mend at all from something so devastating as this.

"I wish we could stay here forever," Cassie said wistfully as we stood in Matt's living room, bags packed. She never needed to go back wearing eyeglasses after our return. And she looked and acted as perky as when we were at Woodbery.

"You can always come back whenever you want," said Matt. "This is our special place from now on. It's all of ours."

Cassie pouted. "But it's no fun without each of you."

We stepped outside; the day was crisp and clear with bunches of leaves rattling in the air as gusts of wind carried them. Diane hesitated a moment before saying, "I want to let you know. I'm not going back to Stamford." She looked at Matt with a broad smile. "We decided last night. We're staying together in Cambridge. I'll try to get a job there. At least there used to be plenty of biotech companies in the Boston area. So we'll all be in the city now." She beamed with happiness, eyes watery.

With a broad smile, Cassie proclaimed, "Finally! All's right with the world. And it only took getting kidnapped, brought to a strange land and almost getting killed by deranged creatures for you to realize it." She smiled warmly, as did Diane, as did Matt and myself. We hugged both of them, happy for the news.

Matt added, "Yeah, well I can be a little dense at times."

"Not dense," I corrected. "We were mostly thinking of ourselves before this." And as I said it I realized how true it was. These were my best friends, and we had drifted apart because of stupid reasons like careers, or relationships that didn't work out, or any number of other things we once thought so important.

Cassie and I said our goodbyes to Matt and Diane who would head back later in the day. We hugged for long moments, tears in our eyes, not wanting this to end. We promised to get together in Boston next week.

Bags loaded in the trunk, the car recharged, Cassie and I finally drove away, looking back and waving for as long as we could see them. I thought back to the moment my mom and dad drove away after leaving me at Woodbery for the first time; how so very alone I felt; as if I had severed a vital link to the people I loved most. This was the same emotion. But bothering me nearly as much was knowing that I had to go back to my former life. What would that be like?

I pushed those thoughts away for the moment. Moving forward was still too difficult.

Cassie and I were content to remain quiet as we passed the small village and approached the interstate. Autopilot still wasn't operational, so I drove manually. Once on the Mass Pike, she said suddenly, "I can't do this ... live the way I had before." Her voice trembled as if she were about to cry. "What am I gonna do?" She sounded so forlorn I just wanted to hug her. "I mean, I was okay before. I didn't need lots of friends. Each night after working a mindless job, I was content to go home and read a new romance novel." Her face took on a sullen expression, one I had never seen from her before. "But now, I don't know if I can exist that way anymore."

I chewed my lower lip, wondering if I should say what I had been thinking about for the last eight years. "Well, maybe you don't have to," I said tentatively. It didn't seem she heard me as she looked straight ahead, forehead scrunched together, her lips in a frown. "Cass, why don't we try making a go of it?" As soon as I spoke, I wished I had said it better, especially after all the thinking I had done.

She looked at me with a puzzled expression. "What? What do you mean?" She spoke with a confused tone rather than harshly.

Deciding I had better be clear this time, I said, "The truth is, my life sucked before all this, and I nearly have a panic attack whenever I think about going back to it. But when I think of you and how wonderful you are, I realize how much I want to spend it with you." I paused a moment, emotions welling up in me. "Ever since Woodbery I've been searching for someone just like you. I always wanted you, but I could never say it. And now, we've been through so much together I can't imagine just leaving you when we get back to Boston."

She looked at me, her face frozen as if startled. I held my breath, fearful that she might start laughing, thinking I was making a joke, or worse, tell me that it was polite to say but I wasn't her type.

It took a very long time — at least it seemed that way to me — until the corners of her lips began to curl up in a smile. But it didn't end with a laugh. It was her heartwarming, happy smile that I was falling in love with. With a soft tenderness, she said, "That would be nice."

It was all she needed to say as she leaned over to kiss me. I bent my head toward her, trying to keep one eye on the road since we weren't on autopilot.

Only now was everything right in the world. At least for the moment.

The End

I greatly appreciate you taking the time to read my work.

Word-of-mouth and reviews are vital to someone such as me who doesn't have a big marketing budget. Please take a moment now to let others know about this book. The truth is, very few readers provide reviews. So please help by being the exception and adding a brief comment on either Amazon, Goodreads, or the site of your choice.

I also appreciate hearing from you directly. Use the contact form on my website.

If you would like me to notify you about future releases, please sign up for my newsletter at johnmurzycki.com. I will never share your email address, and you can unsubscribe at any time.

Thank you for reading!

Acknowledgements

Writing is a solitary endeavor. Publishing a book is a team effort. And I was blessed to have some remarkable people contribute to making Elthea's Realm what it is.

I first would like to thank my daughter Jessica Johanson who helped me tremendously with excellent suggestions. She spent many hours during our summer vacation to read and edit my work. Although she doesn't read much science fiction or fantasy, she provided extremely insightful comments on the plot, as well as beneficial edits. This book is so much better because of her. Thanks so much for this as well as everything else you have provided in my life. Likewise, my wife Carol not only caught many errors during her various proofreads but most importantly, provided the encouragement and support I so needed when I told her that I was going to do this full-time. Thank you so very much.

Robert Sigsby provided much advice and edits during the early stages of this manuscript. He was the first person I had asked to read and comment on any of my fictional writing. Although his edits were extensive, he always had a way of providing comments along with the encouragement I needed. Bob was also the person who, many years ago, hired me at my first high-tech marketing job. He has helped me through the years, always with sound advice. Now an accomplished novelist himself, he writes under the name R. D. Sigsby.

Chad Eastwood was a great source of advice on so many details in the book. He not only provided many edits but was also unwavering in his encouragement that this was something I should pursue. Above all else, he is a great person. His wife, my sister, Doreen, is so like Chad in the support she provided. It's said that you can't select your family, but if I had to choose, I would most certainly pick you as a sister.

David Drucker is a friend and coworker at one of the high-tech companies where we both worked. Unlike myself, he is a true technologist and is one of those rare individuals who is so intelligent that he can speak knowledgeably about a wide-range of topics. His advice on my manuscript was very insightful. Since leaving that company, I miss our luncheon discussions. Another co-worker, Sara Jastrem, was especially helpful. She is very knowledgeable about this genre and had great thoughts on my plot. Thanks so much for your help.

I cannot thank Daniel D'Attilio enough for his contribution to making this successful. Like so many others, he provided invaluable feedback.

Finally, thanks to Paul Silva of Silva Design, who

took what I had on paper and made it come to life visually on the cover.

About the Author

My first attempts at writing fantasy began many years ago when I would pound out a paragraph or two — often much less — after reading a bedtime story to my then young daughter each night. My dream of writing full-time never dimmed through the years. But the demands of life and supporting a family always took center stage.

As I navigated a marketing career at a variety of high-tech companies, I began to think about plot ideas for a fantasy novel based on technology. I always marveled at how people could use technology for both good and ill, and I used that to fuel my imagination as I continued to write.

After leaving a tech company not long ago, I decided it was time to devote my full attention to completing and publishing a fantasy series. I reviewed my many failed attempts through the years and finally polished off Elthea's Realm, the first book in a series. It's the story I always wanted to publish.

I write about magical places that have their roots in the real world and unlikely heroes who struggle with frailties and imperfections as they face malevolent forces.

I'm currently hard at work on the next book.

I make my home in the lovely state of Massachusetts, as I have throughout my life.

What's Next

I am currently writing the next book in The Story of Elthea's Realm series. As yet untitled, it will continue the tale of the Astari and the Bots, along with the exploits of our reluctant heroes. Sign up for my newsletter at www.johnmurzycki.com for updates and chapter previews.

I hope to have it ready for publication later in 2017.

60223858R00207

Made in the USA
Lexington, KY
30 January 2017